HIDDEN WORLD

A LOWER COLUMBIA COUNTY WRITERS ANTHOLOGY

CO-EDITED BY ELLEN JACOBSON, SHARON HUGHSON, MIKE EXINGER, AND JANA MANN

COLUMBIA COUNTY AUTHORS ALLIANCE

Hidden World: A Lower Columbia County Writers Anthology

CONTENTS

PREFACE ... 1

HIDDEN WORLDS OF WRITERS AND ARTISTS ... 3

1. How I Found My Hidden World by Mike Exinger ... 5

2. Not Now, Flies by Sharon Hughson ... 15

3. Search for a Hidden World by Kevin Lay ... 21

4. The Secret Landscape Behind Your Favorite Book by Sharon Hughson ... 27

5. Sculptor's Surprise by David Fryer ... 41

6. The Red Settee by Cate Cross ... 47

HIDDEN WORLDS OF FANTASY ... 51

7. A World that Was by Dawn Shipman ... 53

8. The Eternal Song by Estella Edgewater ... 77

9. The Home Front by Shaun C. Kennedy ... 83

10. Waking the Spring by J. LaRiviere ... 107

11. Into the Depths by Estella Edgewater ... 123

12. Interview with the Gremlin by Buxton Manning ... 129

13. The Music Note by Tamelia Aday ... 155

14. Nondisclosure Agreement by K.D. Jewell ... 161

15. Astera's Radio Astronomy Observatory by Kevin Lay 171

16. Soles Saved Here by Tamelia Aday 181

17. Until the Nightling by K.D. Jewell 187

18. The Fairy Tree by Kathrin Classen 199

19. What Lies Between by Sharon Hughson 223

HIDDEN WORLDS IN PLAIN SIGHT 227

20. The Scent of Goodbye by Tamelia Aday 229

21. Dude and Baby Sister by Jana Mann 235

22. Accidental Inheritance by Kathy Appel 239

23. Ant-ology by Cate Cross 249

24. Don't Ask, Don't Tell by Linda Paul 255

25. Ascent of Wotan by Elaine Kelley 261

26. Do You Like It, Father? by Sharon Hughson 291

27. The Case of the Missing Hot Dog by Ellen Jacobson 297

28. The Backyard: Skies and Visitors by Jana Mann 321

MEET THE CONTRIBUTORS 329

COLUMBIA COUNTY AUTHORS ALLIANCE 337

CONTRIBUTOR COPYRIGHTS 338

PREFACE

Hello, neighbors.

When Ellen and I first talked about an anthology of local writers, the idea wasn't to create the most polished collection or discover the next great novelist. Our goal was simpler — and, we believe, more important: building bridges among writers in lower Columbia County.

After that first coffee shop conversation, Ellen ran with the idea. She took it to leaders of the St. Helens Writers Guild and the Scappoose Library Writers Group. Members were eager to collaborate.

Then something incredible happened. Writers who had been working in isolation—at kitchen tables, in corner cafes, wondering if anyone else loved stories the way they did—joined the writing groups in order to be part of this project. The anthology started building the community we had imagined before a single story was submitted.

Our contributors represent a wide range of experience, genres, and skill levels—from seasoned authors with multiple publications to writers sharing their words for the first time. You'll notice this variety in the pages ahead: some pieces are polished, others rougher around the edges. This reflects our original vision to value every voice.

As the developmental editor for many of these pieces, I've had a front-row seat to transformation. First-time authors have discovered their voices. Seasoned writers have experimented with new genres and forms. But the greatest gift has been watching these writers encourage and support one another—reminding me that though we write alone, we flourish in community.

Within these pages, you'll encounter hidden worlds that may make you laugh, others that may haunt you. A few might even shift how you see the familiar walking path or the house across the street.

Hidden World has connected writers. Now we invite you to discover the talented storytellers living among us. We hope you'll agree that the most extraordinary stories often begin in the most ordinary places—right here in our community.

Welcome to our hidden worlds. We're delighted to show you around.

Sharon Hughson
On behalf of the Columbia County Authors Alliance

HIDDEN WORLDS OF
WRITERS AND ARTISTS

HOW I FOUND MY HIDDEN WORLD

By Mike Exinger

"About how I came up with something to write for this anthology."

I admit that the concept of "Hidden World" as a theme for this anthology initially threw me. When the votes from the members of both writing groups were tallied, it was clearly the winner, though I had ranked it much lower on my ballot (we used ranked-choice voting, so the result was fairer than fair). I despaired, as fantasy and sci-fi were not in my wheelhouse (so I thought)—but I still wanted to contribute. What to do, what to do?

Naturally, my first act was to search online (the kids say "Google it") to see just what exactly was meant by "hidden worlds," and I was not surprised:

> *A hidden world refers to a realm or place that is not readily visible or accessible, either physically or conceptually. It can be a secret, mysterious, or obscure location, a hidden truth, or a realm beyond normal perception. This "hiddenness" can be due to physical barriers like being underground, in the depths of the ocean, or in remote areas, or it can be due to our inability to perceive it directly with our senses.*
>
> Google AI Overview

That screamed *Harry Potter* to me, with dragons and wizards. If you're my age, you could also think "Lord of the Rings." But the last sentence of the description gave me hope—ocean depths and remote areas spoke more of "our" world, because for centuries, what we knew of our world was very small, indeed.

The best real-world (pardon the pun) example I can think of is Christopher Columbus and his "discovery" of the "New World." Leaving out the baggage behind his discovery (and the probability that he wasn't the first, that the Vikings and/or the Chinese were here before him), it's a great example of a civilization flourishing unknown to another civilization at a distance that seemed too great to traverse.

We all know what happened next and the stories that emerged from that discovery.

So, where could I look to find a "hidden world" to write a story about? We've not fully explored the oceans that cover two-thirds of our home planet, and their depths are ripe for the imagination. Even before space travel was routine enough for commoners, authors have written about other worlds on distant planets (and those closer to home, like Mars or the moon).

But I wanted something even closer to home, and there are many, many more worlds that remain hidden from us, partly because we "don't go there." Back when I attended grade school in Southeast Michigan, there was a kid in my class who was oblivious to what everyone refers to as "up north." Granted, where "up north" begins is up for debate, but wherever the line is drawn signifies the start of tall pines and open spaces, a land far different from the citified area we lived in. Because he'd never been there or even seen pictures, he couldn't grasp the concept. For him, "up north" didn't exist. It was a hidden world (until he eventually visited Mackinac Island, and then all he could talk about was the fudge shops, but that's another story).

I remembered this when I lived in Seaside. A couple of the high school students we employed were mystified about my descriptions of Powell's Books and downtown Portland. They had trouble wrapping their heads around a building filled with thousands of books on several floors and a parking lot underneath. They'd never been to Portland (one had never been out of the county, and only to Astoria once), and I guess they never had the curiosity or inclination to go online and check it out. Needless to say, when they finally ventured forth into the previously unknown world of Powell's, they came back breathless with all sorts of stories (and more than a few good books to read).

I've always been an inquisitive person and not afraid to venture into the unknown. I'm no Columbus or Leif Erikson, maybe more of a Captain Spalding (the African Explorer—hooray!), but I've always had a desire to "go there" and see what I could see, and my curiosity wasn't limited to location.

Could this curiosity aid my discovery of a hidden world story? While I've lived in seven different towns in four different states, I've also had a crazy career, moving for work and also switching career choices like some people switch watch bands. I've worked in a variety of industries, including banking, education, marketing research, and the thing I went to school for: broadcasting. My jobs included both the menial and the managerial. I even owned my own business for eighteen-odd years (some odder than others). My hobbies were the same; new words and new worlds were both revealed to me when I got into gardening, and of course, the world of a writer is full of discovery.

And beyond careers and locations, other experiences can be identified as new worlds to discover, adventures of all kinds. Going from "single" to "married" is something many people do (some more than once). Don't tell me that's not a trip worthy of discussion. Having kids, starting your own business...the list is endless.

Moving is certainly an experience, usually one fraught with peril and overtly traumatic, but it can also be educational. If you move to a different state, one of the first things you'll need to do is get a new driver's license. When we lived in Michigan, we went to the Secretary of State's office, but here in Oregon, this is done at the DMV. Other states use the Bureau of Motor Vehicles, Department of Public Safety, DOT, DOL, MDV, and a host of other acronyms. Many other challenges and alternatives exist—sometimes it's as confusing as rocketing to another planet.

If you move to the south, there's a whole new language to learn. During my short time in Louisiana, I discovered the plural of y'all really is "all y'all." If you have a meeting scheduled for the following Tuesday, that's "Tuesday next." And it's not just the South—in Idaho, when repairs are necessary, they'll tell you, "It needs fixed." Pretty sure the state passed some regulation forbidding "to be" in the language (which would make it tough on the folks who run the Idaho Shakespeare Festival).

I'll admit that, like a cat, my curiosity sometimes lands me in hot water...for a while. The five most dangerous words I can utter (and I've done it often) are "Oh, I can do that." Two of my hobbies are living proof.

How in the world did I, one of the most unathletic kids in high school, become a sports professional just a few years later? A new miniature golf course opened in the town next to us, and while I played golf as a teenager, I wasn't very good. But I could putt, and I learned that the course held tournaments every Wednesday evening. There were prizes and trophies, and for some who had "turned pro," cash! The biggest event was the World Championships, offering a top prize of $50,000 back in the seventies (close to life-changing money back then).

I went one night because I thought, "I can do that," and because it was my first time, I played with the other beginners as an amateur. They had the better players go first, so by the time we began, some of the groups were already on their second round. We'd play three rounds in all, fifty-four holes, with the lowest ten scores winning prizes like free pizzas from local vendors, and a trophy to the lowest score. My playing partners were both a decade younger than me and doing this just for fun. We were in the last group, and almost everyone had finished before us. They were starting the presentation of the trophies and prizes to the winners, and I was standing on the seventeenth hole when I heard them begin to announce the amateur low scores.

No one had bothered to check the bottom of the master scoresheet to see if any of the three remaining groups were anywhere close to the top ten. Big mistake, as I had been fifth after two rounds and was having my best round of the night. One of the kids I was playing with dashed to the clubhouse to tell them not to announce the winners just yet because I still had a chance to finish in the top three. All I needed to do was get a hole-in-one on one of the remaining two holes.

Aced 'em both.

That was the start of my illustrious five-year stint as a Putt-Putt Professional (I turned pro a few weeks later and wound up working at the course as an assistant manager). I won several local tournaments, a few out-of-state, and qualified twice for the World Championships (and didn't do too shabby there, either). While it was fun (and profitable), there wasn't much of a story in it for this anthology. There was no "special language" (though a lot of the players did use quite colorful, mostly blue prose while playing). No quirky flora or fauna (a bright green felt carpet in place of grass surrounded by orange-tinted aluminum bumpboards). I'd have to look elsewhere.

How about whaling? I was never a sailor on a whaling ship (I can't even swim), but I learned their art. Scrimshaw is a popular folk art where ivory or bone is engraved with sharp objects. The etchings are then rubbed with a dark pigment (modern scrimshanders use ink). The result is intricate art often found in jewelry shops on both coasts and other nautical locations. Sailors would spend their free time on months-long whaling voyages carving designs on the leftover sperm whale teeth, copying pictures from magazines and periodicals, and then carving the lines with knives or sailing needles used to mend the sails. When completed, they would run the etchings with tobacco juice, soot, or whatever they could find on board the ship.

I got involved when we saw handmade scrimshaw jewelry at a shop on Mackinac Island in Michigan (not known as a whaling port). Besides the jewelry, they offered a do-it-yourself scrimshander kit, and it was cheaper than the jewelry. I uttered a line then that I have since learned to regret—but I continue to utter it. After looking at the kit and speaking with the owner (a veteran scrimshaw artist), I proudly announced, "Oh, I can do that." It took a while, but it turned out I *could* do that. I spent a couple of summers showing at art fairs all across the state, was featured in a couple of galleries, and even taught an adult education class about scrimshaw. But while it was different, it was hidden only until I went looking.

All of this reflection on my past convinced me that a story was there, somewhere. I thought about how writers spend a lot of time and energy "worldbuilding," creating the language, culture, history, and geography used in their story. While you might think this is true only of Sci-fi and fantasy authors, the fact is that *every* story is set in a "world" of some sort. Sure, many of those worlds are mostly familiar to us (just as every Middle-earth Kingdom and Planet X-9 has specific features we can relate to). But a romance on the beach, a mystery in London's East End, even a humorous coming-of-age novel about a teen who wants to be a

DJ set in a small Oregon town in the sixties requires some worldbuilding. That last one is my novel *Heavy Rotation*, and I went to the trouble of drawing a map of the fictitious Oregon town of Maple Falls to help me locate the radio station in relation to the protagonist's home and part-time job (and many of the other businesses mentioned in the story).

And there it was! My "hidden world" revealed itself when I remembered writing that novel. Just like Chuck Moorman, my main character in the book, I had always wanted to be on the radio–a disc jockey–ever since I was in the eighth grade. I recalled how I shocked my parents when I told them I wanted to study broadcasting in college.

"Do you *really* need to go to college to learn how to spin records?" Mom asked.

"No," I said, "but I want to learn about the broadcasting industry. All of it, even if it's just to be a DJ."

Good thing I did.

My DJ days were brief and quite regrettable. I never had a full-time position, and if you ever heard me on-air, you'd know why. Unlike Chuck, I just wasn't that good. I did better when I moved to the news and public affairs department, but in the end, I had to admit that radio wasn't my dream job after all.

At least, not as talent. By luck, I was mentored to try management, and it was in this capacity that I not only had an actual career but also enjoyed being part of the radio industry. Fun fact: because of circumstances (and a lack of staffing), I wound up on-air *more often* as a manager than I ever did before. Of course, it helps to be the one deciding who to put on the air (and by this time, my skills were much improved, too).

It was my time as a manager, overseeing others (and the choices they make), that became the inspiration for my anthology story. The main event in the story didn't happen to me, but I was in a position to witness it. One of my duties as manager of a college station was co-teaching an Intro to Broadcasting class, and one of the lessons was about the equipment students would use. Professional broadcast equipment works differently from the stuff you have at home. If you're old enough to remember those little reel-to-reel tape recorders, you might also remember that you could record on both sides of the tape. In one direction, it only uses half the tape width, so you play one side, get to the end, then turn it over and use the other side. Not so with professional broadcast tape decks. It uses the entire width of the tape, so that anything recorded on a home system would play both sides at once—one side going from start to end, and the other side going from end to start. In reverse.

It sounds hilarious unless you need a grade for your project.

Several wanna-be broadcasters discovered this. Being typical college students, many of them waited until the last minute to do a required project: a recording of themselves speaking, with or without accompanying ambient sound. For days after the assignment was given, the production studio remained silent, unbooked, and then on the final day, everyone wanted in at once...which couldn't happen. One of the students told some of the others that he had a tape recorder at home, and they could all use it and finish their projects. It was not a professional recorder, and the resulting tapes sounded like mice in the speakers (foreign mice at that).

I was sympathetic to a point. From my own experience, I knew that sometimes things go wrong when dealing with fancy electronic equipment. Of course, the reason the students failed the assignment had more to do with their laggardness than a malfunction, but that was the catalyst for my story. All I needed to do was introduce some "other world"[1] elements, and I'd have it.

Fortunately, I discovered such an element and wrote up the story using my pen name of Buxton Manning without further problems.[2] I hope you enjoy it!

---

1. Other world elements? Why, we're right here (hee-hee).

2. At least I don't hide behind a pseudonym. Just you wait. Love, Nigel.

NOT NOW, FLIES

By Sharon Hughson

"It's almost autobiographical. The struggle of being caught between worlds is real."

I deas were flies, and Cathi S. Cribbler could prove it.

Cathi—with a C and an I, which editors never got right in their rejection emails—wrote short fiction. She'd been working on a breakout novel for four years. As she neared the finish line on the 100,000-word behemoth, new and brilliant story ideas hounded her.

The latest idea buzz-dived her on Wednesday morning in the cereal aisle.

Cathi teetered on tiptoes, reaching for gluten-free granola, when a woman behind her said, "The red ones are poison."

Cathi froze.

Red ones. Poisonous.

Her feet flattened on the slick tiles. *A haggard woman behind a rickety cart polished a diamond-shaped fruit. "The crimson ones will kill that shifter who's bothering you."*

An entire love triangle unfolded within her Default Mode Network. Nothing as simple as Team Jacob versus Team Edward, either. No, her gritty, powerful shero didn't need a man. Perhaps she would even—

"Excuse me."

A cart clanged into Cathi's stationary buggy, jerking her from the fantasy realm. Fluorescent lights glared. A woman, whose hunched shoulders reminded her of the seller in her imagination, scowled.

"Sorry," Cathi mumbled and snatched the granola.

Her grab knocked two boxes of an adjacent cereal into her cart. A tax for living half in this world and half in imaginary ones?

Not today. She tucked the extra cereal on the shelf in front of her and sped through the store, snagging the other items on her list.

Back home, after purchasing her family's sustenance for another week, Cathi settled at her desk and opened her laptop. When she woke the screen, the document for her novel popped up over the writing motivation quote serving as her desktop's background.

The cursor blinked. Accusingly? Cathi knew it mocked her inability to write the perfect ending for her book. The adult dystopian set in the bowels of the earth beneath the Roman Colosseum deserved a satisfying resolution.

When her hands flexed over the keyboard, her hapless brain focused on the diamond-shaped fruit and the wrinkled peddler.

"I have to finish this," Cathi told the droning idea.

The old woman cackled in her mind. *"What if the poison isn't meant to kill? What if it transforms instead?"*

Instead of banging her head against a nearby wall, Cathi started a new document. Her fingers flew over the keys, adding bullet points about the story seed, the red fruit, and the romantic angle.

Who eats the fruit? Does it help the shero transform into a shifter? Or can it force a shifter to stop transforming?

Three-thousand words and ninety minutes later, the story's compulsion fizzled. Maybe now she'd find inspiration for finishing her book.

Closing the brainstorming document, Cathi read the final two paragraphs of her novel written at the end of yesterday's session. Her fingers twitched. Creative juices surged like adrenaline. At last.

The front door slammed open. "Mom! Where's my uniform?"

Writing magic evaporated. Cathi's shoulders slumped. Time deposited her into real life.

It always happened this way. Imagination taunted her with sparkling new ideas when what she really needed was a perfect ending elsewhere. She hoped to pitch this novel to agents at a writer's conference in two months, which meant she needed to finish it. Now.

But the dystopian world's dull glow couldn't compare to the shine of the poisonous fruit and spellbinding romance. In fact, the old woman haunted Cathi through the uniform hunt and the drive to the high school softball field.

Later that night, while brushing her teeth, she tasted the bitter-honeyed flavor of the "poisonous" fruit. In place of her favorite reruns, she glimpsed her shero's villainous brother enacting wholesale shifter eradication. She stored that gold mine in the notes app on her smartphone.

In her dreams, Cathi's Spanish-speaking shero navigated the strange marketplace, pursued by red fruit and the howls of a werewolf. Or was it the growl of a tiger?

After her alarm roused her, she scrawled the remnants of the dreams in the pretty flowered journal on her nightstand. Those jots might keep the idea quiet long enough for her to finish the novel.

Once upon a time, she adored this secret geography in her mind. A landscape where boundaries blurred between reality and fiction. Where mundane coexisted with miraculous, and a stranger's casual comment birthed a new civilization. But when the circling ideas kept her from the finish line on her book, the adoration became frustration.

While she washed dishes the next evening, her mind wandered back to the shifter-human rivalry, and her subconscious supplied an answer about the magical fruit. She blurted, "It keeps them from transforming long enough to be killed by mundane means."

An elbow jabbed her ribs. Her daughter tossed her head, and her thick braid slapped Cathi's shoulder. The teenager held a damp skillet like a shield in front of her chest, and the drying towel sagged to her side.

"Are you even listening to me?"

Cathi opened her mouth to lie.

Her daughter's eyes widened and glistened. "You never listen! You're always in your stupid imaginary worlds. It's like I'm not even here."

Whoops. Living between worlds created plenty of tension in her family life.

"I'm sorry." And she was. "This new idea—"

"Forget it, Mom." Venom replaced her daughter's hurt, and silent sulking commandeered the kitchen while they finished cleaning the dinner dishes.

But that emotional charge sparked something. Cathi never understood exactly how unrelated elements suddenly snapped a story into place. But she didn't argue.

She rushed to her laptop and poured inspiration onto the page. Teenage angst fueled a thousand post-apocalyptic worlds, and finally, Cathi typed "the end." One novel finished at last.

"Fickle you may be," Cathi muttered to her muse, "but when you show up, it's dynamite."

And no matter how the flies swarmed, the mysterious realms inside her mind were more than an escape or insanity-maker. Heaven help her, they felt like a calling.

Now, off to see if she could have a real-life reconciliation with her teenager.

SEARCH FOR A HIDDEN WORLD

By Kevin Lay

"Resulted from a game I played to tell a story about something hidden without giving away what it was until the end."

et me tell you a story about writing a story. It's a story about a hidden world. From a writer's perspective, *every* story is hidden until it's written, and from the reader's perspective, that world is hidden until it's read. Being explicitly about a hidden world, I felt I needed to somehow write a story wherein what's hidden stays hidden until the end.

I honestly didn't know how to write about a hidden world without un-concealing it. I continued writing anyway.

Say a world is hidden in a book like the meat of a walnut. You break the story open, and there in each hand it lies exposed. Walnut nutmeats look like left and right hemispheres of a brain, each manifested with a particular solidity. Why did it grow exactly that way? Maybe my tongue could read it best, with the help of a few grains of salt.

But this line of thinking was driving me – I'll spare you the inevitable pun - nowhere. I had another idea.

Excited, I went to my imaginary storeroom of stories, flashlight in hand. I opened the door and switched on the light. At the edge of my vision a bundle of darkness skittered away. That's it! I thought. I was ready for it. I directed the beam of my flashlight to see but it was gone. *Hmmm*, it wasn't going to be so easy.

I switched off the lights and cooed to it. "Don't be afraid, little story. I won't hurt you."

After a minute or so, I pointed the flashlight where the shadow went. Were those glittering eyes, or momentary reflections of suspended dust? Over and over when I tried to see it, the story vanished from that spot and sparkled inside another shadow as if it avoided my focus, quick and very shy.

I *needed* this story. I decided to get a little more methodical and stepped back. There were my completed stories and poems resting on their shelves, disheveled and disordered. I read the titles along their familiar spines and aligned some of them a little more neatly. I saw my published works here and there displayed on their little pedestals, with little USB book-lights attached, illuminating their opening words. So pretty, I thought, there's room for more of those.

The floor was full of bins and boxes of notes and scribbles on envelopes and little books: unfinished things. If I were a hidden story, that's where I would live, I thought. I fetched a little saucer and left out an ounce of milk for it as an offering, sort of the way people used to leave food out for elves.I came back the next day to find the milk was gone.

It became clear that the story was not confined to my storehouse. Over the next few days, I repeatedly looked over my shoulder because something was watching me from a distance, not so much to see if I'm safe as to determine if I'm worthy. I fantasized that after enough time the story and I would grow familiar with one another enough that one morning it would casually reveal itself and let me capture it in a net of prose so loose it could easily escape. But for the moment, I was like a tourist with a camera strapped around my neck hoping to get a snapshot of a UFO or Sasquatch, except rather than a camera, it's my pen. Rather than a spectacle, it's a story.

According to Plutarch, Alexander the Great declared that the wisest, most intelligent beings are yet undiscovered. No doubt it's because they prefer to stay unseen. I realized I had been treating this story like a shy housefly. It was time to treat it with respect.

On a moonless night, I built a fire in a back field beneath the stars. Besides the hiss and crackle of burning wood, the silence held only a chorus of crickets and motors on a miles-off highway.

I practiced finding the most distant object the human eye can see: the Andromeda galaxy. I stared straight up at the bright rocking chair constellation called Cassiopeia and let its end stars point my attention to a greenish blur of light hovering a distance away in the black. I saw Andromeda only if I didn't look directly at it. Like the hidden story it vanished under my gaze, but was willing to emerge into my peripheral vision as a smudge of light. Unimaginable immensity!

I heard something in the grass. Was it the wind?

Between the edge of dark and the flickering firelight I swear I caught a glimpse of eyes. I had it totally wrong treating the story like a shy little spirit - perhaps it was a great being that was curious about me, about humans. Like a coyote or a wildcat, maybe the story crept up to the edge of the light, careful to remain on the side of darkness. I held my breath hoping to see again its wild, golden eyes.

My heart slowed down. I put more wood on the fire to expand the reach of the light - but it didn't help. Acrid smoke got into my nostrils. I let the fire die down, hoping I didn't squander some sparse accumulation of trust.

Out of gratitude and respect, I softly spoke out loud. "You are here, hidden one. I do not forget you. I do not abandon you."

Stars slowly circled in the sky. The crickets quieted. I let the fire dim and slept.

I dreamt I hung in space on a thread. The thread went right and left and attached to other, similar floating skeins. In the dream, I knew I'd made them all. I was a spider on a web I'd built to catch a hidden world. To my disappointment, the web was empty. Nothing struggled against the lines. I failed to catch anything. No world. No story. I decided to end my search and let go. All eight legs jumping away, I saw the situation whole.

My *search* was my hidden story. I'd been building it all along. Although obvious and plain, it was too close to be visible, and now at the end is revealed.

THE SECRET LANDSCAPE BEHIND YOUR FAVORITE BOOK

By Sharon Hughson

"Giving readers a 'look behind the curtain' at the hidden world of publishing based on my journey through its labyrinth."

Inside a writer's mind can be a scary place. Creativity runs wild. Dragons sunbathe on planets with two moons and buff romance heroes arm-wrestle shapeshifters over parking spots. That ordinary grocery run? It somehow involves international espionage and an explosion or two.

Chaos meets creative genius, right? And taming those mental universes into stories you want to read involves navigating a labyrinth most readers never see. A place where things get interesting (and expensive and occasionally soul crushing).

With over 20,000,000 titles in Amazon's catalog and 7,500 new e-books published daily by Kindle Direct Publishing (KDP), even the most captivating stories risk becoming lost in this twisting network of overwhelm.

This essay doubles as your GPS through the circuitous passages connecting imagination to publication (and wouldn't you rather have that than a ball of thread like Theseus?). Consider this a front row seat to the man—and woman—behind the curtain.

Ten Secrets Authors Know

When you pick up a book, you're holding treasure created during a quest fit for a mythological hero. And by treasure, I am talking about gold and precious stones. Your favorite novel might have cost its creator hundreds or thousands of dollars (along with blood, sweat, and tears) to bring to life. Talk about an expensive dream.

In 2015, I didn't care if I sold the first book I published. It was an experiment, a passion project about Mary of Nazareth meant to offer readers a fresh perspective. Should I consider it a success since my bank account hasn't recouped the cost of birthing it into the world? That book you'll find on Amazon? That pretty specimen is the second edition with its third cover, each revision adding to the mounting expenses. *Cha-ching!*

Secret #1: Every book costs money to create—yes, even that $1.99 e-book.

You like that professionally formatted book and its eye-catching cover, don't you? Who wouldn't? Guess what? Someone paid for that. Crisp, error-free text that keeps you invested in the story slogged through multiple rounds of editing.

For my first book, I invested in a line editor, proofreader, formatter, and cover designer. Four years later, I spent more money relaunching it with a new cover to match the series I'd written. *Cha-ching!*

A quality product doesn't always mean the author invested heavily in professional services, but too often if an author cuts corners, readers can tell the difference. A book that felt awkward to read or had a cover that screamed "amateur?" The author probably tried to navigate the design portion of publishing without following the thread to something other than a dead end.

The financial reality of producing a top-of-the-line book shapes your reading list. Many brilliant stories remain trapped in authors' minds because the writers can't afford to pay the piper. Because if they're like me, anything less than perfection isn't going to be shared in public.

You might assume authors write because they're making good money at it. The truth would surprise you.

I've been a full-time author for ten years. The only year I turned a profit came thanks to my side hustle—teaching and coaching—not book sales. You know what the IRS calls a business that doesn't turn a profit after three years? A hobby. Even the dozen romance novellas I published with small presses that hit Amazon's bestseller charts barely covered their production costs.

Which is why I laughed when a writer came to me for coaching with the solitary goal of being published to earn extra cash. As if.

Secret #2: Most authors aren't writing for the paycheck.

When I began writing, I was driven by pure joy—the thrill of bringing imaginary worlds to life. But publishing contracts brought pressure to write at certain speeds and to specific market requirements. The intricate tangle of commercial publishing can drain the passion behind the stories you love.

I lost touch with why I started writing and slid into creative burnout for years. Only when I remembered that original joy—when I stumbled out of the shadows and back to the center of the maze—did my creativity return. Now I write flash fiction for online magazines and return to those fantasy worlds that first captured my imagination.

The authors whose books move you? They're likely writing from that same deep well of passion. Your support as a reader helps them continue following their creative thread through the publishing labyrinth.

Your favorite author's mind probably overflows with story ideas. I have a spiral notebook and a few files on my computer that capture strays so I don't lose them. Most authors have more ideas than they will ever have time to write, which can be a squirrel on amphetamines that derails them from finishing their current story.

Which leads directly to the next secret.

Secret #3: Ideas are everywhere.

And I do mean everywhere. News story? Yes. Overheard conversation? For sure. Poorly executed movie or book? I have an idea (or ten) that would make it rock.

My brain conjures ideas from air, but not all of them have what it takes to become more than a short story. Some fizzle out after a meager few hundred words.

Consider these snippets. Are they meaty enough to carry through a full-length book? Would they find enough readers to make the investment of time and money producing them worthwhile?

1. Recently, a bit of dialogue set off my daydream meter. "Friends, choose to live." It's a line spoken by a Romulan assassin in the Paramount Plus series *Picard*.

   It reminded me of another famous line. "Hello. My name is Inigo Montoya. You killed my father. Prepare to die." (That's from *The Princess Bride*.) Story alert! What if these two men met and greeted each other with their signature salutations?

   Imagine an epic sword fight with flashing blades and dancing repartees. It ended—somehow—in a draw. Mutual respect won. Inigo says, "Friend, I choose to live and fight another day."

2. Once, a large toolbox in the back of a truck compelled me to say, "You could fit a body in there." The friend riding with me thought more than one would fit inside. And so my brain started concocting serial-killing landscaper scenarios.

   Strange. After all, I don't write mystery, thriller, or horror.

3. Ideas care nothing for genre preferences. During my first solo Uber ride, my story brain manufactured an alien body snatching that infested an entire cruise ship. With stories like this in my head, who needs to pay for streaming services?

Enough pages don't exist for me to recount the different sparks that lit a fire of creation in my imagination. Should enough paper or digital memory be found, I would chase another story squirrel. And another. Because new and shiny is always better.

Did you guess that none of these ideas are tales I penned? Maybe they never should be.

Secret #4: Not every story idea has what it takes to become a book.

Traditional publishers once served as gatekeepers, understanding market demands and selecting only the most viable stories. Even then, most published books sold fewer than 1,000 copies—barely enough to justify their existence.

Today's digital publishing maze has removed many gatekeepers, meaning more stories reach readers, but also more unpolished work. When you find a truly captivating book, you're discovering a story that survived both the author's internal editing process and the external standards of the publishing world.

That fantasy trilogy I spent years writing? Those six standalone novels gathering digital dust on my hard drive? They represent paths not taken in the maze—ideas that, for various reasons, never found their way to readers like you.

When you open a new book and immediately become immersed in the story, you're experiencing the magic of a completed creative journey. But what you're reading represents more than the final strand of Theseus's metaphorical ball of yarn.

Ideas alone don't create the books you love. Behind every page-turning novel lies months or years of disciplined writing, even when the author didn't feel inspired. Maybe especially then.

Secret #5: Finished books require more perspiration than inspiration.

That thrilling plot twist that kept you reading until 2 AM? It might have been written on an uninspired Tuesday morning when the author needed either more sleep or more caffeine. But they showed up to write anyway. Professional authors learn to work whether their muse cooperates or not.

I've discovered that consistency matters more than inspiration. When I show up regularly to put words on the page, eventually my muse arrives to "check out" my progress. Sometimes she enhances scenes without major changes. Other times, she demands complete rewrites because she is a story genius. And while I want to strangle her for being late to the party, I'm too busy hugging her for filling a plot hole.

Every writer navigates the labyrinth one word at a time, trusting that persistence will lead them—and ultimately you—to the story's heart.

That polished book in your hands survived multiple transformations before reaching you. I once heard an author say she went through every manuscript ten times before she sent it to her editor. Ten times! It made me tired, but I have enjoyed every one of her books.

The initial draft of any novel is like an entrance to the serpentine web—an accomplishment, but far from the destination. It's a piece of thread that leads to the dark and scary tunnels of rewriting, revising, and editing.

Secret #6: First drafts would horrify readers (even if they weren't horror stories).

Remember that author who did ten revision passes on her novels? That wasn't the end of her editing work.

Traditional publishing companies send acquired manuscripts through three distinct rounds of editing. First, developmental editors fine tune the story and character arc—because no one wants to fall into a plot hole. Once the author makes changes, a copy editor combs through the pages adjusting the prose, grammar, clarity, and consistency. After those fixes are approved by the author—because if the hero has blue eyes on page five, he should not have brown eyes on page 90—the manuscript is formatted, and a proofreader checks for any typographical errors or wonky layouts.

Some independent authors replace the first round of story development with unpaid input from alpha readers or critique groups. They save cash and still find the big problems with their story to fix. Others skip this round altogether, trusting their beta readers to ferret out any story issues.

You guessed it. Beta readers come next. Who are they? Genre enthusiasts like yourself who scrutinize the story for plot holes, pacing issues, and cardboard characters which leads to more rewriting and revising. Each adjustment of the text creates opportunities for new errors to creep in. Typos are sneaky little buggers.

The six-figure authors I know hire professional copyeditors. Once the work represents the author's best fully-edited effort, off to a proofreader it goes—and hopefully the typos are eliminated like ants in a mist of Raid.

This multi-step process explains why books cost money to produce and why some works feel incomplete. Their authors tried to shortcut the revision process. In the puzzling maze, some shortcuts aren't worth taking.

I love a well-crafted story without awkward sentences or plot inconsistencies. Doesn't everyone? That beauty is the result of a manuscript's long, winding, and often arduous journey from maze entrance to center. Minotaurs and traps aside, writers might use multiple skeins of thread during this process.

Here's something that might shock you: anyone can publish a book. If you wanted, you could jump on KDP, upload a document, and make it available for purchase within hours.

But those wannabe authors are so busy wondering if they can do it, that they don't stop to ask if they should. (Echoing the sentiment of Dr. Ian Malcolm in *Jurassic Park* here.) Like those genetic geniuses who shouldn't have cloned dinosaurs, people should think long and hard before publishing their first (or even second) draft of a book.

Secret #7: Anyone can publish a book on Amazon (and boy, do they ever).

Those writers who give self-publishing its somewhat disparaging reputation don't care about professional hoops. They're in a hurry to see their book in print and start earning (they hope) royalties. Amazon's self-publishing platform KDP accepts any manuscript, formats it automatically, and provides cover design tools. Just upload and publish with the press of a button.

Voila! It's magic. Except it really isn't.

While the digital age of publishing has leveled the playing field for a diverse array of authors, the lack of gatekeepers for quality control is one of its biggest detriments. Not that I want someone to decide what tropes and themes are selling (because who doesn't want another vampire romance?), but the traditional publisher's restrictive selection serves a purpose.

Some books need gatekeepers to limit access to publication because they are not ready for readers. I've started reading novels with three grammar errors in three pages, stories that wander through nonsensical plots (if they even have a plot), and books clearly needing professional editing to meet a conventional standard (which sometimes even the big publishing companies fail to meet). Maybe my English degree makes me extra picky, but I doubt I'm the only one who notices these pitfalls.

Amazon profits regardless of quality—the sooner books are published, the sooner their revenue arrives. Their motto might as well be "Publish first, ask questions never." (Well, not questions about the quality of a manuscript – but perhaps the ownership of its copyright. That's a different story altogether.)

This leaves you—the reader—as the final filter in the publishing labyrinth.

When you discover a self-published book that reads as professionally as any traditional publication, you've found an author who invested in guidance to properly navigate the knot of passages. They hired professional editors, designers, and formatters, understanding that readers like you deserve quality work. Or they spent time and effort learning to do these things right—which often meant a financial investment in book formatting software like Vellum or Atticus.

Many readers do judge books by their covers. And they should. Often, those amateurish designs signal less-than-stellar content within.

A top-grossing indie author often builds their own publishing team. They use the same editor and cover designer, exactly as a traditional house does with its employees. You benefit from the symbiotic relationship of these publishing professionals, and they keep each other in business, too.

Unfortunately, predators lurk in the labyrinth's shadows, waiting to exploit authors' dreams, and this affects which books reach you as well as the quality of said books.

When I started writing back in the 90s, only traditional and vanity presses existed. Today's digital landscape creates new opportunities but also new traps. Writer beware. Reader, read on to find out why you should care.

Secret #8: Scammers lurk in the shadows, and they're not picky about victims.

Like hungry velociraptors, vanity presses and many hybrid publishing companies contact unsuspecting authors with fake congratulations. "Your manuscript has been selected!" (Translation: "We accept literally everyone whose credit card isn't maxed out.") For the low, low price of $4,999, they'll guide you through their version of the labyrinth—straight into a dead end.

These companies control pricing and marketing for books they "publish," meaning authors lose control over how their work reaches you. Books become fodder for the feeding frenzy of these predators rather than making it to readers.

Wait, there's more! Even independent authors navigating the freelance maze must dodge the carnivore disguised as a good deal. Sure, I found a decent cover designer on the freelancing platform Fiverr who created lovely artwork for a fraction of traditional costs. But I also paid $100 to a "proofreader" who added unnecessary commas like confetti and caught maybe five actual errors. She needed a warning label: "Danger. Amateur Masquerading as Professional."

The savvy authors? They learn to distinguish between legitimate publishing professionals and Minotaurs in disguise. They connect with other writers who share their ball of thread, pointing them toward designers and editors who know their craft. This community support propels quality stories successfully from imagination to your bookshelf.

Behind every book you love stands its author and a community of writers supporting each other through the maze of publication.

Authors share general business knowledge, recommend professionals, and promote each other's work. This cooperation benefits you as a reader because it helps ensure quality books don't disappear but land on the bookstore shelf or in the library.

Secret #9: Authors are even bigger fans of each other than you are of them.

Go ahead, fangirl over that stellar author. Maybe they'll guide you to their favorite authors. Win for them. Win for you.

Writers in similar genres often cross-promote their work, meaning when you find one author you enjoy, they might introduce you to others who are comparable. This helps readers like you discover new voices and even more great stories.

I carefully curate these recommendations before offering them to my readers. I won't promote books I haven't read or don't genuinely endorse. If I recommend another writer's work, I'm sharing a professional opinion about what deserves your time and attention.

This collaborative spirit means authors don't view each other as competition. There are enough readers for everyone. Your reading preferences might not match every author's style, but somewhere in the publishing maze, a writer exists whose voice, tone, and storytelling will delight and excite you.

Every book you've enjoyed represents an author who refused to quit despite criticism, poor reviews, and well-meaning friends questioning their sanity. They continued navigating the labyrinth because they believed their stories deserved to reach readers like you.

Secret #10: Authors improve by continuing to write and publish—so you have more "good reads."

Your favorite author's latest novel probably surpasses their earlier work because they've honed their craft through experience. Each book taught them something new about storytelling, character development, or connecting with readers.

But let's face it, sometimes your favorite author lets you down. The story doesn't hit the mark. Or the characters feel like caricatures of something you've read before. And that's so disappointing, isn't it?

Don't give up on them. Everyone has an off year. Most authors aren't sharing their cancer journey or loss of a loved one with readers. If those life events throw you for a loop, you can be sure even bestselling authors get stuck in their shadowy tunnels.

As a reader, you have power—more than you might imagine. When you purchase books, write reviews, or recommend stories to friends, you help authors continue their journey through the dark halls of publishing trends. Not because they're reading your reviews (because some authors don't). No, your reviews bring attention to the books and that might attract more readers.

Even a one-sentence review like "Made me ugly cry on the subway" helps authors gain traction in algorithms. And every sale provides capital so writers keep writing, improving, and creating the stories that make you forget you have laundry to fold.

Final Thoughts on this Author's Journey

There you have it—spilled secrets. That book in your hands dodged more obstacles than a reality show contestant. Behind its polished pages lies a labyrinth of possible detours and dead ends that would send mighty Theseus to therapy.

Some paths required financial investment (goodbye, vacation fund). Others demanded creative persistence (hello, 4 AM writing sessions). All of them thrived from editorial refinement. The smartest route through? Community support and a subscription to really fine chocolate.

For an author, nothing is as simple as those first moments when dragons are sunbathing and romance heroes are settling disputes with arm-wrestling matches. Getting those buff shapeshifters and grocery-runs-turned-espionage from our overcaffeinated brains and into your hands requires navigating more knots and tangles than a kitten with a grudge against yarn.

Now you know how the magic happens. Stories that once lived only in a writer's imagination invade your world, ready to mess with your sleep schedule and send you head-over-heels for a fictional person.

The next time you're cursing an author for a cliffhanger or bawling your eyes out over a character's fate, remember: you're holding a treasure salvaged from chaos. One refined by its fiery journey through the perilous and twisted passages of publishing.

Doesn't that make it even more satisfying to read?

SCULPTOR'S SURPRISE

By David Fryer

"Inspired by the Michelangelo quote and the interface between science and art."

The old artist sat in a café enjoying a pastrami sandwich with the perfect mixture of mustard and mayonnaise. He ate slowly while a patch of sunlight moved across his plate and breadcrumbs accumulated.

As he finished, he paused, then scribbled on a notepad next to his plate. He ordered a white chocolate mocha with whipped cream. Finally, his protégé appeared.

"Sorry, I'm late. I was held up with work," the young artist said.

"Not at all. Just finished my sandwich." His advisor motioned to the seat opposite him at the table. "I got your text. What can I do for you?"

The protégé sat, then wiped his forehead with his sleeve.

"I've been having difficulty selling my art these days. The inspiration for my creation does not come easily. I was wondering how you dealt with this challenge as a young sculptor. How did you become such a success? Do you have any tips for me?"

The old artist leaned back, folded his hands across his stomach, and smiled.

"I got pretty lucky. When I was starting out, a geology professor visited me."

"A geologist? Huh, so they helped you pick out the best raw materials?"

"Not exactly. This geologist studied the Renaissance artist Michelangelo, who famously claimed that a sculpture was present within the stone, and his job as an artist was to remove the excess material."

The protégé leaned forward, placed his elbows on the café table, and said, "I've heard this. I think he was quoted as saying, 'Every block of stone has a statue inside it, and it is the task of the sculptor to discover it.'"

"That is true. Well, this geologist decided to start a service that would image marble blocks for sculptors. Using X-ray tomography, she would identify the statue inside the block of stone the sculptor was working on."

"Amazing! Did it work?"

"I was skeptical at first. So, I just gave her a small block of marble to scan. She left for a few days and came back. She told me, 'It's a squirrel.'"

"Did you believe her?"

The old artist sipped his mocha, then furrowed his brow as he set down the drink.

"Not at first. I asked to see the scan of the sample. We went to her lab on campus in the Geology building basement, and sure enough, the density map showed a clear profile of a squirrel. Somehow this shape was embedded in the material, waiting to be revealed."

"Remarkable. What did you do?"

"I picked up my hammer and chisel and, in the words of Michelangelo, revealed the masterpiece inside the stone over the next few weeks. It was one of my most popular pieces, and it launched my career. Squirrels are a symbol of resourcefulness and nature's abundance; it was a hot item in the gardening community." The old artist beamed.

"Was it the beginning of a long-term partnership?"

The advisor nodded, and his hands fell to his lap.

"I kept providing pieces for her to scan, and she would work her geology magic to identify the art inside the raw material. Things were going fine until I sent her a larger piece. She never got back to me."

His hands flexed under the table.

"By then, I was enjoying her company, and we were spending time outside of work together. Her disappearance was a double blow. The geology department office told me she had taken a sudden sabbatical and was unreachable."

"What happened?"

"They didn't say, but mentioned she was scanning my latest marble slab just before her departure. She booked a trip to Florence, the hometown of Michelangelo."

"Did you follow her there?"

The advisor nodded again and flashed a brief smile.

"I closed my studio and spent the summer in Florence, hoping our paths might cross."

The protégé tilted his head and raised an eyebrow.

"Well, did you find her?"

The old artist pursed his lips.

"I studied other works by Michelangelo in the city: the Statue of David, the Medici Chapel sculptures, but also his partially finished pieces, Atlas Slave and Awakening Slave. I haunted the geology departments of the local universities. But our paths never crossed."

His shoulders dropped, and his head bowed slightly.

"Finally, I booked a trip home. But on my last day in the city, as I was stopping for a cappuccino before leaving for the airport, I saw her."

"Wow, such good fortune. Did she explain her absence?"

The advisor shook his head.

"We simply had a coffee together and talked. It was good to see her and connect again. I realized my feelings for her ran deep. I courted her and we married that fall. On our honeymoon, I finally asked her why she left."

"And?"

The old artist rubbed his chin and looked out the window. His lips trembled.

"She said the image hidden in the depths of the stone was a depiction of two people in an embrace. The exact likeness of the two of us. Created when nature originally shaped the stone, several hundred million years ago. It was a masterwork of art, but she could not bring herself to show it to me. The revelation was too overwhelming."

The protégé did not respond. He sat back on the café bench. A fork rang against a plate at a nearby table. Finally, he spoke in a low voice, "To think the promise of your lives together was inscribed in the stones of the earth itself."

Their eyes met, and the older man's shone.

His protégé cleared his throat. "I don't recall ever seeing this piece. Did you sculpt it?"

The old artist tilted his cup and drained his mocha. "I didn't. The whole enterprise made me wonder: are we revealing art, or just following instructions? So, I stopped using the scans. Art, I decided, should surprise even the artist."

His young companion considered this. "Extraordinary. I can see what the experience has taught you. In art as in life, the search for inspiration is as important as the discovery."

"Agreed," the old artist said.

He pulled a bill from his wallet for the meal. Then he stood, clapped his protégé on the back, and they left the café together.

THE RED SETTEE

By Cate Cross

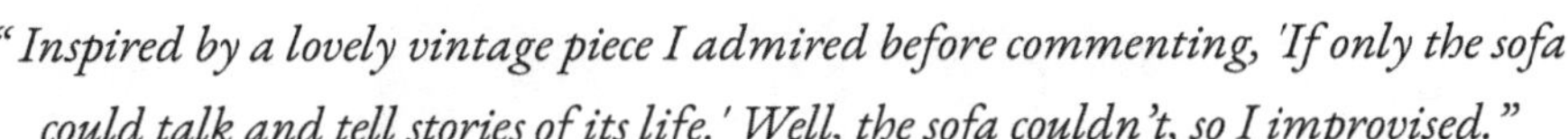

" Inspired by a lovely vintage piece I admired before commenting, 'If only the sofa could talk and tell stories of its life.' Well, the sofa couldn't, so I improvised. "

A woman breathed her last goodbye,
Then drifted off into the sky.
Left behind was not too much;
Some worn-out clothes; an old red couch.
The couch had seen better days.
The clothes were ready to part their ways.

But if hidden worlds could be told,
The couch would start with days of old—

When it was built by rugged hands,
Then shipped away to another land.
Into a room with lighted sign,
Where someone claimed, "That couch is
mine."

Onto a truck, into a house,
The couch was greeted by a spouse.
"We have a settee," the lady said.
"You shan't be using it for a bed."

The settee seated many a guest,
Sometimes even a sudden mess.
A cake, a crumble, a sour tart.
A piece of taffy, a sneaky fart.
A salty sprinkle, a splash of wine.
A naughty cat claw on its spine.

The settee's velvet, now thinned-out
plush.
It's vibrant red, now faded flush.

With owner gone and none to seat,
The couch was taken to the street.
Above the back, pinned to a tree,
A sign was written: THIS COUCH IS
FREE.

The settee worried its time had come,
Until it felt a squishy bum.
"This couch is perfect," the woman said.
"I really *love* the color red."

Into a truck and down the road
The settee went to another abode.
Over a threshold gilded gold,
The settee's secrets remain untold.

HIDDEN WORLDS OF FANTASY

A WORLD THAT WAS

By Dawn Shipman

"Exploring the mythos of the long-forgotten homeland briefly mentioned in my trilogy—the world Argonia's ancestors left behind."

The downhill slope rippled and shook beneath Karwin's feet, causing the young boar's carcass to shift on his shoulder. Scrambling to maintain his footing and not lose the heavy load, Karwin skidded down the gyrating hillside, sliding to a rest against a jagged, hut-sized boulder. Rocks, loosened by the earth's upheaval, bounced down the trail behind him. One—larger than a winter squash—narrowly missed his head as he clambered around the boulder for refuge.

Shucking the boar at his feet, he braced himself against the boulder and waited, panting. The earth's convulsions and the rockslide continued. The pine trees along the ridgeline he'd just descended swayed violently. Finally, all was quiet, but dust wafted in the aftermath of the quake, and mixed with it, smoke. Karwin moved from the shelter of the boulder and stared up at the nearest mountain, Mount Zelle—or *our* mountain—as the inhabitants of South Village called it. The winter snow had long since melted, but streamers of smoke drifted from between its highest peaks into the sky.

Gazing north, he saw several smaller, quieter peaks, but the largest and farthest away, Mount Bane, loomed darkly under a constant cloud cover, as it had for some time now.

Things had been wrong in their land of Smyrna for weeks. This was the reason he'd left his boat moored in the harbor this day and climbed into the hills to investigate. Smoke spewed from their mountains, and the earth shakes were occurring more often—though this one had been the worst. What could it mean?

Dread gripped his gut. Gritting his teeth, he adjusted his bow and quiver of arrows on one shoulder and made certain his sword rested firmly within its sheath at his hip. Returning to the protective boulder, he wrestled the boar onto his back and returned to his path down the hill.

By the time the hillside leveled out, the sun blazed high through the hazy sky, and the straggling huts that marked the outskirts of his village came into view. Beyond those, the sea sparkled in its ever-present, never-silent way. The source of his life, of his family's life, for generations.

"Da!" Elma, his golden-haired firstborn, rushed toward him. Stopping before him, his daughter lifted her eyes to the load he carried. She frowned, her expression the very image of her mother's when Janna was put out with him about something. "What is that, Da?"

He tousled the yellow curls. "You've seen wild pig before. We've eaten it. Don't you remember?"

"Maybe." Her scowl grew deeper. "Did I like it?"

"Yes, you did." He grinned. "And you'll like it again this time. Your ma will turn it into something delicious. Where is she, anyway?"

Still frowning, Elma turned and trotted toward their cabin. "In the garden, of course. Come on!"

He followed his daughter to their little homestead. In the six years since he and Janna had wed, she had turned the shanty into a thing of beauty. Fresh thatch on the roof, flowers planted in the front for no other reason than his wife thought them "pretty." Vegetables thrived behind the cabin, along with the fruit trees she'd brought from her parents' orchard in North Village.

The sea was Karwin's life. Making his living from it was difficult, sometimes dangerous, but he'd thought it was a good life.

He hadn't known what a good life was, what *home* was, until Janna came to it.

She emerged from the cabin now, wheat-colored hair pulled back, cradling eighteen-month-old Jabin, a smile wreathing her lovely face. "There you are, you good-for-nothing," she chided gently. "I wake up this morning, and you are gone, but the boat is moored safely in place, doing nothing useful! Oh!" She slapped a hand against her mouth, eyes huge. "What have you brought us?"

His grin returned. If she wasn't carrying their son and he wasn't carrying a dead pig, he'd gather her into his arms. Hold her tight until she squealed.

She stood before him, eyes closed, inhaling deeply. "My, oh, my! He doesn't smell so good now, but I can change that soon enough. Where did you get him?"

"Far side of the ridge." He lugged the boar behind the cabin and dumped it on the clean-swept earth. "I went up to...well, to check out the lay of the land," he mumbled awkwardly, "and I thought some venison would make a fine meal, but this fellow came along first." He put an arm around her and hugged her tight.

Jabin struggled, and Janna pulled back, smiling. "And did this fellow come willingly at your invitation? Or was there an argument?"

"Oh, he had plans of his own, I think, and he became right unhappy when I put that first arrow in him. He came on the run, then. I put another couple of arrows in and slowed him down a little but still needed my da's old sword at the end. Sure glad I had it."

Janna went up on her tiptoes, kissing him noisily. "Me, too." She sank down, her sea blue eyes becoming serious. "Did you feel the shake?"

"I did." He sighed. "The biggest one so far. And there's smoke from the mountain again. *Our* mountain, as well as Mount Bane."

A frown wrinkled her brow. "I'm worried for my folks. Mort came by. Everyone's talking."

"Did he say anything about Roj and Vince? Have they returned?"

Her face fell. "He didn't say, so I assume they have not."

Karwin took the squirming Jabin from his mother, tossing him into the air. The child squealed his delight at this. Karwin forced a smile, but his mind had journeyed far away. Two weeks ago, great plumes of smoke had been seen billowing from Mount Bane, the peak that shadowed North Village, four days' ride away. That mountain and its village were at the end of the post road that connected the three villages of the land of Smyrna. The post rider who'd been on his monthly trek hadn't returned, so brothers Roj and Vince struck out to see what they could find.

They should have been back by now, along with the post rider. And now smoke was spewing from their own mountain.

Janna leaned over, ruffling Elma's golden hair. "Run, get Oma Treva, please, young lady. Uncle Miles, too, if he's around. If we want a good pork supper tonight, your Da and I need help with this pig."

The child raced off to the far boundary of the family property, and Karwin set Jabin down, who toddled straight to the bristly carcass.

Janna rolled her eyes. "I hope Oma hurries!"

Despite his dark thoughts, Karwin smiled and retrieved the large scalding cauldron from the cabin's porch. He set it in front of the well and returned for the largest of the meat cleavers, a scraping blade, and boning knives. Janna laid the wood for the fire and filled the cauldron with water. Moments later, hand-in-hand with Elma, Karwin's mother, Treva, arrived.

"I'm told I'm needed," she called, sweeping loose strands of graying hair back into its bun. "Ooh, look what you have there. Miles is out on the water, and I was just putting the bread in the oven." Seeing Karwin approaching the boar, meat cleaver in hand, she swept in ahead of him and grabbed Jabin. "Come along, my fine man. Your ma and da have work to do."

Hours later, his brother Miles, a younger, dark-haired image of Karwin himself, according to everyone in the village, strode up to the cabin just as a harsh clanging rang through the evening air. Miles crossed his arms and sniffed appreciatively at the roast pork, new-baked bread, green beans, and fire-roasted potatoes. Then he turned to Karwin, shrugged, and scowled. "Roj and Vince just got back. Town meeting at Mort's as soon as everyone can get there."

Karwin sucked in a deep breath and turned to the women. "Save us some. We'll try to hurry."

"Hold on." Janna skewered a slab of pork for both men, wrapped them in slices of fragrant bread, and handed them over. "Now you can go."

"Thanks, darlin'." He kissed her, and he and his brother strode down the worn pathway that led to the public house, joining the group of men gathered outside.

Mortimer Bean, owner of the pub and self-appointed elder-in-charge, faced the crowd. "Gather round, everyone. You'll need to hear this."

Karwin and Miles elbowed into the crowd, just as Mort waved two other men forward. Roj and Vince, brothers who ran the trading post with their wives, stepped up onto the public house's porch, turned, and faced the assembly. Gasps and murmurs echoed throughout the group. New streaks of white ran through Roj's bronze-colored hair, and dark circles underscored the eyes in both men's lean, pale faces.

Roj, the older brother, raised an arm. "We're all right. I know we look bad, but we're not hurt." He gulped, his Adam's apple rising and falling. He glanced at his brother, then back to the crowd. "It's what we've seen and…what we have to tell you." His eyes darted from side to side, then he swiped a hand over his face. "It's bad." For a long moment, he stood silent, as though confused. Finally, with a defeated shrug, he gestured to his brother.

Vince nodded and turned to the crowd. "North Village is gone."

Karwin's heart plummeted as the crowd erupted into disbelieving shouts and strangled curses.

Vince lifted his hand, pleading for silence. "It's gone. Mount Bane…blew up." He lifted both hands, then let them fall. "I don't know what else to call it. There's a big chunk torn right out of it near the top. It looks like a huge wind swept out of the mountain and…flattened everything in its path. Trees, buildings, the town. Most everything for miles around is covered in that gritty, sandy stuff that started falling here a few weeks back." He raked a hand through his thick, shaggy hair, swallowing heavily. "We think it's ash from the mountain."

"But what about the people?" someone shouted.

Vince's face, already pale, turned ashen. "Except for a few who were visiting kin at Center Village, we couldn't find anyone. Center people have been looking, too."

Karwin's knees felt weak beneath him. Janna's family…

"Was Center Village hit, too?" someone called.

"They felt it—way more than we did—but the worst of the damage stopped a half-day's walk from them. Many had friends and family in North Village." Vince stopped, looked to his older brother, then back to the crowd. "As we did. Our mother and grandparents."

"What about Mattin?" someone else asked, naming the post rider who'd left weeks before.

Again, Vince shook his head. "He'd been in Center Village two days earlier. Left for North. No one's seen him since."

Murmurings broke out in the crowd, and Karwin's gut clenched, but he had to ask. "Has Sue-Ann been told?" Mattin's wife, the mother of a young son, was Janna's best friend in the village.

"My missus is with her now," Mortimer said grimly. "Offering what comfort she can."

How could this be? Karwin covered his ears with his hands, as if that would change the things he didn't want to hear. An entire village leveled? Hundreds of ordinary people, just gone? Disbelief shot through his mind.

"And now our mountain's smoking," someone at the back of the crowd shouted. "Is whatever happened to Mount Bane going to happen here, too?"

This was the reason Karwin had abandoned his boat today and climbed up into the hills, even before knowing what happened at North Village. He hadn't been able to shake the gnawing dread that something was terribly wrong. He raised his hand, forced himself to speak over the shouting and questions. "What are the people in Center Village going to do? Mount Bane hasn't settled down, and Mount Zelle is..." There was no reason to go on.

Roj seemed to have mastered himself and stepped forward. "They're scared to death. Many are speaking of moving inland, getting as far from the mountains as they can, but it's not great land there, either, and a lot of folks don't want to start over somewhere else."

"They'd rather stay there and die?" Miles demanded.

Roj sighed. "They're hoping this is the end of it, that the mountain has had its say and will quiet down now. That things will go back to how they were before."

"And they're willing to risk their lives on their…wishful thinking?" Miles burst out. Several of the younger men in the crowd voiced noisy agreement.

"And what about us? Our mountain's…angry…or something, too." The voice was Emely Vance, a widowed mother of two teenagers. "What are we going to do?"

That was the question, wasn't it, Karwin thought. *What could they do?*

Silence reigned for a long moment, then Roj, his voice shaking, spoke. "All I know is you can't fight the mountain. No matter how long I live, I'll never forget what I saw at what used to be North Village."

Vince reached over and patted his brother's shoulder.

"I think the folks in Center Village have it right," Mort said, after a moment. "They've had longer to think about it than we have. We can stay here and take our chances. Our mountain may just be growling sympathy for his brother up north." He shrugged. "Or we can pack up, best we can, and head inland. Start over someplace else, away from the mountains."

"And away from the sea?" Karwin asked. "From the only life some of us have ever known?"

"But if we're gonna die here—" Miles broke in.

"Now, now," said an unfamiliar voice in the back of the crowd. "Let's hold up here for a bit. I think we're all jumping to conclusions."

Everyone turned, seeking the speaker. Karwin frowned. Narsel Giles, the largest landowner in the area and owner of the only lumber mill. The man rarely attended the town meetings, using his influence, many people thought, to simply overrule any decisions he didn't like later on.

"I'm sure sorry this happened up at North Village," Giles said, waving a hand at Roj and Vince, "But there's no guarantee anything like that will happen here. Nothing's hit Center, and we've had these little earth shakes here from time to time. I remember my da talking about them way back when." He shrugged. "These are our homes. I say we hold tight and see what happens."

"Maybe the folks in North Village waited," Jeb, another fisherman, called out. "Look where it got them!"

"It's just a thought." Giles shrugged again. "You all do as you see fit. But leaving your homes and trying to start over somewhere else is a tough row to hoe. I just wanted to say that so everyone could hear."

Karwin frowned. *What was the mill owner up to? As if anyone would pull up roots and start over somewhere else if they didn't have to.*

"There's another possibility," a quiet voice spoke.

All heads turned, focusing on the grizzled, gray-bearded form of Thomen, a retired fisherman and one of the oldest of the villagers. "My grand-da came from the sea. Washed up on the shore when he was just a lad. His ship had been blown off course, and he wanted to go back, but then he met my Oma, and he never did go back. But till his dying day, he swore that land was out there and was green and beautiful. He called it Argonia." Thomen turned his watery blue eyes upon the men gathered around him. "I've never forgotten my grand-da's stories. We could go to the sea. We could look for Argonia."

❦

Hours later, Karwin lay at Janna's side and held her while she wept.

He'd met this lovely woman seven years earlier while taking his turn as post rider, a task required of all men of age in the three villages. He'd dropped off supplies at Center Village, then made his way to North, to do the same and pick up trade items and mail going back to Center and to his own village, South, by the sea. His father had been struck with fever and died the year before, leaving him, at nineteen, in charge of the family fishing business. He resented any time spent away from the sea and the support it provided for his mother and younger brother.

But the rules were the rules.

He'd stopped at the only inn in North Village, and his earlier frustration melted away when the innkeeper's comely daughter delivered his meal and smiled at him. For the next five months, the days couldn't pass quickly enough before it was time for him to set out again. And at the end of the six months, more terrified than he'd ever been in a storm at sea, he'd asked her to marry him.

Grinning mischievously, she'd said she'd have to think on it, then, at his fallen expression, threw her arms around his neck and said, "Yes."

Later, her father had slapped him on the back, welcoming him to the family, and he'd gained a new mother and sisters, as well.

And now they were all gone.

The lovely little village with its grazing sheep, fruit trees, and happy memories on the flanks of the splendid Mount Bane.

Gone. All of it gone.

And their tough little fishing village could be next.

Janna's sobs slowed and turned to gulps. She turned over, swiped her sleeve across her eyes, and stared at the underside of their thatched roof. "What will we do now? Our mountain is doing the same thing Mount Bane did months ago. Are we next?"

He reached over and took her hand, told her everything he'd heard at the meeting. She tried to listen—he could see it in her eyes—but her heart was far away with the family she'd never see again.

She shook her head and exhaled slowly. "People are really planning to leave?" She narrowed her gaze, bit her lip. "So our choices are to stay here and hope for the best, to cross the mountains and head inland—where there are more mountains—or to take to the sea and look for the mythical land of Argonia."

She'd been listening more closely than he'd thought. "I don't think Argonia is mythical," he murmured. "A lot of people laughed after Thomen said his piece, but when I was just a lad, Thomen would stop by to chat with my da, and he'd tell his grand-da's stories. I think Da believed him, and I know *I* believed him."

He shook his head. "A few of the elders there tonight remembered Thomen's grand-da's tales, and some of them believed them, but it's a long way across an ocean none of us have sailed."

"I don't want to leave our home," Janna cried. "I love our home, but I don't want to die, to have our children die. I don't want to be buried by the mountain."

"Neither do I, but—." A commotion outside the cabin stopped his words.

"Karwin?" His brother called. "It's me and Ma. Let us come in."

He disentangled himself from the bedding and headed to the door, Janna right behind him.

He could see at a glance that Miles and his ma had been having the same conversation he and Janna had just had. His mother was pale and her eyes glazed with tears, but she pushed past him and ran to Janna, throwing her arms around her. "Oh, my dearest, I am so sorry. So very sorry."

Miles grabbed Karwin's arm and drew him toward the door. The two stepped into the darkness. Miles dropped Karwin's arm and swung his own as he paced back and forth. "What're we gonna do? We have to do something."

Karwin nodded, though in the dark it wasn't likely his brother could see him. "I know."

"We can't wait!" At twenty, Miles was more impetuous than Karwin had ever been, but in this case, he was right. Everything they'd heard this night told them any delay could prove disastrous. Land or sea? There were no good answers. And Janna didn't want to leave.

"This whole land is mountainous, wherever you look," his younger brother went on. "We could move inland and die there by exploding mountains just like we can if we stay here. We could go to the sea—"

"I know, but Miles—We have *fishing boats*!" Karwin slammed his hand against the cabin wall. "*Fishing boats!* And we've both been at sea when storms came up. We've nearly died there any number of times. If we had time to build something bigger, well, maybe we might find somewhere to land safely, make a new life." He raked his hands through his hair. "But we don't have time for that. You and I have our boats, Jeb and Smith, Granger and Mitch have theirs, six, total. How're we going to take a whole village out of here? We can't."

Miles stopped him, breathing deeply. "This isn't storm season. And we wouldn't be taking everyone. You heard them. A lot of people want to stay here, take their chances. Others want to go inland." His dark eyebrows narrowed. "They're afraid, but not afraid enough. They haven't seen what Roj and Vince have. Did you see their faces?"

"Yes!" he nearly shouted, pushing himself away from the cabin. "I need to think."

He strode away from his small but much-loved home. There were no good decisions. None. The sea had been his life, providing food and a living for him since childhood, but how could he take his wife and children out onto its treacherous waters?

True, it wasn't the season for the big storms, but with the open ocean, there were no guarantees. There were islands out there—he'd seen them, walked on a few. But they were small and would provide scant protection from ocean storms. They could drop anchor and take refuge for a short time, if necessary, but those little islands couldn't provide a home. And how far was this hidden land of Argonia from those last islands? Even his father, who had fished these waters for decades, had never seen any sign of it.

Of course, the waters around Smyrna were rich with fish, crab, and lobster. Clams were plentiful on shore. There had never been reason to travel beyond those outlying islands. Only a few—the young, adventurous types like his brother—had ever bothered going farther. They had everything they needed right here, and could trade for whatever else they desired with Central and North Villages.

Still, he couldn't shake those long-ago talks with Thomen from his memory. One time, his da had been out on the boat, and he'd been left behind, mending nets. Thomen had stopped by. Even then, the man seemed old to him, but he remembered the light in his eyes when he spoke of his longing to find that land his grand-da had so loved.

Reaching the trail that led to the cabin he'd grown up in, where his mother and Miles still lived, Karwin whirled and paced back. Janna didn't want to leave, and what she wanted mattered. He could hear Miles' impatient stamping next to the cabin, but he stopped on the path, stared up at the waxing half-moon. It would be full in a few days. And then what? Would any of them be here to appreciate its silvery beauty?

Janna loved the full moon. She'd told him, long ago, when they sat together watching it on the grassy hillside behind her parents' house. The house and the people that no longer existed....

He huffed in a breath, looking wildly around him. Was that...? And then there was no doubt. He grabbed hold of a nearby sapling, braced his feet, and felt it clearly—the rise and fall of the land beneath his feet. Voices cried out in the dark, lanterns swayed in nearby cabins. Village dogs howled and still the earth shook. In the forest, a ripping, wrenching sound tore through the air, and an echoing crash told the rest of the story. One of the ancient firs had been heaved from the ground.

"Karwin? Where are you?" Janna's voice, high, frightened.

"Here!" Stumbling over the quivering terrain, he raced to the shuddering cabin, and wrapped her in his arms. The quaking intensified, the ground bucking beneath them like an untrained colt. A bouquet of garden flowers in their earthenware vase slid across the table and fell, shattering on the floor. And suddenly the cabin itself was wrenched to the side, tipping. The lantern swung wildly from the ceiling's inner beam, and from the back room both children wailed for their mother.

"I'll get them," Oma Treva called, and slipping across the jerking floor, hurried to the children.

The shaking subsided, but the terror remained, and soon their neighbors' cries and curses filled the darkness outside. Miles thrust his head into the cabin's open door. "It's shoved your place clean off the foundation. You better grab the kids and get out—the roof could come down."

Standing in the darkness moments later, they stared at the ravaged cabin. Inside, their little lantern shone bravely from its chain, but a final upheaval tore the beam it rested on from the wall, taking the lantern with it. Crashing to the floor, the flame lasted a brief moment, then hissed and went out.

Clinging tightly to Jabin, Janna sucked in a deep breath, sat down next to the outdoor fire pit, and wept.

<hr />

The sun, when it rose, shone down on destruction. Three homes had collapsed completely; others had lost roofs or side walls. Fires, from lanterns knocked down during the quake, destroyed the better part of two homes. People had been injured, but none had died.

That was the only good news, Karwin thought grimly. Above and behind them all, a thin stream of smoke wafted around Zelle's highest peak, as if it were withholding its mirth at their troubles only with great difficulty.

Hands on hips, Karwin surveyed the damage to his home. It could be mended, he knew, but why? So it could be completely destroyed next time, perhaps with them inside? No matter how hard he tried, he couldn't get Vince's words out of his mind: *North Village is gone. Flattened. Buried.*

They couldn't stay here. He couldn't allow his family to suffer the same fate as those in the north.

Villagers rose from their bleary-eyed sleep, disheveled and frightened, some from within their cabins, others, like he and his family, from the relative safety of the outdoors. Miles and their mother had returned to their own cabin, which was relatively undamaged. The children still slept, but Janna was up, stoking the fire in the outdoor pit to heat water for their morning tea. As if this were the start of any normal day.

"I'm going for a walk," he told her. "Be back soon."

She lifted an eyebrow tiredly, then shrugged.

He paced along the winding pathway through the village, searching for a certain hut, hoping it still stood, that its owner still lived. Along the way, he passed villagers—young and old, men and women alike—staring in various stages of disbelief at their damaged homes and property. He didn't stop to talk, finally finding the cabin he sought. It was older than many, broken down and rebuilt many times, but still standing. A wooden carving of a large sailing ship perched against the cabin's rock wall, and next to it, whittling knife in hand, sat the man whose thoughts Karwin needed.

"Pull up a seat." Thomen grinned, pointing to the chopping block next to him.

Karwin sat, stared at the carving of the sailing ship a long moment, then turned to the old man. "Do you really believe Argonia exists?"

Thomen eyed him steadily. "Without doubt."

"Can we find it?"

The old man nodded. "I believe we can."

Anger, fear, and frustration burst from Karwin. "Then why didn't YOU go look for it? Why wait until now? I've got a wife, children. I can't risk them out there on some fairytale!"

The light faded from Thomen's eyes. "I wanted to, but I had a wife and children, too. They were happy here, and they never loved the sea like I did. When Essie died—" He paused, grabbed a short branch from the stack of firewood next to him, and started chipping at it. "After she passed, the kids moved to Center Village—thank the Maker they didn't go to North—and it was just me. I took the boat out a time or two, got out to some of those outer islands, then...just stopped."

"Why?"

Thomen's eyes shuttered, and he turned his attention back to the wood in his hand. Running the knife's blade along its length, he peeled the bark from the light-colored fiber beneath. He paused, staring at the wood, and a grimace ran across his lined face. "Because I was already old. I couldn't fight the sea by myself anymore. I'd waited too long."

"And why should we do this now?" Karwin finally asked. "Why should we seek this lost land? Why not just go inland?

"You can if you want to. Is that what you want?" The old man's glare held him. "I can't answer that for you. All I know is this village is no longer a safe place to live. Mt. Zelle is gonna blow—I feel it in my bones." He looked up from his whittling, stared hard at Karwin. "Now you listen up--because this is important. I'm old. If I die at sea, it won't be the worst thing that can happen. That may not be true for you."

No, it wasn't true for him. Karwin pondered Thomen's words as he strode home later. His possible death at sea had never troubled him. As a fisherman, he'd long resigned himself to the fact that it could happen. Putting his wife and children in that position, though, was another thing altogether.

Miles and his mother were sitting at the fire with Janna when he arrived. Neither looked like they'd slept much.

Miles eyed Karwin. "Where've you been?"

Karwin accepted the mug Janna handed him. "Talking to Thomen."

Janna looked up, stared at him through tired, empty eyes. "You've made a decision, then?"

"No, but I'm closer." He glanced at the lopsided cabin. "I know you don't want to leave, but we can't stay here. Not after last night. And—" He gazed at her, hoping she'd understand. "Thomen is sure we can find Argonia, and I'm pretty sure it's out there somewhere, too." He hesitated, then glanced from her to Miles and their mother. "I don't want to go inland—what would we do there to live? I will, though, if that's what you all want."

Miles opened his mouth, but Karwin waved him away. He already knew his adventure-loving brother's opinion. It was Janna's support he sought.

She bit her lip and looked away. "Wrecked or not, I love our home."

"We will find a place to build a new one," he said softly. "I promise."

Eyes flashing, she snorted and jumped to her feet. "You can't make that promise!"

He gazed up at her. "I can promise to try. I can promise to do everything possible to make it happen."

She stared at him for a long moment, then stepped away and bent to pluck a violet blossom from her tiny flower garden. She held it to her face, closed her eyes, and inhaled deeply. When she turned back to him, her face was pale, but there was a light in her eyes he hadn't seen since before the big quake. "Well, as long as you promise, I guess we'll come along."

Treva leapt to her feet. "Janna! Are you sure?"

Janna held up her hand, her smile broadening as she looked at Karwin. "Yes, I'm sure." She turned to her mother-in-law. "As long as you'll come, too. You will, won't you?"

The older woman hissed out a deep breath. "Of course. But if we all die, I'll never forgive any of you!"

From behind them all, Miles let out a huge whoop.

⸺◆⸺

A short time later, a raucous clanging burst through the morning stillness.

Karwin stood. "Sounds like Mort's ready for us." Shoving a final chunk of bread into his mouth, he waved at his brother, and the two strode down the pathway toward Mort's place.

The solidly built public house appeared to have survived the quake better than most. Mort stood on the tiny porch, a cooking pot in one hand and a hammer in the other. Narsel Giles stood at his side. Other men and a few women—Emely Vance and Janna's friend Sue-Ann—emerged from the woods and joined the gathering crowd in front of the pub.

"I know we're all upset at what happened last night," Mort began, "but Mr. Giles came to me this morning, asking to have a word with you all first thing. Since he's been here longer than most, I thought that was only fitting." He stood back and turned toward the other man.

Giles stepped forward. "I'm so sorry, folks, for everything that's happened here. Nothing like this has occurred in anyone's memory, or has been passed down from our ancestors, but we were lucky. I know some of you lost houses, some folks got hurt, and a bunch of our animals disappeared into the forest, but no one died, and it's entirely possible that rumble last night is the end of it all."

"Are you out of your mind?" someone in the back shouted. "After the news we got yesterday from North Village?" The crowd gathered around the speaker grumbled their agreement.

"Now, now," Giles said, lifting his hand for silence. "What happened at North was terrible, but we don't know there's any connection with that and our...incident last night. It may be entirely unrelated. Most of us have been here a long time, and those who need to can rebuild. We'll all help. That's what neighbors do. We'll go into the woods, find those runaway critters, and bring them back. We can start over."

Karwin stared at the mill owner in disbelief. A quick glance around at the crowd showed he wasn't the only one.

"We can't start over if we're all dead," Miles shouted. "Those people in North didn't have a chance to rebuild. We'd be fools to stay here when our mountain is smoking and the ground beneath our feet is knocking our houses down."

Giles scowled. "All I'm saying, Miles, is that some of us are staying. *I'm* staying, and I know there's others who don't want to leave, either. This is our home." A number of the men standing near Giles nodded in agreement. "My family was one of the earliest to settle here—I don't know how many generations back—and I'm not leaving. I was born here, and I'll die here...one way or another."

"Well, that's fine for you, Mr. Giles," Roj said quietly, "but we're going to get as far from these mountains as we can. We've talked to a lot of folks, and a bunch of us are heading west, away from the sea. Away from the mountains."

"There are mountains over there, too," Karwin pointed out.

Roj sighed. "I know, but they seem quieter than these closer to the sea."

"So," Giles said. "Some of you are heading west, leaving your homes behind. And I'm guessing some of the rest of you, thanks to old Thomen and his wild stories," he sneered at the old man in the midst of the crowd, "are thinking about taking to the sea—looking for the fabled land of *Argonia*." He snorted. "*Dying at sea is a lot more likely*."

Karwin frowned at Giles. He glanced at Miles, who shrugged, a pained expression on his face.

"Well, you're free to go, of course," Giles went on, "but there's something I need to remind you of." The tone in the mill owner's voice drew everyone's attention. "A lot of you owe me money." He scanned the gathering. "You know who you are. You've borrowed to buy land from me, borrowed to build your cabins, borrowed to get your businesses going. Unless you pay me in full before you leave, I'll have no choice but to take your land, your cabins, everything you leave. If you ever want to come back, you'll have no place to come back to."

"You can't do that!" a man in the back shouted.

Giles nodded at several burly men standing at the side of the crowd. "I can, and I will, Mr. Munce," he said, as the men formed a circle around him. "These men here are my employees at the mill. Some of you know them. If there are any problems with me collecting my rightful property, they will...assist me." He glanced at the furious villagers. "Just something else to keep in mind if you're still considering turning tail and leaving your life—and your debts—behind."

Surrounded by his brawny workers, the mill owner pushed his way through the crowd and strode away.

Stunned silence filled the clearing, then erupted as dozens of men spoke at once.

Karwin stepped forward, raising his hand. Thankfully, he didn't owe the man money, but that didn't help those who did. "Hold up, everyone. Calm down." After a few minutes, they did. "We need to remember who the real villain is." At this, even the angriest stopped their muttering and turned to Karwin. "As...unpleasant as Mr. Giles is—"

"*Unpleasant*!" one of the men roared. "What kind of man does something like that to folks who are already down and broken?"

Karwin raised his hand again. "I know, I know, but he's just a man. The real enemy is there." He pointed to the mountain behind him. "It's completely unpredictable. And more powerful than any man. You saw what happened last night. And we know what happened at North Village." He sighed. "And did you really think you were coming back?" He shook his head. "Pretty sure I'm not."

The crowd was quiet once more. "You're going to the sea, then, Karwin?" a voice finally broke the silence.

"I am, Thomen. My brother and I and our family." He looked closer at the old man. "And you, if you'll join us. We'd like to have you help us find your grand-da's homeland. Are you with us?"

Thomen's watery eyes grew bright, and he stood up straighter than anyone had seen him. "I sure am."

"Good." Karwin turned back to the rest of the crowd. "I think it would be best if those who are planning to stay here gather in one group, those heading inland in another, and those taking their chances on the sea, in a third. No matter our choices, decisions have to be made." Remembering protocol, he looked to the pub owner. "Sorry for stepping in, Mort. Do you agree?"

Mort waved away the question. "Absolutely. People have to decide."

The people separated into the groups; some, after listening in at one group, moved to another, but most stayed where they started, their choices already made.

Several gathered in Karwin's group—all the fishermen with their families—but a number of others, too. Two young families and several single men. Both widows and their children. Karwin didn't know all their reasons, and he didn't ask. He explained his plan of heading first to the outlying islands, resting a few days, then setting out again. He also reminded them that all but the smallest child must be prepared to row if the winds turned against them.

In the end, the decision was made. Thirty souls in all, along with their goats, sheep, and chickens, all packed into six fishing boats and their attached dinghies.

Karwin knew that most would not be able to bring everything they wanted, but that discussion could wait until they started packing.

There was only so much room in a fishing boat.

<hr>

The land continued to rumble all that day and into the next, but nothing so devastating as the night of Roj and Vince's return. Karwin sensed the relative peace was a ruse, though. As they packed food and essential goods into each of the boats, he had no doubt the mountain was preparing for a final, explosive act of violence. He just hoped it didn't happen until they were safely away.

Finally, it was time. His fellow travelers stood on the docks, waving goodbye to longtime friends. Most of those moving inland were also leaving that day. Goats bleated, dogs barked. Tears had been shed, hugs given. Narsel Giles and his thugs roved among the crowds, but people ignored them. Most were moving out and moving on with their lives. The mill owner could do as he pleased with the left-behind belongings—if the mountain allowed him to keep them.

Karwin lifted a giggling Elma over the gunwales and set her on the deck, stepped in after her, and held out his hand to Janna and Jabin. His hired man—a young fellow named Sander—was already at the tiller. His mother, Sue-Ann and her young son, old Thomen, and another hired man were already aboard Miles' boat.

Ducking under the boom, Karwin strode to the stern and faced the other boats moored at the dock. Putting two fingers to his mouth, he sent out a sharp, commanding whistle. Each captain waved back. They were ready. Releasing the last line that held the shifting boat to the dock, he gave a thumbs-up to Sander. The summer breeze filled the sail, and the boat pulled away from the dock.

As they reached the channel that would take them out of the harbor and into the open sea, Karwin gave a final long look at the village that was the only home he'd ever known. Then he turned resolutely to the east.

Janna joined him, wrapping an arm around his waist. "We're making the right decision," she said. "I'm afraid, but I know we'll be all right."

He pulled her close, breathing in the salt tang of the sea air he so loved. "I hope you're right. It was the only decision I could live with."

The sea stayed calm, and the winds were good, but as the sun peered over the horizon before them the next morning, something harsh and foreboding filled the air around them. Had there been a sound? A booming?

Karwin whirled. The sky was a brilliant blue as far as he could see, but over the hazy shadow of the land they'd left behind rose huge, strangely shaped clouds. Soon, waves—not huge, but bigger than any they'd seen thus far—began nudging their little flotilla from behind.

Within an hour, tiny sand-like particles began falling down around them, settling aboard the boat, sinking into the sea. Just as they had after Mt. Bane vented its wrath on North Village.

Janna joined him, tears filling her eyes. "I hope everyone got out. I hope...Oh, I hope they didn't all die."

He took her hand. He'd known it could happen—that it would happen—but even so, the pain of it dug a hole deep into his heart. A good number of the villagers had chosen to stay, or delayed deciding, including Mort and the despicable Mr. Giles. Perhaps Zelle had blown in a different direction. Perhaps their people had escaped.

They would never know.

Janna's tears were flowing freely now. "Our world is gone. Like it never was."

Staring at the billowing clouds over their distant homeland, he squeezed her hand. "And now we sail for a new world—a hidden one. One none of us has ever seen."

"Mr. Giles was right about one thing." She sniffed, running a hand over her eyes. "Starting over is hard."

"It is," he agreed. "But we're going to do it, and we'll be fine." He pressed a kiss against her forehead, and together they turned to face the east, the rising sun, and the cool, clean air that accompanied the dawn.

THE ETERNAL SONG

By Estella Edgewater

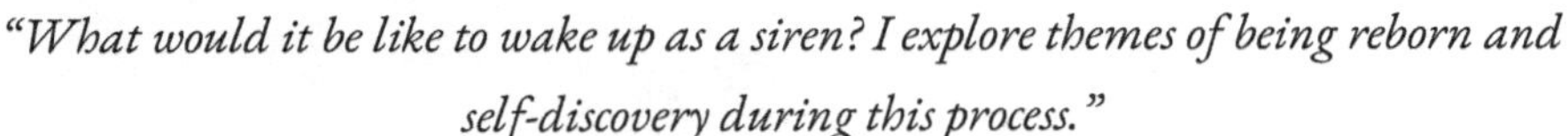

"What would it be like to wake up as a siren? I explore themes of being reborn and self-discovery during this process."

From this sodden cradle, you have bloomed.

A stone monument looks down upon you. Its claws breach the water's surface, just enough for its palm to hold you in the shallows. A tone—a whisper—permeates your thoughts. You have heard them before. Your awareness spears them like a worm on a hook. The earth of this flower's roots, salted with the ashes of you that came before.

Be still and–

Your heart beats color into your skin, puppeting your long thin fingers to push you up. Droplets from your chin mirror the beat of a tune that ripples from the water's surface up to the low curved ceiling.

Call out to–

Salty saliva sprays from your lips as the air strangles you, choking gasps leading your mouth to water. Liquid washes through your insides, expelling from hard bony plates around your ribs, as if you were exhaling.

Become one with–

Opening your eyes, a thin film retreats to the corners of your eyelids. A green tint overlays your vision. You raise your hand, examining obsidian nails that extend your fingers to sharp points. Iridescent skin leads the ink blots of your eyes to ridged collarbones, down a sternum, becoming a gradient of overlapping scales. Each shimmering plate collects into the slender meat of a tail that feathers out to flexible spines, laminated by a thin membrane.

You touch your clammy chest, uncertainty molding dark brows above your eye sockets. You remember dryer skin kissed by the warmth of the sun.

It's okay to–

You find the monument's inanimate stare familiar. From fanning fins, to flaring nostrils and jutting teeth, its body coils down and disappears below the water's surface. A teardrop shaped ornament dripping with algal slime emits a soft glow, and you trace its origin between the monument's crown of horns. It is not the first time you have looked upon the reflection of a god, this time it is a comfort.

You test your tail fin and slap it against the water, watching the splash arc over you in a glittering lattice veil. The water feels too shallow now, you are heavy here. The weight of the air around your body pushes you down. The depths beckon, and you pull yourself to the edges where the monument supports you. Head dipping beneath the surface, the strain on your neck ebbs and your hair feels lighter, so the rest of you slithers after with ease.

Know weightlessness.

The water swaddles you in warmth, soothing the echo of a struggle past. Your tailfin dances with the gentle current, tingling with power that propels you into a somersault. The water's soft melody flows over every scale, unhindered by the stagnant air. Your gills filter the notes and nourish you.

Gruff, jovial voices and lantern-lit dances fill your mind, trying to drown out the melody.

Floating away on the current, sorrow of a life once lived.

Their song–

The songs of your past, you prefer them. They still flow through you. A sea shanty moves your lips but no sound emerges as it plays through your mind over the water's melody.

You run your hand down the monument's body, descending into a rainbow field of coral growing over the stone. The water separates locks of your hair, washing through every strand to fan around your face and neck.

Volatile images of straining sails, crashing waves, and jagged light strikes through your mind. The sea shanty is quieted by rumbling, quaking thunder and your lips still.

Your resolve carried you, not in vain.

See their paradise.

Your new kin, with their inhuman faces, dart through the coral's openings and tunnels. The gleam of their swiveling bodies inspires you to dive further.

Your displacement of the water scatters a school of fish, some of them spinning out, fins flapping to try righting themselves. You weave between towers of coral, following patches of the monument's ridged scales. Soft plants flowering on the sea floor wave at you as you pass over, scuttling crustaceans retreating into the safety of their leaves.

Your blood has always been these waters, they sing to your spirit's roots.

Pulling your tail forward to curl, you arch your back to stop right in front of a forest of seaweed dancing around the monument's body. The coral tapers off here, and looking forward and above, the green towers so high it fades out of sight. The unknown above coaxes a prickling warmth in your heart, rippling out to your fingertips.

Don't stray from–

You swim slower, keeping your gaze forward now. The monument's path spirals upwards into a hollow, music trickling down from a twinkling light. It allures you. Further ahead, the water proceeds into darkness. You contemplate the path.

The darkness echoes what you once called liberation. Waves lapping at barnacle encrusted wood and musty ropes, sea spray stinging dry cheeks and dampening clothes. An endless sky and infinite horizon all within reach. That is a different freedom. A painful freedom.

From the light above, a new freedom calls.

You are found, spirit anchored anew.

You bask in the song flowing over you from above, letting it wash away the last remnants of waterlogged lungs and a drowning form.

Forget all that you were.

Your tail propels you up towards the light. Your vocal chords vibrate in time with the music, the melody interweaving with your mind.

Accept what you have become.

Let the world become only the sea. Only I.

You reach a new surface, this new freedom which I offer.

The glistening ridges of waves become my glimmering scales. Interlocking white mountains become my teeth, seeping bubbling breath. Black moons against yellow nights become my eyes. I watch your fingertips brush the bulb of a lonely star, my light.

My eternal song is yours.

THE HOME FRONT

By Shaun C. Kennedy

"Personifying the self-confident, argumentative impulses I observe in humans as tiny, powerful faeries in order to recognize and tame them within myself."

B edtime was always a battle between the twins and their father, Kyle. Kelly ran through the house saying he was a wild rhino, and Cindy chased him trying to echo Kyle's commands to calm down. A strategic switch from the Savannah to an iceberg convinced the rhino to become a seal, and that's how the twins ended up in the bath.

After the bath, the assertions come that seals don't wear pajamas, so they are moved to the rainforest and become monkeys. Once the duo had taken their baths and put on their pajamas, the ritual stalling began. Bedtime is the number one leading cause of dehydration among children under ten. The monsters in the closet need to be tamed. There were too many blankets, then not enough, but no such thing as just right.

Then finally, the battle was over with their father the winner, two small children tucked into their beds and fast asleep. Kyle went down to the living room to watch one episode of television not specifically made for those learning the alphabet. The same routine every night, day after day.

Until today. Of course they would save the worst for the last few days, as Kyle's wife, Nell, was on a business trip. Kelly started right after the call for bedtime by complaining that a butterfly was bothering him. That's where the running started. Cindy corrected him that it's a moth, because butterflies don't come out at night. She asked Kyle to back her up.

"I'll look it up once you are both safely in bed," he assured her.

Bathtime went as expected. Two five-year-olds splashing as wildly as they could, trying to stir up energy to stay awake, until Cindy piped up, "Oh, what a colorful moth!" Kyle wasn't falling for it.

Finally, the two little ones were dressed and tucked in. There were demands for water, but when Kyle returned with two cups, both kids were hiding under their blankets. Bedtime is the number one leading cause of dehydration among children under ten. The monsters weren't in the closet today, they had flown out into the hall.

The kids eventually fell asleep after Kyle sang them a lullaby. After tucking them in, Kyle took a moment to catch his breath and went down the stairs. That was when he saw them on the dining room table.

At first, he thought they were butterflies, too. They had colorful, iridescent wings. But upon closer inspection, they were three tiny girls, curled up, asleep. Kyle emptied the glasses he was holding into the sink, then used them to capture two of the three sleeping girls. They all sprang awake, and the two captured creatures began to bounce around inside their glass cages as the third flew in zig zags around the living room until finding a vent and disappearing into the night. After about a minute, the *ting, ting, ting* of bouncing off the glass slowed down, and the frightened creatures fell to the table, panting.

Kyle leaned in and looked closely at them. Each was about one and a half inches tall, with two-inch wings. The wings possessed an iridescent rainbow effect, causing them to change color depending on the angle from which you looked at them. Generally, they were either purple, blue, or orange, with only the most oblique angles giving red. Their bodies were very slender, with long legs and arms, but hands and feet that were not only small because the creatures were overall tiny, but even tiny in comparison to the rest of their bodies. They wore tiny dresses that were knit from spider silk and hung loosely from their bodies, with one single strand going over each shoulder and then crossing like an X in the back.

Their heads were unusually large for their bodies, and their eyes unusually large for their heads, just on the edge between being cute and creepy. They had ears with no lobes that came above their heads to a point. Instead of eyebrows, they had long, feathered antennae like a moth would have. Each antenna started at the middle of the creature's forehead just above the eye, and then extended out before gently curving up where it separated from the temple. Their antennae matched their hair: one was golden yellow, the same color as buttercups. Her hair hung down around her head and curled up at the shoulders, making her head look like some sort of yellow lily with only one petal from the back. The other was bright red, but almost light enough to be pink. Her hair was up, and from the back she looked like a red thistle blossom.

Kyle leaned in to look closer at the creatures. Once they realized they were being watched, they curled up as tight as they could in little balls and avoided eye contact with Kyle as best they could. Kyle grabbed two pieces of tissue paper and started to lift the opening glass with the golden-haired girl just a tiny bit off the table. Once again, she started zipping around in her glass prison while Kyle carefully passed the tissue under the opening, then set it down again. She continued to bounce around the glass, banging her head against the sides and bottom of the upside down glass until Kyle had completely secured the tissue in place with a rubber band. He repeated the process for the second one, then turned them both over. He grabbed a needle and prepared to poke a small hole in the top of the golden-haired girl's enclosure so she could breathe, but he was afraid of hitting her.

"Slow down!" he almost shouted after a moment.

She cowered in the bottom of the glass, but before she could have time to start causing trouble again, Kyle stabbed the needle into the top. She let out a tiny, high-pitched scream as soon as she saw the needle poking through. Kyle put three holes in very quickly before stopping. She kept screaming, but Kyle held up the needle so she could see it.

"You're fine. I'm done."

She crawled as close to the needle as she could, looking at it reverently. She looked up at Kyle with a face full of awe. "You saved me!" she squealed.

Kyle did the same with the other glass with the same results. Kyle looked at the tiny creatures again, only this time, instead of cowering, they knelt on two knees, looking at him with a combination of curiosity and reverence that one would need eyes that large to replicate.

Finally, Kyle asked, "Who are you?"

The golden one answered. "I'm Nod."

The red one stammered a few moments later, "I'm Winkin."

Kyle picked up the two glasses. "Are you real?" he asked.

The two creatures looked at each other for a moment, then shrugged. "I don't know," Winkin said.

"What do you mean you don't know?" Kyle asked, his frustration pouring out.

"I'm sorry!" Winkin cried. "I didn't mean to upset you! Don't hurt me!" She pressed her face to the floor of the glass and hugged her knees.

"It's okay. I'm sorry, I didn't mean to frighten you," Kyle said. "I've never seen anything like you before. Where did you come from?"

Winkin looked up slowly. "We came from the woods."

Kyle was skeptical. "I have been in the woods a lot. I've never seen anything like you."

Winkin stood up and put her hands on her hips. "Of course not! We hide! No one has ever seen us!"

"No one?" Kyle asked.

Nod stood up and put her hand on the glass. "My sister is insolent and ugly. You can ignore her."

Winkin sprang to her feet. "Don't listen to her! She's a liar! And besides, she's the ugly one! I'm obviously the pretty one. You should just let her go. Or better yet, just squish her."

Their attention switched from Kyle to each other, and they began to bicker in a way that only siblings can, making faces and calling each other names, each trying to talk over the other.

Finally, Kyle said in a small but firm voice, "That's enough!"

They stopped their bickering instantly and turned their curious, reverent attention back to him.

"There was a third one. Was she your sister as well?"

Nod shook her head violently. "No! Mother had her a year before Winkin and me."

Winkin looked up at Kyle again. "You don't need to know anything about her. She's ugly and mean and stupid. I am pretty and smart and nice, and I will take care of you."

This conversation was getting confusing quickly. "I'm sorry, I'm not sure I followed any of that," he said. "Did you say she had the same mother as the two of you?"

They looked at each other a moment, then back to Kyle, nodding. "Yes," they said in unison.

"But she's not your sister?"

They very slowly shook their heads in unison.

"Does that mean she has a different father?"

"We don't have fathers!" shouted Nod.

"Fathers are for humans," humphed Winkin.

Kyle was sure he was lost now. "No fathers. Got it."

Kyle looked at the tiny girls. They looked back at him. After a few minutes of being quiet, they both went back to kneeling on the bottom of their jars and looking at him with looks of curiosity and reverence.

Kyle shook his head. "I'm really tired. But I don't feel right about leaving you in these jars all night. What do you eat?"

"We eat honey!" both girls yelled, jumping to their feet and pressing themselves against their respective jars. Then the chattering started again, each one trying to say how much hungrier she was than her sister, and how the other one didn't deserve any honey.

Kyle went to the kitchen and found a small eight-ounce bear with honey. He put some on two spoons, and then came back to the girls. He carefully measured to ensure that the spoons would fit entirely inside the jars, opened the tops, put the spoons in, and then closed the jar tops again. The tiny creatures dug into their little offerings as if they had never eaten before. Kyle turned off the light and went to bed.

Kyle set his alarm to go off an hour before the kids got up. He wanted to get the little captives to a more secure place before the kids were ready to help.

When the alarm went off the next morning, Kyle had a night's sleep to consider what to do. He remembered that there was an old bird cage in the garage, and he brought it inside. He placed the tiny girls' jars in the cage, then pulled the tissue paper off their jars. Slowly, the girls fluttered their wings and rose into the air, out of their jars, and started to look around the cage.

"Winkin, Nod, are you two okay in there?"

They started to flutter in opposite directions. One said, "Yes," though it was not at all clear which one had spoken. Kyle waited a moment to see if the other would speak, but then he couldn't even be sure that both hadn't answered in unison.

Kyle went to check on his kids. Sure enough, they were just waking up. "Kids, I need you to come with me," Kyle said. "I think I caught your monster."

Blurry-eyed and still groggy, the two five-year-olds followed their father like ducklings following a duck hen. Kyle came into the living room, and the two tiny girls were at the television, poking the remote, cycling through streaming services.

Kyle's voice caught in his throat, "What..."

Winkin and Nod looked up from their project, then quickly flew back to the cage as if frightened. Winkin lifted the gate of the cage to allow Nod in, then Nod held it while Winkin flew in. They let the gate crash closed, then sat down crossed-legged on the floor with their hands in their laps, trying with all their might to look innocent.

Kelly screamed. Cindy jumped into her father's arms. "Daddy, what are those?" Cindy insisted.

"Aren't they what you saw last night?" Kyle asked.

Kelly was the one to answer. "Yeah. But they are kinda creepy. Why are they in a cage if they can get out?"

"I can't get out!" Nod yelled. "That was all Winkin's idea!"

"No, it wasn't!" Winkin yelled, jumping to her feet. "I can't get out! Don't listen to her! She's ugly and a liar!"

Nod jumped to her own feet. "Don't call me a liar! You're the liar!"

As the two bickered in their tiny, high-pitched, and incredibly cute voices, Kelly and Cindy slowly approached the cage. Kyle stepped up behind his children.

"Did you say your name is Winkin?" Cindy asked.

Winkin turned to look at Cindy. She fluttered her wings and rose into the air, looking the small girl in the eyes. "Yes. I'm Winkin. That's my sister Nod."

"I'm Kelly," the boy said, looking over his sister's shoulder. "This is my sister Cindy."

Nod lifted into the air and hovered next to her sister, face to face with the children. "It is nice to formally meet you."

"How old are you?" Cindy asked.

"Why?" the fairies asked in unison.

"I'm five," Kelly said. "But you're so small. You must be like, two or something."

The tiny girls looked at each other, shrugged, then lowered back to the floor of the cage.

"I need to take the kids to Playgroup," Kyle said. "Will you two be here when I get back?"

Winkin and Nod nodded, then shrugged. "If you bring honey," one of them squeaked, though again it wasn't clear which one.

"What about the other one?" Kyle asked. "The one you said isn't your sister? Will you be able to convince her to stay?"

The two looked at each other again. "Do we have to?" they asked in unison.

"Of course not," Kyle said. "I just thought it might be nice to get to know her as well."

The girls sighed and shrugged. Their wings and antennae slumped with their shoulders, and they looked at the ground, giving some little chatter between them, but Kyle couldn't quite make it out.

Two kids were dressed in record time, and Kyle took them to Playgroup before stopping at the grocery store to pick up some honey. He decided to err on the side of caution and get a gallon of honey. Then he went home, eager to learn more about his tiny guests.

He was not remotely ready for what he walked into. Winkin and Nod were out of their cage, on the coffee table in the living room. Between them was another tiny creature, one of her wings broken, a silver antenna off at an odd angle, silver hair disheveled, with a thread wrapped around her securing her arms to her side. Winkin and Nod were sitting on the other girl's back to hold her down as the other one screamed and thrashed.

Kyle instinctively ran forward and pulled Winkin and Nod off, then untied the other. The new one stumbled, trying to get up, but ended up on one knee. Her tiny dress was hanging off one side, and was torn on the sides.

Kyle held back Winkin and Nod as the new one caught her breath. She looked up at Kyle. "You saved me!" she declared.

Kyle processed what he was looking at. "I couldn't let them keep hurting you."

Winkin gave a harrumph. "We didn't hurt her that bad."

Nod crossed her arms and leaned her back on Kyle's arm. "Yeah! She'll be fine if a frog doesn't eat her."

The new one cowered at the mention of a frog. "I can't run from a frog!" She looked panicked.

"It's fine!" Kyle said, trying to sound comforting but realizing that he sounded condescending. "You can stay here. There aren't any frogs here."

"Just kids," Nod said in a teasing, sing-song voice. "Kids that play in the mud and bring home frogs."

"There will be no frogs!" Kyle assured the now nearly hysterical newcomer. "What is your name?" he asked, hoping desperately that this would change the subject.

"I'm... I'm... I'm Lilly," the new one answered at last.

"Hello, Lilly. I'm Kyle. It is a pleasure to meet you, though I wish the circumstances were different."

Both Winkin and Nod turned to Kyle, mouths agape. They started chattering so fast that Kyle could only pick out small phrases as they tried to yell over each other with no idea which one said which.

"How can you like her?"

"She's broken and ugly!"

"You wanted to talk to her, so we made her stay put for you!"

"She was ugly before we hit her. She'll be ugly when she's all healed up, too."

"Why are you being so mean to us?"

"I thought you liked me!"

"I feel sorry for her," Kyle explained. "She's hurt and needs my help."

The other two stopped their chatter. They looked severely chastised. Then Nod held her arm. "Lilly bit me right here, and it still hurts."

"No, it doesn't!" Winkin countered. "You're fully healed."

"Nuh-uh!" Nod retorted. "I'm hurt all over because she bit me right here!"

"Nod," Kyle interrupted the bickering. "Do you feel like I'm ignoring you for Lilly now? Are you jealous of Lilly?"

Nod tried to shake her head no, but then hung her head as she said, "Yes." Then, after a breath, started in. "But that's stupid because she's old and ugly and stupid and mean and she bit me so I'm the one that's really hurt here, not her."

"Nuh-uh!" Lilly yelled back. "I'm the one who's really hurt, and Kyle saved me! So there!" With that, Lilly stuck out her tongue at Nod.

"Stop it!" Kyle yelled. "I would protect any of you. No more fighting!"

Nod and Lilly stopped talking, then looked up at Kyle with their giant eyes full of tears. "We're sorry!" they said in unison.

Lilly kept going. "Please don't squish me. I promise I'll be good."

Winkin flew up and landed on Kyle's shoulder. "She's been naughty and made you mad! You should squish her! And Nod too. I'm the only good one of us. You should just keep me."

"No!" Kyle said, trying to turn to look at Winkin. "And don't you ever suggest that I squish anyone ever again. That's a horrible thing to suggest."

Winkin lifted into the air, looking aghast. "What did you say?"

"I said I'm not going to squish anyone!" Kyle tried not to yell.

Winkin crossed her arms. "But... she's broken, and ugly, and she's so stupid!"

"You shouldn't talk about others that way." This bickering was getting old.

Winkin floated down to the table, then once she landed and her wings stopped fluttering, she ran her fingers along the top of her wings. "How dare you speak to me like that!" If looks could kill, she would have Kyle dead in her sights right there. "Do you know who I am?"

"I don't care," Kyle said. "This is my house, and in my house we treat each other with respect and kindness."

Her nostrils flared, and her eyes grew red. "Oh? Your house? If it's your house, I guess I'll just have to take it from you, then!" With that, she threw a handful of the dust from her wings at Kyle.

Kyle held up his hands, guarding his eyes, and then looked at her. He was just about to ask if that was all she had when he felt his hands getting sticky. He looked down at his hands, and his fingers were fusing together, almost as if the skin were taking the form of mittens instead of separate fingers.

Several thoughts passed through his mind at once. Was this what she intended? How was this happening? Could this be undone? Above all of these, piggybacking on all the adrenaline he already had in his system, was the singular thought that drove his next actions, though: who was she to attack him in his own home?

Kyle brought his hands down hard on the table. Winkin dodged, zipping one way, and then another. Nod flew up into the air, and hid behind a picture on the windowsill. Lilly, broken and incapable of flight, dived behind the flowers that were on the table. Winkin threw another ball of dust at Kyle, but this time he dodged. When the dust ball hit the chair Kyle had been standing in front of, the wooden chair turned into a sort of thick liquid and started to slowly melt.

Kyle reached out and managed to grab Winkin by the feet. He pulled her down and held her on the table. He tried to be careful, since he didn't really want to hurt her, but he was also starting to feel like this might be a bit scarier than he initially thought. Kyle brushed her hands back and used his thumb and forefinger to pin them to the table and shouted, "That is enough!"

Winkin struggled for a moment, flapping her wings and flopping her legs, trying to get any kind of leverage that would break her free and resume the battle against Kyle. After the moment had passed, she stopped struggling.

Kyle watched her breathing hard, her thorax almost tripling in width as she sucked in air like you'd see in a cartoon, with her yelling between breaths. Then, all at once, like someone had flipped a switch, the struggling and the hard breathing and the violent yelling all stopped. She flopped to one side. Kyle let go of her wings and let her roll into a fetal position on the table. She started to cry.

Kyle sat back down in his chair without thinking, and when he noticed that it was once again whole and solid he checked his hands to see that they were also back to the correct configuration.

Nod and Lilly came out of their respective hiding spots. "Is it over?" Nod asked.

"Yes," Kyle said.

Lilly jumped up and down. "Kyle is our new leader! Hooray for Kyle! Down with Winkin! She was always mean anyway."

"Wait," Kyle said, looking at Lilly. "Do you mean that the way she was treating you when I came home is how she treated everybody?"

Lilly seemed a little confused by the question. "Of course."

"But that's okay now," Nod said, flying close by. "Because you beat her, and that makes you our new leader."

Winkin was just starting to stand up. "Nuh-uh. This was his territory to start. I'm still the leader outside."

"Well, we're welcome here, so there!" yelled Lilly before sticking her tongue out.

"Anybody is welcome," Kyle said. "As long as they can live by my rules. No fighting, be nice to each other, and be nice to me." He let that sink in for a moment as Nod slowly descended to the table. "Now, who wants honey?"

All three of them started jumping up and down, yelling, "Me! Me! Me!" before hurling minor insults about how stupid and ugly the other two were, so the speaker should get all the honey.

Kyle didn't have the energy for any of that, so he just went to the kitchen and got three spoonfuls of honey. When Kyle came back into the room, Nod and Lilly were examining Winkin's hands. Winkin was trying to pull her wrists away as if embarrassed.

"What's wrong?" Kyle asked.

"You broke Winkin's hands," Lilly said.

"Shut up!" Winkin said. "It was not my hands, it was my wrists, and I'll be back when I get a little honey."

Nod just laughed. "If you get any honey. Kyle is our leader, and you're hurt, and he knows how stupid and ugly and useless you are, so he's not going to give you any honey."

"Nu-uh!" Winkin said. "Kyle, feed me first to show them that I'm not as broken as they think I am!"

Kyle felt a little insulted that they thought he would bypass the care of someone in need, so he laid down the spoonfuls of honey. "First, one for Winkin, then one for Lilly, finally one for Nod," he said.

The three ate in silence. In a way, it was good that Kyle got to see what happened. He learned some things about his little winged friends. As they ate, Lilly's wings straightened and her cuts healed. By the time she was done eating, she was fluttering her wings and lifting into the air again. The same thing happened with Winkin's wrists, but it was less visible because her hands were so small.

Another thing happened, though. Both Nod and Lilly, who seemed so brave and sure of themselves moments after Kyle had pinned down Winkin, were now acting skittish and scared. They held their spoons like a leprechaun protecting his pot of gold. Winkin, in contrast, was sitting up straighter and eyeing the other two between bites. When Winkin finished, she stood up, walked over to Nod's spoon, and reached down to take some.

"Stop that," Kyle warned.

Nod looked at Kyle with giant, pleading eyes. Winkin looked back at him defiantly. "No."

"Winkin, I don't think..."

Winkin wasn't waiting for Kyle to finish. "Stop! Kyle! You'll listen to me from now on!"

Winkin took a bite of Nod's honey in defiance of Kyle's instruction.

"Winkin, I'm letting you stay here, but you've got to follow the rules of this house." Kyle was getting exasperated.

"I make the rules!" Winkin said. Then she lifted into the air and looked Kyle in the face. "I told you to feed me first, and you did! That means you listen to me!"

Kyle reached up and grabbed Winkin's wings. Her eyes grew to fill her entire face, and Kyle brought her to eye level. "I fed you because I felt sorry for you. Do we need to fight again to show just how much I don't answer to you?"

Winkin started shaking her head. "No," she whimpered.

"My house, my rules. I want you out of my house until you can learn that. Do you understand?"

Winkin nodded again, and Kyle set her on the table. Winkin took a bite of honey, which was enough to right her newly pinched wings, and with that Winkin flew off.

Kyle now turned his attention to Nod and Lilly. "This house is now a safe haven for you. Anyone who can live by the rules of this house and not fight and not make a mess is welcome. Winkin can't live by those rules, so she's not welcome." Kyle thought about it for one second, then added, "And no hiding. My kids want to see you."

Nod and Lilly jumped for joy, and Kyle started getting things together to get Kelly and Cindy from Playgroup. Finally, Kyle thought that all these adventures were coming to an end. With only two of the tiny creatures to keep track of and the worst kicked out, Kyle was sure that things were going to get easy.

He picked the twins up from Playgroup, and they were both eager to get home and see their new friends. Of course, the Playgroup teacher had just assumed that they were talking about a new imaginary game or book or television show, and Kyle wasn't in the mood to fix their error. He knew he wouldn't be believed if he backed up the story his kids told, but he also didn't feel he had anything to prove or anything to hide. On the one hand, if everyone just thought his kids had an active imagination it didn't hurt anyone. On the other, he didn't start out with the intention to keep them secret and didn't care if people saw them. He thought bringing them in for show-and-tell would be a bit difficult if they resisted, but if the kids wanted to do that in a week or two after things had settled in with Nell, he would try.

Kyle and the twins walked through the front door, and Kyle yelled out, "Nod! Lilly! We're home!"

As Kyle helped Kelly out of his jacket, one of them flew right into his face. "Welcome home!" the tiny voice squeaked.

Kyle stumbled back, trying to focus and see who it was. Gold meant Nod, silver meant Lilly. Except what Kyle saw was purple. Purple hair and antennae, fuzzy and wild. "Who are you?"

The newcomer looked offended not to be recognized, folding her arms in front of her. "Well I never! Nod said this house was a sanctuary as long as we don't hide from you, and you don't even have the common courtesy to know my name!"

Kelly laughed. "A new one?"

Cindy reached up, holding her hand flat. The new guest landed on her hand. "Hello. I'm Cindy. What's your name?"

The newcomer sat cross-legged in Cindy's hand. "I'm Nikki."

Kyle tried to process what he'd just heard. "Nikki, did you say that Nod invited you here?"

Nikki turned, glaring at Kyle. "Nod does not tell me where I can and cannot go. Nod cannot invite me or dismiss me from anywhere. I'm here because I want to be here, not because stupid ugly Nod said so."

"Yes, okay," Kyle said, trying with every fiber of his being to choose his words very carefully. "But you want to be here because it's a sanctuary from Winkin, right?"

Nikki fluttered her wings and flew up to Kyle's eye level again. "Of course! It's not like I go looking for houses to live in all the time or something."

Something in the way she avoided eye contact while she said that was a little unnerving, but Kyle was on a mission and decided to ignore it.

"Did Nod tell anyone else that this was a sanctuary?"

"No," Nikki said. "Everyone else heard it from Lilly."

Kyle took a deep breath. "Who is everyone else?"

"Umm..." Nikki thought for a moment. "Tessa, Clair, Margaret, Kendra, Kathy, Abby, Rose, Bobbin..."

Kyle interrupted. "Are they all here now?"

"No, silly!" Nikki said. "They're not invisible! You'd see them if they were here! They're in the kitchen."

Kyle tore through the living room and into the kitchen. Sure enough, there were about two dozen of the tiny creatures, busily looking through the cupboards like they owned the place. Two boxes of cereal had been dumped out, and the contents were strewn across the floor. The gallon of honey that he'd just bought was tipped over, running down the counter onto the floor where several of the tiny creatures had gathered to start taking tiny handfuls and licking their fingers. All the silverware was across the floor, except for one paring knife, which was pinned through one tiny wing, holding the owner in place on a cutting board. The fridge door was open, and all the contents were on the floor.

Kyle stepped forward and unknifed the poor, stuck girl, and as she looked dreamily at him, thanking him for saving her, he unceremoniously plopped her down next to the spilled honey to eat and heal. "Who did that to you?" he asked.

She licked honey off her fingers. "You did! You saved me!"

"Who put you in danger to start with? Who put the knife through your wing?"

The healing girl shrugged. "One of them," and she gestured wildly to the whole kitchen. "You should kick all of them out. It can be just you and me and all this honey!"

"Do you know which one of them particularly put that knife through your wing?"

"Of course!" she said. As she ate, her green hair and antennae started to grow, and Kyle got a sense of just how extensive the damage she suffered. Her hair grew until it was twice as long as her body.

"Point out the one that did that to you."

The green-haired girl looked around the room. "I don't see her."

"Do you know her name?"

She looked indignant. "Of course I know her name!"

"What is it?" Kyle asked.

"It's Buttercup."

Kyle raised his voice. "Will Buttercup please come forward?"

Several of the small girls circled around Kyle. "Why do you want Buttercup?"

"Buttercup is ugly and gross!"

"You don't need Buttercup for anything. I can do anything she can."

"I'm prettier than Buttercup! Just ignore her!"

"Enough!" Kyle yelled. "I want everyone to go into the other room. Get the twins, and go to their room with them. I need to clean all of this up, and I get the distinct impression that none of you are going to help!"

One by one, every tiny eye filled with tears, and slowly they turned and flew out of the room. Kyle heard the twins going up to their room, and then he turned his attention back to the kitchen. This was going to take a while, so he got straight to work cleaning the kitchen.

Two hours later, Kyle went up to the twins' room. They were chasing the tiny creatures around, everyone giggling, apparently caught up in the throes of some kind of game of tag. Kyle watched from the door for a few minutes, then cleared his throat to catch the attention of at least his kids. The twins stopped running, grabbing onto their father's hips. "Daddy! They are so much fun! Can we keep them?"

"Let me talk to Nod and Lilly first," he said.

All the creatures kept playing in the absence of the twins, though decidedly more rough and tumble than Kyle would prefer. They would collide mid-air, falling to the ground in a tangle of pulling hair and twisting wings, but lightened up when they caught sight of the humans in the room. Kyle called out a little more loudly, "I need to talk to Lilly and Nod!"

All the tiny girls stopped their wrestling and chasing each other and turned their attention to Kyle. "Why do you want Lilly and Nod?"

"Aren't I prettier than Lilly and Nod put together?"

"Lilly is stupid and Nod is ugly! Play with me instead!"

Cindy pulled at Kyle's shirt. "Daddy, you can't do it like that. You'll make them jealous!"

"How am I supposed to do it, then?" Kyle asked, feeling overwhelmed.

"Like this," Kelly said. Then, turning to the room, he said, "I need everyone's attention, please! I need to know who can answer a question!" All the tiny voices stopped, and they all looked at Kelly. He cleared his throat. "Who knows where Lilly and Nod are?"

Every tiny hand in the place went up. "I do! I do!" they all yelled, trying to be heard over the din.

Kelly laughed a little. "Do you, really? Prove it! Where are they?"

And in an instant, every tiny hand turned and pointed directly at Lilly and Nod.

Kyle made eye contact with them. "Lilly! Nod! Come with me!"

A clamour of jealous voices decried how unfair it was that they got to go with Kyle, but he ignored it. He didn't have time for this nonsense. Lilly and Nod flew to him, landed proudly on his shoulders, and stuck their tongues out at everyone as they left the room with Kyle.

In the living room, Kyle gently lifted them off his shoulders. "Where did they all come from?"

"The forest," Lilly answered happily. "We told them that this is a sanctuary from Winkin, and they all came to get away from her under your protection."

"I meant a sanctuary for just the two of you!"

Lilly and Nod recoiled for a moment at the harsh change in tone. But then they recovered. "Well, if you didn't want us to tell, you should have said something. We didn't know, and we can't banish them. You'd have to fight them one at a time to banish them."

"I don't want any fighting!" Kyle growled. "Can't you understand that?"

Both girls shrugged, and Kyle couldn't tell which one said, "Then they're here to stay. Get used to it."

"They made a mess of the kitchen and now the playroom!" Kyle said.

Nod flew up and landed on Kyle's shoulder again. "So?"

"I don't want to have to clean this up, too!" Kyle said.

Both girls shrugged. "Too bad," Nod said. Then Lilly, looking like she was thinking something through, echoed her a few moments later.

Lilly lifted into the air. "I thought you were bringing us out here to tell us how much prettier we are than all the others. I don't need to stay here and be insulted. I'm going back to the playroom, where at least Kelly and Cindy know how to tell us we're pretty."

Half a beat later, Nod lifted off Kyle's shoulder and said, "Yeah! What she said!" before flying after Lilly.

Kyle followed them, feeling somewhat defeated. When he opened the playroom though, what he saw amazed him. The room was almost completely cleaned up, with the tiny girls carrying toys and games back to their proper locations. As the last few things settled into their place, Kelly yelled out, "Everybody wins!"

All the girls except Lilly and Nod let out a cheer. Lilly and Nod looked just as confused as Kyle.

Cindy ran up to Kyle. "Daddy, we know how much you hate cleaning up, so we told them that the first one to get the whole room cleaned up would win, and then look! They actually cleaned! They aren't so hard to work with, once you know how to handle them. Can we keep them?"

Kyle looked at Kelly, who was also pleading. "Fine, we can keep them," Kyle said. "But you two get to explain all this to Nell in the morning!"

"Deal," the twins said in unison.

A few hours later, the twins went to sleep. No struggle. No extra water. They just lay their heads on their beds, closed their eyes, and fell asleep.

Kyle lay down to sleep, and the next thing he knew his alarm was going off. Time to get Nell from the airport. He went downstairs, and the house was completely quiet. He looked into the kitchen. Not a tiny, winged body anywhere. He looked in the bathroom, the playroom, and Nell's study. Nothing. Other than the fact that the kitchen was nearly devoid of food, there was absolutely no evidence of what had been going on all day yesterday.

Kyle showered, and then the babysitter arrived. Kyle wanted to warn her, but she was just the sixteen-year-old girl from down the street. What was he supposed to say that wouldn't make him sound crazy? He did warn her that there had been an incident in the kitchen, so she would need to order in for breakfast and lunch, and he left her the money to do that. That was all he could bring himself to say, though.

Kyle drove to the airport and waited in the parking garage to get the text from Nell that she was ready for pickup. The text came two hours later, and Kyle drove to the pickup location. She threw her luggage in the back seat, jumped in next to her husband, gave him a kiss, and then immediately started talking about the trip. The whole drive home, she droned on and on about the new products that were coming out and how the company was gearing up for a major change, and this was going to be her year. Kyle made no attempt to interrupt her.

They pulled into the driveway, and Kyle grabbed the luggage. The babysitter was sitting on the couch, the remains of a lunch pizza on the coffee table. "The twins are in their playroom," the babysitter said. "They have been for hours. I went to check on them once, and they told me to leave, so I've just left them alone."

"I guess I should go say hello," Nell said. "After all, I did marry their father."

Kyle paid the babysitter, ignoring the playful jab at their relationship. No sooner had the babysitter left than Nell let out a scream from the playroom.

Kyle ran into the room, and sure enough there were dozens of tiny guests playing with the twins. Nell stood in the middle of the room, turned to Kyle, and said, "What is going on here?"

Kyle shrugged. "I have no idea. Why don't you ask them?"

Nell turned to the closest little flying girl and said, "Hello."

The little thing made eye contact, then flew straight to her. Nell held out a hand, and the tiny creature landed there. She gave a curtsey and responded, "Hello," back.

"You're very pretty," Nell said.

"I know," the little girl answered. "I'm the prettiest and the smartest and the kindest there's ever been. All the others are stupid and ugly and mean."

Nell smiled at that. "That's not a very nice way to talk about your friends."

"I don't have any friends," she said.

"Can we be friends?" Nell asked.

The little one lifted up and started fluttering around. "Well... you're not very pretty. Won't you be jealous of me?"

Nell suppressed a laugh. "I promise I won't get jealous." She paused, considering for a moment, then added, "I'm not smart enough to be jealous anyway. But I'm so dumb that I end up being really nice."

The little one floated down, and Nell held up her hand. "Alright. I'll let you be my friend, then. As long as you don't get jealous."

"I promise," Nell said. "I'm not smart enough to be jealous. You know what else? I'm not smart enough to remember your name."

The little thing started laughing. "I haven't told you my name, silly thing! But I already know your name. It's Nell. You're Kelly's step-mom. Which is like a mom, only alive. Because I guess human moms are dead, and that's why humans have dads and why human dads have to get their kids step-moms."

"See, I knew you were smarter than me," Nell said. "But shouldn't you tell me your name if we're going to be friends?"

The little one thought for a moment, then said, "I'm Ty. It's a pleasure to become friends with you."

Nell nodded respectfully. "Oh, I think the pleasure is all mine. Can I go talk to Kyle for a bit, though?"

Nell and Kyle left the playroom, and as soon as the door was closed, Kyle asked, "How did you do that? It took me forever to get anything out of them, and you had Ty sitting up and doing tricks almost instantly!"

Nell just rolled her eyes. "You've only dated girls. I recognized in an instant, they're all id. Like men, only slightly worse than average. So I just treated her like I would treat a new boyfriend."

Kyle felt really offended by that. "I'm not at all like them!"

Nell crossed her arms and looked him straight in the eye. "Oh, really? Is that why you gave me a detailed description of these things while driving home? Took it upon yourself to make sure I was fully prepared for a house full of... whatever they are? Because you, unlike them, are concerned primarily for my mental well-being and not entirely self-focused?"

"I..." Kyle wanted to justify himself, but she did kinda have him pegged. "I'm sorry. You're right. I should have warned you. Or at least tried."

Nell gave him a playful kiss on the nose. "Yeah, right. Like I'd have believed you. No, all things considered, this was the best way. I just wanted to see you squirm." Nell thought for a second. "So, they're all id, like I said. That means there's probably a leader. Probably the toughest and most aggressive of them. Have you figured out which one that is?"

"Yeah, that would be Winkin. Except, I kicked her out."

Nell processed that for a second. "Did she go willingly?"

"Not so much. Things got a little violent for a minute."

Nell took both of Kyle's hands. "Then, Dear, I think you're their new leader." Kyle nodded, trying to nonverbally admit that he kind of figured that out already. "But don't worry," Nell said, giving him another kiss. "I find it kind of attractive that you have an army of tiny, rude, fighting fairies at your command. Even if you need me to wield them."

WAKING THE SPRING

By J. LaRiviere

"Inspired by the hidden worlds within the human spirit—the private realities we keep behind closed doors and what it's like to emerge from them."

Their sanctuary was a monument to derelict human life. The computer keys no longer made clicking noises. Silver and red foil wrappers littered the desk like forgotten present bows. Their body by the window had not made it out of bed for days. Beside them sat sealed jars, lids screwed tight enough to cage the smells. The floor was carpeted with cotton and polyester piles of clothes. Shirts, pants, boxers, bras, socks, all softened the places where their feet could avoid touching the wooden floor or the rough carpet. They couldn't remember what was underneath. Beside them was a sculpture of possessions in the shape of a naga. A long serpentine tail made of gnarled blankets nested around the back of their bed, and a stuffed rabbit with an upside-down-Y mouth acted as the head of the human-snake guardian. Orange light reflected off the black-bead eyes into their own.

The computer pinged with notifications, tiny alerts, and alarms requesting action. A knock. "Good morning," her voice came through the door, scratchy sounding, with a watery tremor that couldn't be cleared with a cough. She did not enter their room.

Pastel shapes on white curtains were becoming more and more gray. The air was so stale they wondered if they were already a rotting corpse waiting to be discovered. They pictured their skin melting into the plastic-made textiles beneath them, polymerizing into something irreversibly changed. All of the oxygen left in the air was drawn into their body. They had to have breathed it all by now. There couldn't be more left here. They exhaled.

Not eating became easier. Their stomach, they imagined, was coated with a fungus. A white packing-peanut-consistency growth blooming through their intestines, stopping their rectum, climbing the trellis of their esophagus to exude out of their mouth, so when their body was found strangled, the finders could say definitively, "Yes, that is what killed her, something real."

They rubbed their forefinger against their thumb. Their skin hurt. The tenderness like someone had ripped the first epidermal layer off with duct tape. Their body shifted on the dingy mattress and their cheek sought the familiar yellowed pillow with feather stuffing. Burrowing deeper, the comforting darkness of their eyelids let their body heave a sigh.

There were flies.

They thought their hair must be matted with broken wings and dead bodies. A sliver of sunbeam between dust-covered shades made all bodies of living things fly towards it. Buzzing vessels battered against the invisible barrier crafted to keep them divorced from the source, until eventual weariness left the diptera to crawl, to drop. Mounds of small black corpses on the windowsill made up a mountain of death above where their body lay.

Today, the only movement in the room was the cooling fan. The gentle thrum of the dead-air-coated computer was the pulsing heartbeat they relied on.

Their body was six feet away from them.

Children think the monitor is the computer. Ignorant people think the display is the mechanism. When there is nothing to see, then it is dead. They were already dead because there was nothing to see. What did they look like? They hadn't seen their own eyes in years. Eyes to see, ears to hear, and teeth to hurt. The sun was up.

They couldn't bring themselves to unplug the computer, the ever-running thrum of activity. Particle-clogged vents effortfully made to live, lungs made to breathe stale air, the machine was the last preserver of where they'd been. Arteries and veins were like the copper and gold wires running the mechanism, and they could not tear them out despite their fantasies.

Water was the only clean smell. A story their mother read to them as a child said that if a boy didn't clean his room, to shut the door and send a garden hose up through his window. So the green snake came now, sputtering before spurting into a five-gallon paint bucket that remained clean because of the motion. The bucket filled some, and the animal of their body pushed up onto its hands and knees, scapulae reaching for each other before it crawled towards the watering hole.

Chilled wellwater splashed into their nose and eyes and maw. They bared their teeth and kept their body wet, minerals dripping down their neck. Gargling in their throat made them cough and hack. They waited to puke up their stomach, their spleen, their liver, kidneys, bladder, lungs, appendix, and for their larynx to prolapse and their vocal chords to bite their uvula.

Their diaphragm hurt. They collapsed onto the bed. They stared down into the dark water of the scrying bucket. Inching closer and closer. Nose, philtrum, lips, eyes, submerged in the water, and they waited for their body to inhale. They waited. They waited. Today could be different. Today could be. Water splashed onto the floor, wetting the cotton and plastic clothes, displacing the growing mold, as they tore their face from the option of death.

Today was different. They grabbed the flowing hose and jerked it towards their mouth. The stream burst into their cheeks, over aching exposed bones. Water stopped flowing and drained back into the snake of the hose, gurgling. They watched their body's hands tremble. Twin river tendons rippled under their skin. Six hundred and fifty muscles moved as one animal. Biceps and shoulders burned with contraction as they lifted the hard-plastic bucket up into the air and baptized the water over their body. Shock trembled the body's limbs and the weight of the empty pail fell and hit the floor like a silent film.

They lay back on the soaked mattress, wet blankets, rubbish, and rabbit-faced bedmate. Every muscle seized as they convulsed in laughter and screaming hysterics. Shoulders contracted then opened as their torso arched, levitated. Blood pumped their heart, pounding in their eardrums. When the broken human sound ceased, all of the world ceased with it, replaced with the relief of warm dream-filled sleep.

Cycle after cycle of water uncontained. Their room became a bog, the croaking of their voice calling like a creature that lived in a natural world.

Their computer's lungs quit on them, its fan no longer hummed.

They cried.

They'd lost the last tether.

Clarity took its place. Their face leaned to the side and saw the sea of waste beside them. Terrain of their isolation with the graveyard of versions of a person. The room that held the toilet was within view. It also had once held a bathtub and a sink, both had been covered. Wherever there was space, they had filled it with garbage and nothingness formed into matter. Nothing. All of it was bursting at the seams and none of it mattered. The tail of the naga moved. They spoke to it with echoed words,

"Be not long to speak, I long to die."

Go to the bathroom, the naga said to them.

They did not move. They slept.

Waking was a wet peeling thing. Their body had already begun to melt. Weakness, born of pressure, created a posture of restriction on their coccyx.

The naga imitation looked at them with dark-pool rabbit eyes.

They did not move. They slept.

Waking hurt the body's eyes, lashes glued together with sickness.

The naga waited for them.

They did not move. They slept.

Waking broke open their dissonance, prattling out of them like a cadaver's song.

The naga cradled them.

They did not move. They knew the smell of urine.

The portal to the room with the bath was open and dark. Orange lights around the room grew dimmer and dimmer. Their eyes found the topography, as in their ear they felt the naga whisper of the way. The road, the path, all laid out before them. They only needed to move. Their hundreds of muscles felt coated in thick mycelium fascia, an abandoned house crawling with cobwebs made of hardened cement. A net entangled under their skin waiting to be cut free, but she had taken all of the sharp things. Their teeth had become soft.

Water flooded the space over their clothes. They watched the sputtering hose splattering against damp, mildewing fabrics. The room hosted new life born of lack. Without intervention, they would see it flourish, living decay.

Come to me, said the naga.

If they died on the journey, they would become more of the landscape. More of the decomposition. Entropy could break them down and reveal the true core of their being. Cerebral spinal fluid could water the crops of their potential. It was too late while they were alive. They were a vulture with a crushed rib cage, without even the energy to get nourishment from their own carcass.

"Cowards die many times before their deaths." The body's voice could only produce words that were not their own. Quotes from a past life with a love of language. They hadn't loved anything in this life before they had constructed the naga's idol.

The room's alien space, created by another life, came into focus. They were the foreigner in an inhospitable land they were not bred for. That which had made them had not known how to create a being who would thrive in this environment. Living was impossible. Just as it was impossible to get to the bathroom.

But they started to imagine the body rolling onto the floor with a wet splat. They would go while the hose ran and cold water would run over their skin like the river, where their body was thrown, when they were left for dead. They wouldn't need to be in it, the body. They could rise above and taint the light-bulb-less bowl that hung over the room. The body would give out, even in this vision. Bones unable to support the weight of them, legs not able to uncurl from the fetal forty-degree angle. They would scream, and like all screams it would be ignored even by the ears of the body which disparaged the sound.

Imagination came to them with relative ease. They had been imagining their death for years. So much that at times they thought they were a ghost bound to this realm. Witness to their own diminishment.

They remembered a different past, a different future. One where the body was *their* body and their heart touched their fingertips and the sun shone from their mouth. Energy, movement, momentum, spinning like an endless top leaping off the table. Arms raised above their head to the sky and sun. Teeth splitting their face with merry ivory keys and pink life. Soft hair, supple skin, and dark curls untangled. Their mind had conjured wonderful things, kaleidoscopes and gentle hands, blankets and music, sweet spoken words and promises. It had not fed the ouroboros.

The stench of rot, where inorganic fibers soaked up the matter of red flesh life, had dulled their senses.

Tonight could be different.

They moved the body.

Their fingers touched the edges of sleeve-cuffs over their wrists. The shirt, soaked with water, sweat, and oils, lay against them like a second skin. They peeled it away and pulled their hands in, like a hermit crab into a toxic painted shell.

The cool tail of the naga brushed their legs and slithered up their spine. Webbed fingers brushed their matted hair away from their eyes. *This is not you. This body, this blood, this skin, this breath, this immutable form,* said the naga. *Go to the bathroom. Look in the mirror. See what you carry around. We will wash it off. Remove all that is not you. I will help you. I care for the waters of you. You are my body.*

It was real and here for them.

They traced the raised bumps of the ceiling with their eyes. Every part of their skin felt sensitive, both soft and rigid at the same time. The clothes they wore restricted their movements. If they undressed, they feared that all of them would come away with the filth. Changing began with rocking. They moved their body gently from side to side. The garment containing their legs slid down slowly. Fabric sloughed off dead skin cells and shed hairs. Pits of shiny wet dermis made the body jolt as the wounds were passed over. The body's hands moved for them as they ascended back up to the ceiling to observe the hatchling peeling the shell of their adornments off. Out of body, they could almost see the true naga.

The body's eyes, shiny and dark, stared into the space between spaces. Hands with fingers like anemone sensors felt where to close and draw in. Left behind was a dirty thing which had once been wild. The palms were strong keratin and hugged their biceps. Looking again through the eyes, they saw paper skin webbed over thin bones branching the tops of their feet. They felt the naga at their back. The smooth, scaled tail soothed the base of their spine and false ribs.

Unfurling their legs felt impossible. Each centimeter of movement, sliding their foot, tore the net of fascia that had locked them bent. Pins pricked them like heavy rain rippling over a pond and waking the water. Flow returned and made them lightheaded. They looked out over the battlefield. They lay back down.

They did not move. They slept.

Waking did not feel real.

The naga was silent.

The season changed.

Silence beneath the noise held them. Insects buzzed, and shadows crawled over the bed as the light moved. Dust motes like dancers entertained their eyes. Water flowed and collected, they had managed to contain it again. They wet their skin and crawled to place the pads of their fingers on the windowsill. Touching the green skin of the garden hose, they felt movement within, rushing. The cracked open window pinched it in place. A gap, enough to slide their fingers and top of their palm through, let the light kiss their raw skin with sunbeams. They touched their warmed hand to the yellowed pillow and pressed their cheek to it.

Once you decide, the journey will be easier. You must not look back, it will keep you confused. Now that you have seen me you cannot unsee me. You can carry on as you were but I will be here. And you know now, that I am here as I've always been. You will never be unknown again. I can help you, but I cannot move you and you remain yourself. Once you decide, you will have the strength to move and the way will be clear.

"Too sullied flesh would melt, thaw, and resolve itself into a dew," the body protested.

If inaction were all that was required there would be no suffering. There would be no reason to know.

They looked to the faraway water-stained floor.

She spoke through the door, "Good night, my baby."

Her voice was like an icepick in their brain. They coughed and retched, and the fit threw them from the bed to the floor. Organ-warm wet clothes and decay unhinged every stitch of their flesh, a demand to feel. They couldn't flee the body as they tried to tear themself apart. Vehicle-lifting-strength kicked out their legs and rolled them away.

More, there was always more, it never ended. Spine electrocuted with madness. They realized they were screaming when they choked on the spore of something disturbed. Hacking, begging. The entrance to the room, long barricaded by paper plates, black trash bags, and infestations, rattled as she beat a fist on the door, calling the name of their body. The body wouldn't stop. They were lit up with the energy of an overtired infant. Wailing. Wailing. Wailing.

The body moved them.

It dragged them across the bog, through the muck that coated their skin. Her voice was closer now, but she did not speak words they understood any longer. Her soul's voice was always tired, sad, buffered by the waste she could not bear to push past because of the years she refused to look at it. Too much holding on. She stopped reaching for them.

They moved the organ of their tongue over cracked lips. Their eyelids closed. There was silence.

The door to the bathroom had never closed. The sea of clothes, rot, collections, memories, all poured into it and painted the floor. They dragged the cadaver of themself to the opening and fell in with the forgotten worthless things. There was nothing in the bathtub. They had not remembered that. They remembered something born there.

Webbed hands gripped over the edge of the tub. The blue and violet scales were exactly as they had imagined the naga. Monitor-black hair pulled half up emerged over the edge, then two large eyes with narrow indigo slit pupils. Those eyes found them on the floor, the body seeking refuge. The naga said, *Come into the bathtub.*

Their own words cried out, "That is not what you promised!"

When sorrows come, they come not single spies, but in battalions, the naga said.

"If I could bear this, I would live." They wept.

If I lifted you to me without your word it would be for nothing.

"You are unfair." They raged.

I will always wait for you.

"I cannot, I cannot, I cannot." They lay still.

In the corner of the room, behind a pile of towels and empty soap bottles, was the mirror. The mirror's surface was the brown tiled floor beneath the tub, the blue and green striped wallpaper, the sea of decay outside the door, and them, on the ground. Naked, bruised, sore, matted, trembling, diminished. They could not look at all of those things and the mirror. It had once been a whole piece, lined with a painted border, but now pierced a pile of belongings with its diagonal snapped edge. The mirror itself was fragile glass, it possessed a shimmer when light touched it and ate more when light did not.

They turned their eyes to trace the map of the body. They were meant to be the charge of it all: Eyes, nose, lips, cheeks, teeth, eyebrows, forehead, ears, hair, throat, collarbones, chest, lungs, heart, ribs, arms, wrists, palms, fingernails, stomach, spleen, kidneys, liver, hips, sex, thighs, knees, calves, ankles, feet, toe-nails, arteries, veins, bones, muscles, and that which they could not name. To feed this body, to move this body, to steward it from step to step– they were given this being to care for. They did not want an animal, a child, to bathe. They moved the body's eyes to look at the tub. There the naga was. They made vibrations in the body's throat.

"You who know me," they said, "help me, please."

The concrete tension of their body fractured and became water. They were the flowing streams and the relaxed pond reflecting a breeze. The naga's touch brushed their shoulder, tracing down their arm to their hand, and it cooled the flaming rawness of their skin. Casting their eyes upon the scaled human-like face, they raised their other arm to be pulled into an embrace.

Pulled from the floor, as if they weighed nothing, and placed into the empty porcelain space. The faucet turned on and shocked them, then they became the water. The naga lay half beneath and half behind them. They felt the strong tail beneath their seat, their legs rested on it, their back against the steady rising and falling chest which regulated their own breathing and heartbeat.

Gossamer yet steady hands touched their face, brushing their cheeks and forehead. Water poured over their hair. Their own hands were guided to touch their scalp to help dislodge the dirt and oils, letting the waste be washed clear. The naga lay their hands over the body's belly. Their belly. It massaged their head and untangled their hair.

They remembered when they'd closed the door. She had come by and knocked before entering their room to find them under the fluffy comforter on their bed, head hidden beneath the pillow. She had sat at their feet and placed a hand on their body until they had uncovered their head. She promised that they could weather the storm together. She soothed them, each strand of hair she guided away from their face was a reassurance. The days would pass, there would be a new dawn, she promised. They could cry, and when the crying ended they would feel better.

But they did not cry in front of her, she hadn't known that they had already left their body. The naga laid each strand of hair free of entanglement. The shedded pieces dropped away outside the basin of the tub.

"It hurts," they said.

Yes, said the naga.

"My hurt is a bouquet of thorns piercing each other."

The hurt is not you.

"The body hurts."

The body holds what you do not let flow. I am here to help you flow again. A river cannot be stabbed, but a dammed lake becomes diseased.

"I cannot ever be well again."

You cannot live as you are and be well.

"I don't know what to do." Their being shuddered, and more tensions relaxed from them as the truth was spoken aloud. "I don't know how I got here."

The naga put soap in their hands. They returned to themself. They found their skin with their touch. Their breath expanded the lungs of the body. Their body, their lungs. Their soft animal self.

"Return to yourself," the naga said.

Slipping back into the body, the weak vessel, the neglected home, how could they? How could this have been done to them? Inaction as violence against themself. Their toes, their feet, their ankles, they remembered living there, their legs, their hips, their stomach. They rolled up into this form they had once fully lived within, and felt the pang of deprivation. It hurt too badly, and they fled to the ceiling above, gazing down at their form and that of the beautiful naga who cradled them like a baby.

The naga looked up and saw them. *"Sing yourself back into your body."*

The body knew a folk song. Tones first and a halting melody that stopped to shudder the body and let tears fall. The naga held them, it remained the silence beneath the song. They did not drift back down, they emerged behind the eyes. They filled their throat and chest and arms and head, turning their gaze up as if they could see where they'd been. But now here they were with living hands and lungs and blood and flesh. They curled their soapy fists and let their voice open their throat more. It was them. The sound reflected off the tiles and resounded against them.

"I am here," they said, and they turned to look at the naga.

The naga's face had beautiful eyes that reflected the light of their own. Scales, like on its tail, shaped crescent moons around its eyes, and its mouth smiled with all cuspid teeth.

"You can make it through the door," the naga said. It reached up to cup their face between cool palms.

They bowed their head forward, and the naga touched its forehead to theirs. Sorrowful peace washed over them. They kept their eyes closed and felt the naga melting beneath them like snow off boots placed near a hearth.

They looked around the bathroom, sitting alone in the tub. With new hands, they touched the edges of the bath, and the water sloshed as they strained to stand on their own two feet. Clinging to the basin, they stepped out. The floor of towels and possessions absorbed the droplets raining off their body. They did not need to look in the mirror to know themself.

"I am," they said.

The ceiling felt familiar, it beckoned them up. Repulsive rot met their feet because there was no floorspace to support their step. Bottles, disposables, boxes, clothes, waste, discards, and once precious things were beneath them. They touched the foundation of obstacles they'd built, wobbling on unbalanced skeleton legs. It was suffocating, and there was a mountain in front of the exit.

They collapsed to their knees at the sight. One could not bear the suffering of their mind alone. They were too weak. They felt they were slipping from their body. Looking to the bed, the purpose for this room, there was the imitation of the naga. Sculpted clothes as a curved tail, with the head of their childhood companion taking the place of the naga's face, something loved into realness. Bead eyes reflected the light of the room.

They could return to sleep. They could imagine pulling themself up and lying against the clothes and touching the silk of the rabbit ears. It was painful there, but they knew where the darkness rested in the corners, where the sliver of light hit, and water came once a day in a single stream. When they did not give in to despair, the prize was maintaining their head above water. Nothing more. There was no final victory. They wanted to stop swimming, but they didn't want to drown.

They began to sing again, the same folk song, something ancient and ancestral. Each note strengthened their hand as it reached for one of the rocks of the mountain. They pulled it away. They reached for another. A pizza box, a lemonade can, a cotton t-shirt dress, a sympathy card, dead flowers in plastic wrap, a paper shopping bag, an electrical cord, a shoe, a burnt candle, a phone, a trophy, a piece of foil, and plastic and garbage and plastic and garbage. They kept singing, looping, louder, quieter, whispering to themself. Each item plucked the web strings of their body. Taut tendons ached and vibrated, muscles strained, and their voice grew softer. The song continued in their body when it would not pass their lips. *Here, Here, Here.*

There was the floor. Forest-green carpet. There was the door. Dark-brown wood. The pads of their fingers touched the portal, tracing the grooves of the rectangular panels. They grabbed the cool silver handle as they exhaled. One foot, then the other, they rose to their feet. Straight legs, two hands holding the way out. They opened their mausoleum door, the effort of prying open a cracked geode.

Clean air baptized their body. They closed their eyes. Breathing here didn't strangle them. There was space here. Burning light. A red vision through their eyelids swirled with fractal kaleidoscopes. The patterns lingered once they opened their eyes.

The hallway was wider than they remembered, dark wood and a red river of rug running the length to another door. They crossed the threshold, and their door closed behind them. Here in the in-between they had to rest, sitting against their door, it looked the same as its twin across the hall. There could be anything behind it, space and matter.

They used the wall to stand, it kept them upright as the floor met their feet. The song still thrummed a mantra in their cells.

Down the hall was a coat, and below it a pair of slippers. There was sound out here, a shushing white noise outside and behind the door at the end of the hall. Their skin tingled as the artificially-made air blew over them from a vent. Shoulders raising, they curled their chest and hugged their body. They found the softer rug an even path beneath their feet.

Each step eased their body's pain as curiosity kept them moving to the end of the hall, shoulders relaxing as they brushed the coat's hydrophobic-polyester material. The coat was sleek and had a beautiful violet exterior with an indigo satin lining. It hung around their shoulders and kept safe their arms, like a blanket. It smelled like something alive, smelled like her, peaches and cut grass. Something like they were.

The slippers on their feet were soft like rabbit fur. Each step they took was gently cushioned. When their heart beat quickly, they squatted down and hugged their knees, their forehead pressed against the wood.

Out there, where the flies were meant to be, they could go there. Stacking their spine back up again, they held the handle of the way out. The door was locked. They turned the mechanism, the cracking cued the order before chaos.

The *pitter-patter* percussed the earth with the song of their atoms, beckoning. Being the harmony, they opened the door and met the rain.

INTO THE DEPTHS

By Estella Edgewater

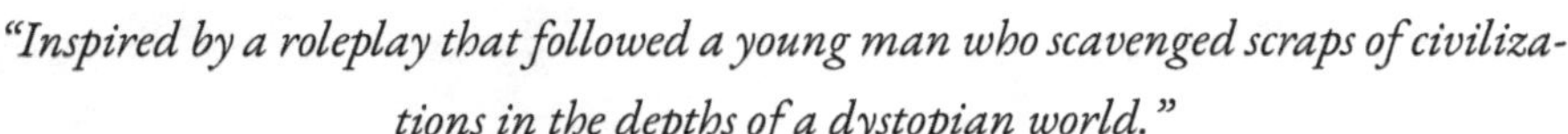

"Inspired by a roleplay that followed a young man who scavenged scraps of civiliza-tions in the depths of a dystopian world."

His boot kicked loose stones over the edge of a chasm that filled his horizon. Beyond, a darkness eating through the world left threads of land clinging to the planet's core.

He tightened the buckles of his harness holding fast two climbing axes. Securing his makeshift reel of wire rope and its spring-loaded grapple hook on his hip, he withdrew one of his two remaining flares and dropped it into the chasm. He counted heartbeats until the black gradient swallowed its glow.

Somewhere in these depths was hope for refuge. His feet propelled him off the cliff's edge.

Freefall.

The wind deafened his ears, goggles suctioning to his eye sockets, as he dove into the heart of the chasm. Craggy walls closed in at the edges of his vision as the red glow of his flare appeared. A suffocating dread washed over him in layers of sweat, unhindered by the tunnel of wind enveloping his rapid descent.

The flare bounced as it landed. He twisted his body and launched the grapple hook towards the wall in an arc. Its claws caught the stone, dragging before cutting into a ledge with a spray of rock. The reel on his hip grew hot as the wire unrolled at blinding speed.

He unhooked the pair of climbing axes from his belt, choking their handles and catching the wall. His shoulders strained as the descent threatened to tear his arms from his body. Red-hot lines trailed from his tools while he eased the steel toes of his boots against the wall. He tucked his chin before the wire snapped taut. The reel on his harness stressed the leather, trying to hold his weight. Between his legs, the burning flare revealed the ground inches from his heels.

Exhaling, he rested his forehead against the wall and coughed. His burning palms relaxed around the hafts. Blisters bubbled across calloused skin under the freshly torn palms of his gloves. He sucked in through his nose and yanked his axes free. Kicking out from the wall, he detached from the reel.

His landing on the foliage caused a ripple of light to roll outwards as it crunched underneath his feet. Every blade of grass bloomed with a purple glow that faded like settling water. He took another step and a new ring of light birthed from it, revealing the silhouette of a grove where trees arched over a small crater filled with dark shimmering water.

The flare sputtered out, leaving the grove's blueprint in his mind's eye.

Lips pressed together, he stopped drawing breath, lungs burning. He peeled away the edges of his goggles, unable to stifle the suction release that echoed.

He froze, muscles tensing at the sound of something clawing the rocks above. The ping of his grapple hook being yanked from its anchor point sent him diving away, as chunks of rock fell and shook the ground. Light burst out from the crushing weight, before his grapple hook plunked down amongst the debris.

His harness strap secured his drumming heart in his chest as he stood and approached, eyes scanning the unnatural jagged grooves in the stone. He snapped his gaze upward towards a clambering sound and then silence. A swallow caught in his throat.

Static floated across his vision as he tried to adapt to the dark. He reached for his final flare and its red light fought fresh shadows dancing in his periphery. Backing away from the fallen debris, his steps carried the weight of pebbles dropping into shallow water.

His back hit a solid surface. Aching fear settled behind his optic nerves, distorting his surroundings. He turned, blinking through the haze to reveal the gnarled, twisted trunk of a tree. Purple veins glowed, etching across curled branches that ended in long locks of flowy hair. A pirouetting phantom rose from his memory and embodied the tree, their laughter echoed on repeat like a broken record. He reached out to brush his fingers through their soft hair. Instead, he touched the weeping leaves sprouted from the motionless tree.

A rustling coaxed his heart out of its bony prison as the faint glow of a small creature caught his eye. The round, fluffy bobble, no bigger than his fist, had a black nose at the front of its body below two oblong ears. Its stubby legs made it waddle when it moved.

The corners of his mouth turned up as more puffballs moved through the grass. He followed alongside them, watching the rhythm of their glow with each of his steps until he arrived at a hollow mound nestled amongst the trees. At its bottom, there was a hole just big enough for the puffballs to fit through but its peak surpassed his waist. He swept his hand over the familiar patterned ridges of the mound. Once home to a large tortoise, it was now blanketed in creeping lavender moss and a shelter for these little rodents.

The tortoise shell sat close to the crater, and the light of his flare shone along its edge, where the weeping leaves of these bowed trees touched the surface of the water. Crouching down, he used the tip of one of his axes to break the surface tension. Viscous liquid clung to the metal, coating it when he pulled back. His tongue tried to wet the inside of his parched mouth as the syrup dripped down. He gritted his teeth and stood, fighting away the despair creeping in at the edges of his resolve.

Walking the perimeter of the crater's pool, he found the edge of the grove where it transitioned, leading into a maw of stone. He stopped as a warm breeze kissed his cheeks, steadily pushing around his body, before the inhale drew him closer.

There was no refuge here.

He raised his flare to cut through the black veil, brandishing his axe. Two smooth black orbs stared back at him from within and devoured the light.

INTERVIEW WITH THE GREMLIN

By Buxton Manning

"Inspired by a remembered incident from my days teaching intro to broadcasting."

There are so many ways our future can take an abrupt turn, a sharp curve, a different direction. Some give credit to the stars, others to fate or divine providence, but for me, it was an unplanned disruption from a group of individuals better known for mischief.

Being a journalist, specifically as a television reporter, was a lifelong dream of mine. The summer before I started kindergarten, I watched the TV news from my father's lap. What was being said was well above my grade level, so I merely watched the pictures and the talking heads. The news anchors held no appeal, but the on-the-scene reporters—they were different. Their ability to speak clearly and compellingly, no matter the situation or location, mesmerized me. Whether standing in front of a five-alarm fire or at the scene of a bank robbery, they always looked so cool and calm and, to me, heroic. Something struck a nerve, and I knew I had found my life's calling.

Growing up, all the other boys emulated their athletic heroes. Kobe, A-Rod, Tom Brady. Me? I wanted to be like NBC News' Lester Holt. Yes, it was awkward, but it didn't stop me from pursuing my dream. In high school, I became involved with the school newspaper, a practice I continued in college, while also reporting for the on-campus cable channel and pursuing my journalism degree with a double minor in history and economics. In my small amount of free time, I hung out in one of the two newsrooms. My social life was zilch, but I was career-focused. I got a summer job tending bar at one of the dance clubs next to campus to help pay the bills, but outside of studying and my two journalism gigs, that was my life, and I loved it.

Once I graduated, I took my degree and my desire and went job hunting, but quickly found out that desire and limited experience weren't enough: I got no offers, not even entry-level. After a few months of failure, my dad began mumbling about me still living at home and not being gainfully employed. I needed to do something, and quickly, so I took my other talent—bartending—and found work at Sue's Brews, a local pub that happened to be a hangout for some of the media folks in town. I made the best of this lucky coincidence and started recognizing faces and voices so I'd be sure to chat them up while serving, hoping to get an "in" somewhere.

Bernie Sholtz was a regular at Sue's, though he had neither face nor voice that was broadcast-worthy...or recognizable. He was the chief engineer at KNIN-AM, a news-talk outlet in town. It's a rule that every station has to have someone responsible for the station's technical infrastructure, which means ensuring compliance with all FCC rules and maintaining the station's equipment. Years ago, a chief engineer's position was full-time, but now, with so many technical improvements and everything being digital and computerized, most stations share a chief engineer. Bernie split his time between KNIN and two other stations: a religious station and one that broadcast in Spanish. He spent most of his time at KNIN, and says he liked it better than the other places because he's not that religious and doesn't speak Spanish, but I think it's because he's a news junkie.

Sue knew him well and told me he was a bachelor and a bit of a loner; whether by his own choice or everyone else's, she couldn't say. The joke in the bar was that his three best friends were Jack Daniels, Jose Cuervo, and Captain Morgan, but I learned that wasn't true; Bernie was strictly a vodka man. He'd change it up, though; Black Russians one week, White Russians the next, and sporadically Moscow Mules. Notice the plurality here? Bernie never had just one drink. Come to think of it, I can't remember a time when he stopped at two.

He usually drank by himself, but now and then he'd hang with some of the KNIN sales folks, or sometimes he'd mosey over and chat with the on-air staff and reporters. They're two different worlds—sales and talent—think back to those old reruns of *WKRP in Cincinnati*. They speak different languages, have different goals, and as you might expect, dress differently, too. My observation added a fourth deviation: salespeople drank hard liquor, while reporters were craft beer people.

Bernie never wavered—at least, in his choice of drink. He came in around six and sat at his regular spot at the bar, nodded a greeting to me or whoever got to him first, ordered up, and then drank. By nine or so, someone had to pour him into a cab or ply him with coffee so he could walk the seven blocks from Sue's to the apartment he called home.

It was during one of his White Russian loner nights sitting at the bar that he asked me a question that wasn't like, "Can I get another?" Bernie was usually polite when he wasn't plastered and rarely spoke except to order, so I almost dropped the vermouth bottle I was using for a chocolate martini when he grumbled, "What's a kid like you doing working here? Whadja go to school for just to be a bartender, eh? What do you really wanna do?"

This was the first time he'd spoken more than two sentences to me, if you don't count, "Gimme a drink and make it with the good stuff. Use the Grey Goose. And make it a double." I had time to recover while I finished and delivered the martini, then went back to where he was sitting.

"If you must know," I said, "I want to be a world-famous TV reporter."

He gave me a look that made me wonder if he forgot he was the one who asked the question. Eventually, he said, "Like Brokaw? Anderson Cooper? Good luck."

"No, actually. A reporter, not an anchor, though I used to idolize Lester Holt."

"He's an anchor now. Well, he was."

"I know. I liked him better when he wasn't behind a desk. He got assigned to all the hot spots: Iraq, Somalia, Northern Ireland."

"It gets pretty hot in here." He laughed at his joke, then pointed a finger at me. "Listen, if you're serious and don't mind not being on camera, I'll see what I can do about getting you on at KNIN."

"Radio? Gosh, I dunno."

Bernie pounded the bar with his fist and let out a laugh-snort. "Gosh? Did you say gosh? Oh, hell, I've *got* to find a spot for a guy like you, just so they can teach you some new four-letter words."

A week later, I found myself in the office of the news director, who waved off my lack of professional experience once he saw my college transcripts. He made me read some prepared news copy, and although I didn't have much prep time to review it, I must've done OK because he said, "Bernie told me he thought you might have a knack for this, and frankly, we're short-staffed right now. I can't pay much, but the job's yours if you want it."

It wasn't TV, and it was only part-time, but I considered it "a foot in the door" and figured I'd gain some experience; eventually, I'd make a name for myself, then move on. That was the plan anyway. I kept working at Sue's to make ends meet, and I was lucky they were extremely flexible in scheduling me around my radio hours, which were crazy. I was on call to go whenever they sent me to cover whatever it was they wanted me to cover, so I had to be able to leave the bar within minutes. In addition, I did weekends on-air, mostly reading headlines and weather in between the syndicated shows.

I kept hoping I could go full-time, but I knew I'd have to earn my promotion. Most of my assignments were fluff pieces, covering some organization's fundraiser, local high school basketball, or an evergreen piece on "how to stay cool during the upcoming heat wave." The biggest story I'd covered was a community protest about the lack of sidewalks in a neighborhood. Hardly top-of-the-hour stuff. What I needed to do was land a scoop, do something big, so they'd recognize my talent.

I'd been there about six weeks when I overheard a police call on the scanner just as my shift was ending on a Sunday. There was a reported hostage situation, and the police were closing the streets and advising residents to stay indoors until everything was resolved. I wrote up the details so that the newscasters who followed me would have the information to read during a broadcast, but then the weekend editor said, "Why don't you head out there and broadcast live on the spot? You can call in with your phone and report if there's breaking news."

I grabbed one of the station's new digital recorders as a precaution and headed out the door. At the very least, I could ask questions of someone in charge at the scene when there was a resolution, then bring the interview back to be used for later broadcasts and on Monday morning's drive-time show. This was it! No cupcake story this time, but genuine news and my big chance!

Well, it might have been, had either my phone or the recorder worked.

I confess that in dealing with the station's equipment, my skills were deficient compared to the other reporters. Most of them had a broadcasting education or had worked for years in the industry, whereas I was straight out of J-school with no tech training whatsoever. I thought I'd be on television, and TV reporters usually had camerapersons with them when they were out on assignment, so a knowledge of the technical stuff wasn't necessary. I didn't even understand everything about my smartphone (it was smart, I wasn't), but when the hostage situation quickly escalated and the police moved in, I grabbed my phone to call the station so I could go live with what was happening.

What was happening was that my phone refused to dial. I kept entering the station's number (I still hadn't gotten around to setting up the favorites in my contact list), and…nothing. By the time the cops were bringing out the unharmed hostage and the bad guy in cuffs, the moment was lost. But I still had the recorder. I went over to someone in uniform who looked like they might be in charge to get a summary of what happened. This way, I have something to take back to the station to air during the next newscast.

I asked intelligent questions. He gave me crisp answers. It took just three minutes, and I was thrilled with the results. I raced back to the station, went into the production studio, plugged the recorder into the soundboard, and…pfffft. Nothing.

I could have sworn I did everything right during the recording (not an easy assumption to make with a device that has a 92-page operating manual). The recording levels were going up and down while we were talking. I *saw* it, and I *know* it worked then. But now it was all static, and I was crushed.

I did the next best thing and wrote up a summary for the newscast, then recorded the summary so they'd have that, too, but I knew what the news director would say when he heard it: "That was a dry report; all canned stuff. Where are the actualities? Didn't you speak to anyone there? You need to do better."

That's pretty much what he said when he saw me later on Monday, though he added some extra verbiage—the four-letter kind Bernie was talking about. He also made it clear I'd never get off the part-time fluff-stuff train at the station until I could bring home a story worth talking about. That hurt worse than the cursing. My dream was slipping away, and fast.

That's what I told Bernie that night when he stopped into Sue's. Normally, I'm as quiet as he is when I'm tending bar, but I had been feeling low all day and needed to let it out to someone. We got into a conversation when he first came in, when he ordered a Vodka Collins, something he'd never ordered before. I asked him why the change in beverage.

"Supposedly, it was invented by Ted Majeski of United Press International back in the '60s. I met Ted when I was working for a newspaper in DC before I got into radio. Found an old UPI teletype ribbon in storage today and thought of him, and so I thought I'd change things up." He looked away and then mumbled, "Just like I did when I switched careers."

I didn't get that, but seeing he was in a talkative mood, I told him about my in-the-field screw-up on Sunday. I thought maybe he'd offer me some words of wisdom based on his decades of experience.

Imagine my surprise when he told me it probably wasn't my fault.

"It's the gremlins, most likely," he said while making a face as he sipped his drink. I couldn't tell if he didn't like it or if there was some other reason for his grimace.

I grimaced back because I was hoping for something more than a lousy joke from him. He saw my face and added, "No, I'm serious. Gremlins foul up everything."

"I know things break occasionally," I said, "but maybe it *was* my fault. I could have bumped one of the buttons, and if I'd forgotten to set the 'hold function' on the recorder to lock them in, they wouldn't have—"

"No, kid, listen to me. It. Was. Gremlins."

"C'mon, you're a techno-wizard, and you—"

He put up his hand to stop me, then took a big gulp of his Collins. "What I'm trying to tell you is that gremlins are real. They exist."

I didn't know a lot about gremlins, just what I remembered from cartoons and that awful Spielberg movie. All made-up stuff—so why was he blaming my failures on them? I was starting to wonder about Bernie. First, he orders a new drink, and now this bunk about gremlins. Maybe he had a few before he came in? It didn't make me feel any better about my problems, though I had to admit I forgot about them for a few minutes. I left Bernie to himself while I was waiting on other patrons, but after a few minutes, he flagged me down.

"Gimme another one of these," he said, "and I can tell you don't believe me, do ya?"

I ignored the poke, but when I came back and delivered his drink, I said, "Of course, I don't believe you. That's just silly. Gremlins fall into the same category as leprechauns, fairies, gnomes, and such. Not real—imaginary. I don't get why some people need to blame made-up beings for life's misfortunes."

He was about to say something, but I cut him off. "I was hoping you could give me some feedback on what might have happened to the equipment, why everything failed, both my phone and the recorder. The boss says if I can't deliver the goods, my time at KNIN is gonna be short. I need that job, and I want to do better. Bernie, what happened? Why did my phone and the recorder fail me? What did I do wrong?"

"I told ya, it was gremlins. Whatever you did, they undid. For whatever purpose. They pick their times for the screwiest reasons, but they have their motivation for it."

"They have a motivation to be malicious? That makes no sense."

"You'd have to ask them, not me. I gave up trying to figure 'em out long ago. I just know that they're real and ain't much you can do but go with the flow."

With that, he grabbed his drink and headed over to where a couple of the KNIN salespeople were sitting. I was fine with that; if he wasn't going to help me, or even take pity on me, well...the heck with him. He never came back to the bar that night, finishing his drink and leaving shortly after.

Once my shift ended, I headed home, feeling horrible. Once home, I contemplated making myself a drink from my bar, just to help me sleep through the night, but I feared a hangover. I checked my phone for any last-minute emails and Facebook posts that couldn't wait until morning. I saw a weird, unrelated response from someone I didn't know to a post I had made a few days ago.

Nigel

> So you don't think we're real, huh? Be at the corner of Ninth and Sunset at 3:30 tomorrow afternoon.

I didn't know anyone named Nigel, and couldn't figure out what was meant by the taunt. I was just about to delete it when a second message popped up.

Nigel

> Bernie's right, you know.

Bernie's right? About what? Bernie was old enough that he'd probably worked with hundreds of people in the industry, and I searched my brain for anyone I knew who might be friends or acquaintances of his named Nigel, but came up empty. It could have been anyone. And just what was it that Bernie said that I didn't think he was right about? The only discussion we'd had was about the technical malfunctions and...wait, *about the gremlins*? Was Nigel saying Bernie was right about gremlins being real?

And was he calling me out to prove it?

I clicked on Nigel's profile to see who he was, but all that came up was a generic icon and no information. No hometown, workplace, schools, family...or friends. Nothing. A blank slate. I sat there trying to figure out how to do a Google search...I mean, what the hell do I search for? "Gremlins named Nigel?"

But as I sat there, a third message appeared:

Nigel

> Don't bother looking for me, you already found me (hee-hee). Ninth and Sunset, 3:30. I'll be carrying an umbrella.

While that response was totally weird, it was enough to whet my journalistic curiosity. I didn't know what to expect, but I knew I had to be prepared for anything, so the next morning I checked the Internet for background info. Wikipedia reported their presence on British Air Force safety posters during World War II, and a whole slew of media references, including that stupid Spielberg film. Nowhere did I find anything about gremlins being real; in fact, quite the opposite. That clinched it—I had to see Nigel.

I double-checked everything on my phone to ensure it was working, and also stopped at the station and checked out a digital recorder for backup. No one asked me what I wanted it for. I assumed they figured whatever story I was covering, I'd screw up just as badly as the hostage situation, so it wouldn't matter.

Initially, I wasn't thinking "story." I just had a simple curiosity about who Nigel was, why he was sending me coded messages, and how he could have known (or guessed) that I'd try to find out more about him. It was strange, spooky—as if he were looking over my shoulder while I typed...or as if he were IN the computer, watching my every move.

I called Sue to see if I could take a longer and later lunch than normal that afternoon, and when I told her it was for the station, she readily agreed.

"I hope you get something worthwhile so you can get on their good side again," she said, having heard about my hostage fiasco from the other KNIN employees at the bar.

That's when it really sank in—if I could pull off an actual interview with a *real* gremlin, then THAT would be something that could be my big break.

I arrived at the corner of Ninth and Sunset about fifteen minutes early, parked in a public lot a few blocks away, and still had time for a quick look around. There was a drugstore on one corner, a coffee shop on another, a Subway, and a bank. If someone had been waiting until I arrived, they could've been anywhere. I considered killing time until the appointed hour in the coffee shop, but thought better of it since I was already nervous and getting a coffee would've made me more jittery. I felt foolish just standing on the corner, but I couldn't think of anything else to do, so...I stood and waited.

And waited.

And waited.

By 3:45, there had not been a single individual who came along with an umbrella. In fact, there hadn't been anyone at all who stopped there. Simply a couple of dozen souls who moved briskly to complete whatever business they had elsewhere. It was a sunny day, with no rain in sight, so anyone with an umbrella would have been conspicuous. But no one came. No one stopped. No one even paused to look around as if they were looking for me.

I decided this was some lame joke, perpetrated by persons unknown, and I knew Bernie had to be involved somehow because Nigel mentioned his name in the post. I felt horrible because I liked Bernie. The way things were going at the station, he was just about my only ally. Nuts. I was tired from standing around, I was mad at being stood up, and I felt like kicking something, but there wasn't anything except a lamppost.

Disgusted, I headed back to where I'd parked my car. When I got within a few feet of the driver's door, a figure popped up on the passenger side near the hood. It was wearing a long coat and what I'd call a big Outback hat, and that's all I could see, so I really couldn't tell much about the individual except...he carried an umbrella. It was plain to see and pointed skyward as I approached the car door.

"You're a patient one," a voice from under the hat said. "That's good, because you're going to need all the patience you've got by the time we're through."

I was startled, but kept enough of my wits to realize this was Nigel. At least, I hoped it was and not some random weirdo who just happened to be standing by my car. There was only one way to find out.

"Are you Nigel?" I asked in my best newsman's style.

"You know, it would have been safer had you asked me who I was rather than assuming I was the one you're looking for. Are you going to let me in?" He pointed to the car with the umbrella in case I forgot that was how I was supposed to recognize him.

Rather than open up, I said, "How did you know this was my car?"

He laughed. "If you haven't guessed by now, I know everything."

That was unnerving, and I hesitated a bit before unlocking the doors. He got in right away, but I just stood there for a moment before committing myself. When I finally got in, I still couldn't see much of Nigel; just the coat and that hat pulled down over his face. He'd opened up the umbrella and placed it in the seat well to cover his legs...if he had legs.

I mustered up my courage and said, "There must be a reason you called me out, and I'd appreciate knowing why. You weren't where you said you'd be, then you surprised me here. I have to know what's the purpose behind this meeting and if you're going to be straight with me from here out, because if you're not, or if this is some kind of joke, you can get the hell out of my car right now."

He didn't respond right away, but he didn't move to get out, either. Finally, he shifted a bit and said, "All right, I apologize for not being on the corner. I knew you were there waiting, but I didn't feel like being a public spectacle—too many people walking by. And I saw you arrive, so I knew it was your car, lest you think I'm some sort of omnipotent being. Though I am." Then he nodded forward as he chuckled, "You'll see. Let's go for a drive."

Having doubts about my safety, I nevertheless started up the car and eased out of the lot. As soon as I got onto Sunset and headed west, I regretted not starting either my phone recorder or the station's unit. Maybe I could hold off asking the big questions until I had a chance to turn them on. I didn't want to miss anything he said, but at the same time, I wasn't completely trusting either. Then there was the usual late afternoon traffic to consider. Maybe I could stall, say I wanted to get a coffee, and then—

"Pull over if you want to turn on your recorders," he said. "It won't do you any good, of course, but go through the motions. You won't hurt my feelings."

How did he DO that? Could be just a lucky guess, right? Still, I found a parking spot on the street and did as he said, and once both recorders were on and positioned on top of the console, I drove on. I wasn't sure if I could drive and ask questions at the same time, so I decided against getting on the highway. I needn't have worried, since Nigel anticipated my first question and took off.

"No, I'm not human. I just appear to you that way."

"What are you, then?" I asked.

He laughed. "A gremlin! No, seriously, I am."

I was tempted to say, "Just tell me what you want to tell me since you're the one who set up this meeting," but my good journalistic instincts took hold and I said instead, "What do you really look like if you're not human?"

"Good question. Gremlins are part of the *persona-littleus* species, which includes elves, leprechauns, fairies, sprites—all the smaller folk. So you were right when you told Bernie we're in the same category. But..."

He stopped and then made a low-guttural sound that shook the insides of the car so much I had to slow down. "Oh, sorry. That just slipped out. I knew I had to contact you when I found out about what you said to Bernie. That really cheesed me off something fierce."

"What, being like a leprechaun or a gnome?"

"Arrrggh, leprechaun is bad enough, but never, ever, say we're gnome-like. Bothersome, pesky people. Filthy, too. We're more like elves in that we're helpers, but in appearance, we're more like...well, something like leprechauns. It's the ears. But they're the real mischief makers, and they always work alone. We work in teams, and we can modify our appearance to fit the situation. That's why I appear human to you. We try to remain unobserved and out of sight, but now and then someone gets a glimpse and then tries to describe what we look like. It's always ridiculous, like in that movie where we're supposed to be Furbys."

"Then what about all those old war posters with the pointed heads and ears? Isn't that accurate?"

"I need to give you a bit of backstory before I tell you about that. See, we've been around since forever, but the word 'gremlin' didn't enter the vernacular until about a hundred years ago. It was between your world wars when one of us was accidentally exposed. This was 1929, in Malta, involving that damned Royal Air Force—they're the ones who popularized the idea later. They were having equipment problems due to shoddy machinery that wasn't being properly maintained. There had been accidents and a couple of serious crashes. One of our operatives was spotted near a plane that later had a nasty mishap, and rather than search for the real reason, they blamed us."

"But why were you there?"

"That's the rest of the story. Gremlins are what you might call influencers."

"What, like on social media?"

"Hardly. Just the opposite. Our role in society is to make sure things happen the way they're supposed to. We were there to get the RAF pilots to take pre-flight inspections seriously. That's why they were having all those problems. Right after the first war, the fly-boys had a feeling of invincibility. When they flew those older biplanes and crashed, there were injuries, but only a handful of pilots lost their lives. As the technology improved and planes traveled faster, there were more serious accidents, and the deaths were starting to mount. There were mechanical breakdowns in flight that could have and should have been averted. Our job was to tinker with equipment so that they'd have to stop and inspect the entire plane before take-off to ensure everything was in order."

Outside, I remained stoic, my best journalist face showing nothing but seriousness, but inside, I was giddy. This was fantastic! I don't mean like "unbelievable," though in a way it was, but it was going to make the kind of blockbusting interview that's often award-winning. A glance at my phone and the recorder showed they were working just fine. I asked, "So what happened?"

"One of our operatives didn't disappear quickly enough before the crew came into the hangar. One of the pilots told everyone he saw a gremlin, then another pilot with a literary bent put it in a published poem, and the rest is history. And we were only trying to help."

"That's hardly been your reputation. Gremlins are always depicted as trouble-makers, mischievous imps who sabotage equipment for nefarious reasons."

"That's the Brits for you. Always have to have someone to blame. That was the reason they used a leprechaun-like figure when they created those posters. It reminded them of the Irish, and you know what they think of *them*."

I had been driving south on Leggitt, heading out of town. I wanted to stop somewhere so that I was less distracted and could really listen to what he was saying. Then I could respond with better, more inquisitive questions.

I started to slow down near a park, but he grumbled and said, "No, don't stop, keep going. I like your car, it runs well for its age, and I'd hate to create a malfunction later. Don't give me a reason. Drive on."

I did as he suggested and then asked, "You said you're like the others in your species, but there are lots of stories about fairies and leprechauns that go a lot farther back in history."

"That's not really a question."

"Well, I guess I'm curious why it took so long for gremlins to be discovered, if that's the right term, when there have been reports of fairies and elves that go back centuries."

"We weren't nearly as active before the Industrial Revolution. Our specialty is technology, so there weren't a lot of reasons for us to get involved with humans back then. Fairies and elves had other missions, other priorities. They've taken a back seat to us now since everything today is technology-driven, though we were the brains behind a lot of what the elves were doing."

"Like what?"

"You know the old story of the shoemaker and the elves? We were there."

"That's one of Grimm's Fairy Tales, and there's no mention of gremlins."

"Yeah, the Grimm brothers..." He stopped and shook his head. "The Roald Dahl of their time. Of course, they were just re-bottling old stories, trying to get rich off of them. Copyrights weren't a thing then. And anyway, they got it wrong, so..."

"What do you mean, they got it wrong?"

"The shoemaker and some of the other peasants were having tremendous issues, suffering at the hands of an oppressive landlord. The elves were intervening on behalf of the local merchants, but couldn't figure out a way to help until we suggested—"

I confess I tuned him out a bit while he went on, talking about supply-chain issues and leather shortages. I don't know why it hit me like it did, but one thing I've always been pretty good at is sniffing out nonsense, and the more he went on, the more it sounded like pure drivel. Bunk. It was like what my grandfather would do when I was a kid and asked him questions. He'd just start blathering, making it all up as he went, until my mom intervened and told him not to fill my head with rubbish.

This sounded like similar garbage. Even though I was driving, I felt like I was being taken for a ride, so I interrupted him and said, "Just a moment. This has gone on long enough. This story is...I mean, all of this sounds like baloney, just a bunch of words. Not a speck of truth. How do I really know you're what you say you are? You're intervening, helping elves, not humans. Why, I've heard better stories at the bar from the guys who can polish off a fifth of whisky like soda pop. I'm gonna stop this car right now and—"

I had taken my foot off the gas and was about to hit the brake so I could pull off on the shoulder, but as soon as I did, the engine started sputtering. The Camry was about all I could afford out of college; it had 120,000 miles on it, and the exterior was a bit dinged, but it had run OK for me. Their V-6 engine was notorious for having a problem with excessive carbon buildup in the intake system, and at first, I thought maybe I was overdue.

But before I could worry about the engine, I noticed my passenger was shrinking. At least, that's what appeared to be happening. The top of his Outback hat was now level with my shoulders, and the coat was folding up like it was going to be put into a laundry bag. As the car continued to sputter, I pulled it over to the shoulder and stopped, just as the hat sank into the wadded coat, as if Nigel had completely disappeared. Yet he was still there—well, his voice was.

"Don't bother to get out. We'll be OK in a moment." As if by magic, the passenger window lowered, and he yelled, "Hey, Reggie—are we ready to roll again?"

I didn't hear a response, but then he said, "Right, good job," and the window rolled back up. During the entire conversation with whoever Reggie was, there had been a brisk wind blowing through the open window, and it made me snap to.

I was tired of being played with. "I suppose you're going to tell me Reggie is also a gremlin, and he's the one who made my car falter? Where is he? Why can't I see him? How do I—"

"I told you we work in teams. You're still doubting me? Just what kind of evidence do you require? Do you want me to have Reggie set the engine on fire? Have him tamper with the brakes? Oh, don't worry, we won't let any harm come to you. That's in our conduct protocol, like your doctors with their 'do no harm' code." He cleared his throat with a loud, "Ahem," and then said, "Unless there are unforeseen circumstances, but I don't think it will come to that."

I sat and stewed, but couldn't think of a response. Truthfully, I had no explanation for what had just happened except for the one Nigel offered. Coincidence? One helluva one if it was. No, I had to admit that this was reality. That is, if the engine started up again, and of course, it did. I stewed again for a moment before putting the Camry in gear and easing back onto the road.

With no particular place to go, I drove on, going about five miles below the limit. Nigel had yet to resume his taller, human-like appearance, and that was fine with me. I peeked at my phone and the recorder on the console, and both seemed to be working normally, so I resumed our interview. "You said something about unforeseen circumstances. Just what do you mean, and how do you avoid catastrophes? You're in the business of causing trouble and wreaking havoc if your reputation is to be believed."

"Like I said before, humans like to blame others when stuff goes haywire. They fault coworkers, friends, enemies, whoever is convenient, and when it doesn't seem like there are other humans around to blame, then...well, that's why we try to stay out of sight."

"But there are always problems with technology. Things break, wear out, and come apart. How can—"

"And that's where we come in. We're not there to wreak havoc, but to teach lessons. With the planes, we were trying to make pilots pay more attention to their pre-flight inspections so that worn-out parts could be replaced before there was a problem. We crippled enough of the plane so it couldn't take off, so they'd *have* to stop and check everything. We had to do something drastic once the Nazis started the Blitz of London. That would have been bad for everyone—humans and the rest of us."

I gave him a side-eye. "Teach lessons? Give me another example."

"Easy. Computers."

My BS-meter went into the red again, and I didn't want to let him off the hook so easily. "I need more of an explanation."

"Sure. Granted, it wasn't our idea, but we helped make them what they are today. Take the mouse; that was us."

"How so?"

"Well, we didn't invent it, but we made it popular. Trackballs had been around since the sixties, but the idea of using them with a computer didn't catch on until Bill Gates and Microsoft. We left a deck of cards out on a table near where he and his engineers were working, and set them up as a game of solitaire. One of them took the hint, and pretty soon they added mouse capabilities to the software. The idea was to teach people how to use a mouse by playing a game; then they could move on to other tasks that used to be accomplished with a keyboard."

"Oh, come on."

"No, seriously." I heard him grunt, and then the window rolled down again. "Reggie!" he yelled, and the car started to sputter.

"OK, OK, I believe you," I cried, and I thought I heard a couple of giggles as the window rolled back up and the engine purred again as if nothing were wrong.

As we motored along, the Outback hat began to rise and the coat filled up so that Nigel returned to his earlier form. I assumed this was some sort of exclamation point to prove he was what he said he was, so I grudgingly accepted everything as fact and contemplated my next question.

Before I could ask anything, he interjected, "You realize the computer mouse was one of those times where there were unforeseen circumstances that resulted in unexpected consequences. We had no idea people would misuse their valuable time playing a stupid game rather than doing their work. That's something no gremlin would ever consider. A gnome, sure. Vile things, really. A complete waste of oxygen."

"What do you have against gnomes?"

"Don't you have better questions to ask me? There's not much time."

I hadn't thought there'd be any rush to end our interview. I didn't have to be back at Sue's until five-thirty, and Nigel...who knew? Do gremlins punch a time clock? Have time management issues? How would I know? Did it matter?

But he had a point about asking better questions, so I said, "Let me think for a moment," and considered my options. What did I really, really want to get out of this interview? Something meaty, something big. Then, I found inspiration.

"You said you were behind the computer mouse," I said. "What other technological inventions can we credit to gremlins?"

He didn't answer right away, and for a moment I thought maybe he wasn't there. Or worse, I made him angry for some reason. I started to slow down, and suddenly he said, "No, no, keep going, I heard you. I'm thinking. Before I tell you, I just want to say for the record that we had nothing to do with AI. Got that?" He raised his voice, "Gremlins are not responsible for Artificial Intelligence."

Speaking normally, he said, "AI is going to be the death of your race, you know that?"

"Oh, I don't know about–."

"I know. Anyway, we don't invent. We don't make things, we just, um, motivate humans to do the right thing when they work with technology. Like with the pilots, making them more careful. We did something similar with computer programmers so they'd make better computers."

"Like what?"

"Don't get mad when I tell you. Promise?"

I wasn't about to blow this interview now, so all I said was, "Fire away."

"We came up with the idea of bugs. Minor glitches, so they'd be extra careful with their coding."

"You mean like viruses?"

"No!" he yelled. "That was those damned gnomes. All we did was make sure that there was only one way for programs to be coded. Like back in the old keypunch days, we'd change a colon to a semicolon on just one line on one card, and that would make the whole program bomb. It was fascinating to watch them pore through those cards to find the one thing that made it crash. We just carried that practice over to personal computers and then the Internet. But no, not viruses. That's the gnomes. They're responsible for bots, too. And those stupid ads on YouTube."

His story sounded silly, just like everything he'd told me so far, but I knew better than to say anything. If only I could activate the camera on my phone, I could—

"Hey, listen," he said, "I hate to cut this short, but Reggie and I need to be moving on. There's a car wash up ahead on Nineteenth. Dash in there."

I headed for the car wash, but I still had questions, not the least of which was why, if he and Reggie needed to go somewhere, they'd do it from a car wash. Like so much of what he'd said, it didn't make sense, and I told him so.

"I didn't expect you to understand," he said. "Gremlins exist for a purpose, and that purpose is to help humans make better decisions. We do it at the macro level, of course, but we also affect individual lives."

"You mean you intervene with people one-on-one?"

"Yeah, in the same way we do with the big jobs. We set up situations so that...well, take your coworker Bernie. Who do you think set out that UPI ribbon so he'd find it and think of that guy and then order that drink and get talking to you? We got the ball rolling."

"But to what end?"

He let out a sound like a little girl's giggle and said, "Yeah, that's the part I can't tell you about. You'll find out eventually, and to tell you now spoils it."

I was hardly satisfied with that, so I suggested we drive back to the parking lot so he could explain further. He just grunted and said, "Just pull into the car wash here. Don't argue...unless you want to fix a flat tire on your way home. When you get to the rinse cycle, crack my window. Don't worry, your interior will survive a little water. Then you can go wherever you want and don't worry about your recordings; they're secure as ever."

Feeling stupid about this, I nonetheless did as I was told. I pulled into the car wash, paid the attendant, drove up to the hitch, then drove in silently. I wanted to ask Nigel one last question, but couldn't think of what to say. When we got to the wash cycle, I saw the hat and coat deflate and debated whether I should open the window at the rinse cycle or not, but as I was thinking this, the car started backfiring, so I quickly hit the switch to lower the window.

Water poured in, no doubt one of Nigel's unexpected consequences. Once we were under the dryer, I rolled the window back up and took another peek at the recorders. Still going strong. At least I had that. Was he still here, or did he and Reggie leave?

As soon as I got out of the wash tunnel, I pulled over to the vacuums and parked. First thing I did was check under the coat and hat, then the umbrella, and naturally, there wasn't anything there. I threw it all in the back seat and grabbed my phone. I turned off the recording function, set it for playback, and listened.

It was all there. I listened to the beginning of our interview for a few minutes, then realized I still had the station's recorder going, so I stopped that and reset it to the beginning. Same thing—it captured every sound (a lot better than my phone, I had to admit that), and even though the inside of the car was a small pond, I couldn't have been happier. I renamed and saved the sound file, knowing I had the scoop to end all scoops with the evidence to back it up.

I raced to the station. Even though I wasn't scheduled to work until Wednesday, no one was surprised to see me. Staff wander in and out, even on their off days, sometimes just to hang out or shoot the bull, to work on an evergreen story for broadcast later in the week, or to work on an audition tape to find another position at some other station. That's the nature of radio. Even when you're content and think everything is fine, you keep looking, just in case.

I wasn't worried about that now. My previous botched job would be a distant memory once I put together my interview with Nigel. I went over to a vacant computer and wrote some continuity that could be used once I packaged the recording into an interview. I'd have to take the recordings and splice them up, using Nigel's answers and cutting out all that background noise (and the times when he threatened to blow up my car, though I'd mention that in closing). Both production studios were in use, so I couldn't do it now, but I needed somewhere to put the recorder. I'd hang onto my phone for backup. I saw Bernie in his office and realized he had a locked cabinet. Maybe I could use that?

I went over to his door and knocked gently. "Hey, Bernie? Can I get a favor?"

"Whadaya need, kid?"

"I need to dub this interview off the recorder, but the rooms are taken and...uh, I don't want anything to happen to it, right? Can you lock it up somewhere until I come in on Wednesday? I have to get to work now and can't wait."

"Sure. I can pop it in the file cabinet, and I'll lock it up when I go."

"Can't you lock it now?"

He took the recorder from me, and just before he put it in the cabinet, he turned to me. "OK, sure. Wanna tell me what it's all about?"

"Maybe later, when I've got the package complete."

"Big deal, then?"

"Oh, yeah." I didn't dare say another word for fear he'd think I was crazy.

He came into Sue's later that night, like always. I didn't get a chance to serve him, and then we got busy and he left early for once, so I never got the chance to talk to him. Would I have told him about it if I had the chance? Not sure, but he was the only one I would have trusted with the tale. I almost said something to Phil, who was working the bar with me that evening, and that's only because he caught me looking at my phone during a slow moment. We're not supposed to use our phones while we're working, but all I was doing was just checking to ensure the recording of Nigel and me was still intact.

I was at the end of the bar and had the volume low, not really listening, just making sure nothing had happened to it, when he slid over to where I was and said in a low voice, "Hey, what's going on there?" like I was watching porn or something. I didn't want to get in trouble, so I told him the truth—that it was an interview I did for the station. He looked crestfallen, said, "Oh, huh," and went back to work, as did I.

The next morning, I was up early and checked my phone. Still there. Even though I wasn't due at KNIN until noon, I went in two hours early to work on my gremlin story. I got the recorder from Bernie, confident it had been in his locked cabinet since I left it with him, and walked proudly into one of the open production studios, ready to make history. I plugged a cord into the recorder and the opposite end into the soundboard, and then searched the files on the recorder for my interview.

And it wasn't there.

I had cleverly renamed the file ME_AND_N001.wav, and it should have been the topmost file since it was the last one created. There were several other files, but not mine. Just to be sure, I listened to them all, just in case. No luck.

Somehow, someway, the gremlins had deleted my recording. So what? I still had my phone, and it never left my side! I grabbed a different cord for my phone, plugged it in, found the recording on my phone (tough luck, gremlins!), and turned it on.

The first thing I heard was Phil's voice: "Hey, what's going on there?"

After that, I heard bar sounds, then my voice saying I wasn't watching porn but listening to an interview I did for the station. The recording had changed from my interview with Nigel to the conversation I had last night with Phil at Sue's.

I probably sat motionless in my chair for a half-hour, and might still be there had no one needed to use the studio. Another reporter, seeing that the "On-Air" sign wasn't lit (and me just sitting there), came in and asked if I was finished.

Boy, was I.

I pocketed my phone and took the defective recorder to Bernie's office. He was working on an old Zenith radio, the kind with vacuum tubes. It's a hobby with him, fixing up old antique radios and selling them to collectors. He stopped what he was doing and said, "Grab that screwdriver off the desk and bring it to me, will ya?"

It was like he could read my face. "Didn't work out, did it, kid?"

I shook my head.

"I'm not sure what to tell you," Bernie said, "though I can relate. I didn't do well in my first career choice, either. Wanted to be a newspaperman, and was one for a while, but soon found out I couldn't compete with the big boys. Couldn't write my way out of a paper bag. So much red ink on my stories, you'd think the editor bled to death. Got talkin' to a radio guy, he tells me to try radio even though he knows I ain't got the voice for it, then he tells me about the other side of it all, and I always liked to tinker with machinery, so I study hard and get my first-class license, and bang! I'm a radio engineer. Maybe that's what you should do, too."

"You mean change careers?"

"Nah, I mean learn engineerin'. That way, you can still be in radio. I'm getting too old for this stuff. You can take my place when you get up to speed. But you'd better hurry. I ain't gettin' any younger."

Quitting KNIN was like a breath of fresh air. We parted amiably, like two star-crossed lovers, knowing it was for the best. My folks weren't thrilled about my decision, partly because it meant I would still be living at home, but they came around once I told them of my long-range plan. I started taking classes last week, and Bernie is trying to get me some part-time work as his lab assistant at KNIN. He promised me he'd teach me everything he knows as long as I keep the Grey Goose in stock. That's not a problem, and besides, he doesn't need to teach me *everything*.

I already know about the gremlins.

THE MUSIC NOTE

By Tamelia Aday

"Introducing a character starring in a future novel."

The letter arrived at the height of summer. Weathered paper, brown, fragile—his name, in lacy loops, decorated the top of the page—Glendale Picky.

He trudged back inside. At eighty-three, the spring in his step had waned. The sun soaked into his bones, and the wind revived his skin. His hair, which he'd grown tired of cutting, drifted across his eyes.

He closed the door against the hot breeze and eased into his torn, red recliner.

Glendale sliced open the envelope and pulled out aged paper. A bar of music graced the top, followed by the notation to repeat.

"What kind of gobbledygook is this?" Disappointment surprised him. What had he expected? A love letter?

The piano, covered in dust, mocked him from the corner. Glendale shuffled to the scratched wooden bench, propped the paper before him, and squinted at the faded notes. He flexed his arthritic hands before they stuttered along the keyboard.

Glendale swayed to the unexpected quality of the sound and repeated the bar. His fingers lost their stiffness, and his back straightened.

A foggy ray of sunlight shimmered through the room, and the music expanded—full and deep. His hands paused. Stillness, like before a storm, weighted the atmosphere, and a high-pitched note reverberated throughout the room. The blinds rattled, and the door flew open.

"Blasted heat," Glendale muttered, shaken from the outburst. "Some kind of freak tornado?"

As he stood, the air cooled. Trees surrounded him instead of walls, and a bubbling creek played in the background. An underlying timbre rose from a bed of ferns that covered the ground. A wisp of the music echoed. Youth and vitality surged through his body.

He held his arms as though he and a partner waltzed within the green haven. Taking a step back, he bumped into another piano, this one almost invisible in the brush. A sheet of paper drifted onto the keys. He grasped it.

"Another one." His fingers now flowed over the keyboard with ease.

The notes tumbled and twirled through the air, and the forest vanished.

Balloons and colors popped, and a birthday cake sat at a far picnic table. Classmates from the fourth grade surrounded him. He glanced down and found his legs unmarred, no varicose veins, but the smooth skin of a boy.

"Glen!"

Someone handed him a bat. A piñata dangled. Now blindfolded, he twirled and swung. *Thwack, thwack, thwack*—candy fell and scattered, cheers followed by laughter. He flung off the blindfold, ran, jumped, and laughed.

Shouts rang from the street. "Glendale!" A glint of sun sparked against the metal of his bike. He hopped on and pedaled as fast as he could.

The air shifted as a faint song approached. A girl sauntered along, transistor radio held to her ear, a high-pitched note belting from the speaker.

Glendale found himself back inside his house, his hands old and his nails discolored. He drifted off in the recliner, but awoke to a knock on the door.

"Marina." He startled and took a step back.

"Glen." She brushed past him. "I received a letter." She handed him the cracked paper, with a glance at the piano. "I don't play."

He unfolded it, set it on the music rack, and his fingers strutted across the keys. The sound differed from his letter. A melody in a minor key—a warning.

Trees accented a lake. Marina's hair shimmered, and her skin glowed with a summer tan. Her eyes sparkled, reflecting off the water.

Muscular strength, the kind he once had, filled him.

"We're young again." She spread her arms out and lifted her head to the sky. "We must stay here."

"Doesn't work that way, Rina." The nickname slipped off his tongue. "We can't stay in a time we've already lived."

"Your logic bores me."

"You'd go back—to this?"

"Absolutely. We could improve on it. Enjoy what we missed."

Glendale hesitated. He and Marina—together as he always imagined.

She stepped closer and ran her hand through his hair. "Stay with me."

Something wasn't right. The night air sizzled. Her words meant nothing, and he found he'd lost his longing for her.

Chatter in the distance distracted him.

"It's the lake gathering."

They strolled toward the crowd, led by the smell of hot dogs. Fried cinnamon bread blended with the scent of water—intoxicating, comfort mixed with danger.

He stopped short. Under the gazebo: a piano, black and elegant, lured him toward the stage.

"No." Her fingertips dug into his arm. "Don't go."

"Marina, this isn't real."

He edged away. Her hand fell to her side. His steps matched the rhythm of the piano, its melody drowning out the laughter and voices. He caught a glimpse of Marina watching him. Her image wavered, then vanished.

Chemicals mixed with a flowery scent assaulted his nose. He stood among lettuce and bananas at the grocery, old once again. This time, he didn't mind the slowness or the hint of pain in his joints.

"Glendale?"

He turned. His friend Trudy appeared beside him.

"I'm making tacos." She held up the shredded lettuce. "At your house, like old times?" She smiled as though holding out an olive branch. Oh, right. They'd had a rift—a stupid quarrel.

"Maybe I'll try a peach pie." He offered a truce. "Improve my baking skills."

Her laughter chased away the dim surroundings. "Glendale Picky, I know when you're conning me. Grab a few peaches. I'll show you how it's done."

They arrived at his house and set the bags in the kitchen. "I got this letter." She handed him the worn stationery with the notes written along the top. "Should we play it?"

Glendale glanced at the bar of music. "Nah, this rhythm makes no sense." He went to the sink and lit a match. The paper burned at the edges and poofed into flames.

Trudy's laugh filled the room—better than any song he'd played. "I admire a decisive man."

He started the coffee while she cooked. "You know what, Trudy? I wouldn't change a thing. You, me, tacos, and peach pie."

NONDISCLOSURE AGREEMENT

By K.D. Jewell

"Arach has been with me for many years, and this story was short enough to keep him contained."

The echo of their shoes scuffing along confirmed to their ears that they were indeed in an enclosed space, but that was the only evidence. Travis wondered how Ben was moving forward at all as he stumbled blindly, following Ben's sounds.

"Seriously, do not call him Eric," Ben insisted, leather jacket flapping softly. "It's Ah-Roc. Arach. He really hates it if you say his name wrong."

Travis scoffed audibly into the pressing darkness, but his mouth started to go dry. Ben was no pushover. Ben was the guy who walked in and bought a round of drinks, the guy who had 'friends'. Ben was not the guy who worked on things like pronunciation.

Bluish pools of light came through the high windows, spreading across the floor, sending Travis' thoughts down a long, lazy river. Monsters lived in deep, dark rivers. Travis heard Ben huff out a sharp breath, the kind of thing you do when you're trying to physically rid yourself of anxiety.

"You know I appreciate this," Travis whispered. "With the restaurant burning down, the staff disappearing... I'm really in a bad spot. It'll be good to work again."

"Just let me do the talking, okay?" Ben said, whirling to face Travis with his eyebrows almost touching his greasy hairline. Ben trapped his stress between his parallel hands. "He's going to ask who you are and if he speaks directly to you, then you can talk. As little as possible."

Travis nodded. "Got it."

Ben turned, about to proceed further into the dark, then spun back around. Travis jumped a little.

"Even if he asks a loaded question— as little as possible."

"Yeah, okay," Travis groaned.

His nonchalance did little to uncoil his tightening intestines. Ben scowled at him but finally, FINALLY continued on. Mistily, something you almost had to watch with your peripheral vision at first, a tiny orange glow began to float in the distance. It flared and ebbed, blazed and dimmed, as though breathing in long, metered breaths.

It was a flame in the darkness, but how big was it? How far away? Travis imagined a furnace, a crematorium, until the acrid scent of cigarette smoke snaked into his nostrils. Travis flexed his hands and found his palms sloppy wet. Ben stopped like a dropped sack of cement, Travis blundering into him.

"You brought a guest?"

The voice was younger than Travis expected, more like his teenaged nephew than one of his bosses. His brain went instantly to Brad Pitt from Snatch, though this character's accent was an understandable Irish lilt. Ben's frame trembled in front of Travis, a gasping breath broadening his tense shoulders. The hairs rose on Travis' neck.

"He's from my old neighborhood," Ben explained. "He's a good guy. No one to worry about."

The ember at the end of the cigarette flashed, dulled. "Do I sound worried to you?"

"No, no you don't, I just meant—"

Travis leaned around Ben, peering into the shadows to get a look at who or what his new employer was, the one causing Ben to quake in his leather zippered boots. Ben had hinted to Travis many times about how beastly his boss was, but it wasn't until a particularly intoxicated evening that Ben finally confessed what his boss actually was: a dragon.

Travis steeled himself for the terror, the awe, the magic of laying eyes upon the mythical creature. The scales, the horns, huge teeth, claws, wings, and fire. There had to be fire as well. Travis was prepared for a fairytale, but not for what he saw.

"You're Eric? Seriously?"

About ten yards ahead of where they'd stopped stood a slightly built young man who looked like he could be anywhere from a mature seventeen to a childish twenty-four, but certainly nothing more than that. His youthful, practically lineless face was in sharp juxtaposition with his short slate gray hair. Ben grabbed feebly at Travis' arm as Travis strolled out from behind him to take better stock of Arach. Travis towered four or five inches over him, looking the youngster up and down.

"Come on! After all this buildup? You're so nervous about this little guy?" Travis pointed to Arach as he looked back at Ben. He couldn't understand why Ben had gone so pale. "All that talk, man. What a load of bullshit. I came all the way out to the docks to see a dragon, and this is what you've got? Is this a joke?"

"For your sake, I certainly hope so," Arach replied, taking another drag.

The young man's eyes flashed a brilliant golden yellow, like a pirate's treasure, but maybe they'd just caught the light of his cigarette.

"Are you even old enough to smoke?" Travis scoffed.

Arach shrugged. "I am a fire-breathing dragon. Smoking is nothing by comparison and a poor substitute."

Travis tilted his head, raising a skeptical eyebrow. "You're going to play along with this too?" He shook his head, glancing over his shoulder to Ben. "I cannot believe you pulled this over on me. Dragons. How drunk must I have been to even consider that you were telling the truth?"

"Please," Ben's voice was hardly a whisper, as though his breath was too scared to leave his lungs. "God. You have to stop talking."

Travis hummed, glancing from his stiff, wide-eyed friend to the casual young man taking a long drag. Arach's eyes were most definitely gold. Must have been some kind of contacts.

"A good guy. What an interesting thing to say," Arach mused. He shrugged and spun on his heel, signaling for the pair to follow with a flick of his finger.

Ben smacked Travis hard in the back of the head as they started after the retreating Arach.

"What did I tell you?" Ben hissed. "What was the one, single thing I made sure you understood before we came in here? I told you at the bar that if you wanted to get in on what I do, you have to play by the rules. His rules."

Travis fluffed himself up, confused by the relief he felt once Arach's back was turned. He hadn't realized how tightly he'd been clenching his jaw or how sweaty the back of his shirt had gotten. He rolled his eyes at Ben's scolding.

"Rules? He's some nutcase proclaiming he's a mythical beast from Harry Potter or something, and you believe him. Why? What the hell are we even doing here?"

Ben went silent and hustled, spotting Arach holding open the back door to the warehouse, waiting for the pair of them. He held his cigarette pressed between his lips, murmuring around it.

Arach took another drag. "Do you have any idea how inconvenient it is to get around when you're bigger than a house? Ridiculous. All these Ring cameras and radars make it so I can't even get in a good fly anymore."

Ben nodded, slipping out as far from Arach as he could manage and Travis found his own body pressing to the far-side of the doorframe. And when Arach smirked at him, Travis could not account for how his heart jumped. He remembered the time when he was ten and the neighbor's rottweiler had cornered him in his garage. He'd wanted to cry out, to run, but he'd been paralyzed.

Travis' stomach crawled up towards his quivering mouth, making it drip with fear. But why? What was he so afraid of? A chain-smoking teenager in some empty building? The dog had foamed and growled, hackles raised, but Arach hadn't so much as said an unkind word. Arach stood by, holding the door, as mild as his cigarettes were advertised to be.

Travis sidled up to Ben as Arach walked by to take the lead again. The rows of cargo containers felt like a cattle chute, ground lit up by the reflected floodlights on the wet asphalt. Out in the open, Arach should have seemed smaller. Travis' mind stuttered when he observed the man's shoulders and jaw squared, perhaps now a bit taller than Travis himself.

"Well, Benny," Arach began, "since you've taken it upon yourself to expand the payroll, I can't help but think you owe me for my flexibility." He faced them again, his feet solidly in a large, shallow puddle.

Travis didn't notice at first. He was so distracted by the subtle alterations Arach had undergone before his eyes that it was several moments before he realized what was being reflected in the dirty asphalt water. It wasn't some gray-haired young man, flicking ash from the tip of a cigarette. It was a monster. Steely scales shingled every inch of his skin, great black claws glinted from what had been hands, a crown of horns adorned a head full of pointy, pearly teeth, and those same brilliant golden eyes glowed out of the reflection. Travis looked from the person in front of him to the image in the water, horrified, not believing what he was seeing.

Arach smirked. "Curious why you might shit yourself?"

He snuffed his cigarette in the puddle and walked towards them. He was certainly bigger, now a few inches over Travis. Each step Arach took rooted Travis ever more firmly to the spot, his desire to flee rivaled only by his paralysis. Then Arach was a mere arm's length away and he inclined towards Travis like he might just take a bite.

"Because I'm a dragon. That's why." Arach started up another smoke and burst out laughing. He slapped Travis on the shoulder much harder than his physique suggested he could, then half playfully, half irritably shoved him into Ben.

"If I wanted to kill you, I certainly wouldn't monologue first. I've been around more than a few hundred years, I managed to watch a movie or two." He flicked his cigarette to the pavement, jamming his hands in his pockets and heading to a dingy red cargo container about ten feet away.

"I'm so sorry, Arach," Ben sniveled. "He won't be an issue again. Whatever you want, boss."

"Ben," Travis whispered, eyes bulging. "Ben. Ben."

Ben locked his eyes on Arach who looked on, bemused, waiting to see what was happening. Travis' body started to quiver uncontrollably.

"His reflection, Ben. Did you see his reflection?"

"Yes, Travis," Ben growled. "He's a freaking dragon. How many times do I have to tell you?"

A smile slit Arach's face, nothing friendly about it. "Have we settled it now? Can we move on? The task I have for you has a ticking clock attached." He took a drag, waited for any further protests, then nodded sharply. "Capital. Do you see this red container here?"

"Yeah," Ben nodded.

Smoke rolled out of Arach's nose.

"You see those fellows there?"

Ben and Travis followed Arach's pointing finger. They would have no matter what. They would have looked anywhere he told them. Travis squinted into the shifting darkness between two other containers, about ten yards away. He made out an arm here, a crispy face there. He recognized a sloppy stack of slightly singed bodies and ice cracked down Travis' spine as he stifled a yelp. Arach paid him no mind.

Ben simply slumped. "Yeah."

"I want those" -pointing to the bodies- "put in there" -gesturing back to the shipping container. "Floor to ceiling. I want the whole thing very neat. Then, I want you to deliver it to Dreki."

The next cigarette ignited by merely touching Arach's lips. Its glow was lost in the golden overflow from Arach's brightening eyes. "She needs to know what happens when she crosses me." He snorted ruefully, catching Travis' doe-y stare. "You get it, right? We go out to eat and get the option of indoor or outdoor seating, so I ask her where she wants to sit and she tells me she doesn't care. The second I head outside, it's 'Outside? But I'm cold. Why do you want to sit out there?'"

Arach ran a hand through his hair. "So, we sit inside and then it's too loud or too crowded or too close without a mask on, and I keep telling her that she's a freaking dragon, she can't get freaking COVID. Then I'm the asshole who ruined dinner." Arach muttered something to himself. "Honestly. No pleasing her. Maybe when she realizes her bitching caused an entire restaurant staff to get cooked and lost her the best pasta primavera in the city, she'll be more appreciative of what she's got."

Ben nodded sympathetically while Travis attempted to keep pace with what he was hearing. Travis forced himself not to look at the reflection in the puddle or the corpse tower composed of his former coworkers. There was no longer any doubt that sweat was not the only thing running down his leg. He was grateful for the darkness and the wet ground. Arach sighed, focused back on Ben.

"By Friday. Got it?" His eyes scanned the perpetually dawning city sky. "And send her some flowers. No roses. No boring lilies, she hates the smell. Container of bodies and then, maybe an hour later or so, make sure she gets something with calla lilies and hydrangeas."

He turned to leave, then changed his mind, pointing at Ben. "Make sure you get the paperwork for him. He needs to sign before you two leave."

With a final stern pass over his audience, Arach walked off without another word. Ben folded his arms, silently lamenting the size of the pile as Travis watched Arach until the tiny, languid pulse of the cigarette finally disappeared.

"What the hell just happened?" Travis burst out.

Ben slouched, appearing exhausted before any of the physical labor had even started. He shuffled his burly frame to the cargo container and yanked open the door.

"What happened was exactly what I told you would happen. I'm not sure what you didn't understand about being a dragon's personal assistant."

"I'd say, *hmm*," Travis pondered sarcastically, "the part where dragons exist."

Ben threw up his hands, his jacket squeaking in protest. "Why would I say that was my job if it wasn't true? I prefer black leather to straight and white, thanks," he snapped. He slapped his hands to his sides. "A few bodies here and there is one thing, but good grief, a whole container? This is going to take all day. Dreki's place is all the way uptown."

Ben moved to the closest body, taking hold of the stiff, stinking arms. He stared at Travis, eyebrows raised in expectation.

"Well? Are you going to help?"

Travis crossed his arms. "I know those people. This was the restaurant I worked at, Ben."

Ben dropped the corpse, a puff of ash fluttering up from the impact. "Yeah, Travis, I know. And here Arach was hunting down that whole staff, so I asked if you could just work for him instead. Get it?"

It had not occurred to Travis that this ghoulish working interview might actually keep him alive. He shuffled over to Ben, picking up the legs as Ben regripped the arms. They hauled the flaking body to the back of the container and dropped it. Recalling Arach's instructions for neatness, Travis straightened the body against the wall and made sure the arms laid tucked in by its sides, legs pressed together. The two men got in a rhythm, loading the bodies, tidying them, then getting the next one.

Ben pressed his hands into his lower back and leaned, stretching himself out. "Don't let me forget to get you the employment paperwork."

Travis nodded, dazed by the whole ordeal. Paperwork made sense. "How did you ever get this job, anyway?"

Ben sighed, shaking his head. "Craigslist."

ASTERA'S RADIO ASTRONOMY OBSERVATORY

By Kevin Lay

"Life isn't confined to water and carbon. What if invisible energies were alive?"

Each evening, Astera kept out of her parents' smothering attention by heading up to her attic bedroom. She had her own books there, her own devices, even her own Wi-Fi. She was an astronomy undergrad, in love with the stars.

Years back, for Christmas, Astera asked for a radio telescope.

"A *radio* telescope?" Her father was a little mystified. "Astera, do you want a radio or a telescope?"

"Father, it's both. It's not an optical telescope to see through. It's a radio that I can tune to *listen* to them."

Because her father thought it might distract her from high school boys, he got her one. After a few years, Astera upgraded to a radio that not only could listen but could also transmit. It employed SDR, or 'Software Defined Radio', which allowed her to design her own radio protocols. She named it Arrow, after ARAO (Astera's Radio Astronomy Observatory).

Astera sat with Arrow most every night, exploring meteor showers, storms on Jupiter, and even distant pulsars. She also connected with ham radio buffs all over the globe, much to her father's disapproval. He was beginning to believe people used these radios to be secretive and fretted she'd involve herself with shadowy men, revolutionaries.

Her mother would say, "Don't be ridiculous, Harry!"

Astera was developing a new radio waveform to share with geeky friends so they could talk in private. She didn't care that it was possibly illegal. For now, no one could receive it, which was OK. She figured it was harmless to let Arrow keep transmitting her experimental radio protocol while also listening to outer space.

Late one night, Arrow dutifully scanned the skies as always, speaker sizzling quiet pink noise and transmitting periodic, possibly illegal HELLOs into outer space. *Moby Dick* lay open beneath her desk lamp, and a cup of honeyed tea was in her hand. Astera savored Melville. Ishmael just declaimed:

'There is a Catskill eagle in some souls that can alike dive down into the blackest gorges, and soar out of them again and become invisible in the sunny spaces.'

She set the cup down and closed her eyes. Imagining she was such an eagle, Astera glided off into a trance. As she soared into the world between dream and awake, she heard Ishmael ask:

What is your name?

Such a pleasant voice, Astera thought. It asked again.

Hello. What is your name?

"Astera." She answered out loud and woke herself up. She opened her eyes and looked around.

Greetings Astera! Thank. You.

The voice was coming from the radio. Immediately, Astera regretted speaking her name out loud to a stranger.

"Who's there?" she demanded. Quickly, she checked Arrow's settings. Thank god, transcription was enabled. There wasn't time to think. The messages came in quickly.

Dear Astera, I sit far far above you smiling, hovering at the edge of Earth's atmosphere. My tail catches your signals which ripple up my body like delicate unfolding fire. My skin tastes their nuances. I shape my wings to feel their meanings surge across them.

Astera couldn't speak. No way this happens.

My family and I touch wingtips as we hover. We surf Earth's radiance for nourishment. We are invisible to humankind.

It was too much for her to follow. Surf Earth's radiance for nourishment? Invisible?

Every frequency and modulation known and unknown can be sensed by our tails, depending on how they're coiled. I love to hang mine down in spirals.

How did it know English? Astera wondered. She had heard of lucid dreaming and thought, 'I'm having a lucid dream!'

Neither do I understand how we mirror each other through words. Perhaps my heart has learned your language, and fate has bridged us, who knows why. But know, O Astera, that I care for you. Indeed, I reach down to say thank you.

Astera was spooked. Was it reading her mind? She jerked herself upright.

"I can't believe this! Is this some kind of joke? How did you get on my channel? This modulation technique is secret!"

She thought of the physics teaching assistant who helped her get started with Arrow. "Bernie—is that you?" He was cute and had a sorta creepy crush on her, she could tell. "Who *is* this?"

We are energy dragons, come to sip dynamic information that pours out from your planet. Our tails reach towards Earth's surface like lightning that listens rather than thunders. Our grateful heads beam outward above the atmosphere and into the noosphere like petals on a spherical flower.

"Dragons?" She threw her hands up. "Wait!" She remembered that Chinese love dragons. "Are you from China?"

If a signal tastes of information we quantize it and eat its least significant bits. It doesn't harm the message. Our bodies scrub the other bits as they go by and pool the message in our family's heart. We take only enough for our family to thrive.

"Listen, I don't know who you are, but my parents are very protective."

Silence.

Astera looked at Arrow's display and read a little bit of the transcript. "Impossible!" she yelled. "Stop it, Bernie! I've had enough. You've gone too far!"

She lowered her voice. "But really, why on Earth would you pay attention to me?" Her eyes kept scanning the transcript, trusting that at some point it would sink in.

Every planet is unique. Earth is a gargantuan blossom who attracts us to taste her, and in that I'm like a cosmic bee, a pollinator of her energy. I'll soon carry it to other systems, other planets.

Astera didn't believe Bernie could make this up. Besides, she didn't share the new protocol with him. What if this were real? She decided to play along for now.

When she took what she was hearing half-seriously she was alarmed. "How many of you are up there, up there in your — hive?"

Not so much a hive, I'm more like a polyp on a galactic coral reef made of electro-magnetic energy. Like humans, we grew up with Earth and over aeons co-adapted. In the larger design, you and I are cousin symbionts of Earth, Astera. We were here since the beginning.

"We're cousins? Symbionts? You sound like a predator!" Her heart raced. "Or a parasite!"

Be at peace. A healing balm to you!

A cool breeze sparked to life inside Astera's chest and she wondered, *Where did that come from?* She breathed it in. While exhaling, she let a spacious, minty sensation shift her whole presence. Healing balm indeed. Maybe there really *was* something real out there.

She murmured. "Thanks."

As always, I listen. My tail is covered with feathery antennae that sprout like spokes from a spinning axle. My wings fine-tune as my tail tastes everything in my field. Each day, I collect information to toss into our family pool.

Astera was fascinated. She asked, "You have a family pool?"

Everyone in my family contributes what they catch into a shared heart of intelligence. Once inside the family pool, these bits soak and spin and join together. Self-selecting structures mix in a nutritious informational soup. We farm enough information to sustain our migrations through the galaxy. In abundant years, there's enough pooled food for frequent festivals. What falls directly into my mouth is mine. To me, the tastiest signals are the most spiritual – the ones with the lowest bit rates.

"You eat information?" Astera asked. "From out in space?" Astera wondered what her geek friends would say.

Yes. It's not the content of information we typically care about, only its absolute energy. Modern humans generate a great deal of information and don't seem to notice how much of it spills out into space. Radio, TV, wireless data, it's all very tasty. It shouldn't go to waste.

"I'm only transmitting at 5 watts!" Astera replied.

Dear Astera, I can taste the power of the signal but it doesn't nourish as much as the energy in the information. Though I can choose to interpret the content of the information, what feeds me is what you might call its entropy per unit of time, like a temperature. Information has structure, and that structure is latent energy I metabolize.

"I certainly hope you have more to eat than my little signal."

Albedo is my base, my basic nutrition. Every day, I gorge myself on the rich noise of solar winds sluicing the Van Allen Belts. When night comes, Earth's shadow is a safe abyss of refuge. We normally sleep then, unless night-lightning is underway, when we make festivals and distant friends fly in to play.

Should she tell her parents? She knew this was big.

"Why are you thanking *me*? Seems you should be talking to someone important."

Tonight the field is quiet. I heard your unusual modulation and frequency. My heart told me to answer with the same kind of wave.

Astera, let me tell you a secret! Long ago, my kin and I made a hobby of staying awake near the poles each night to snack on auroras. They are a welcome change of diet after so much albedo and lightning.

One night, the auroras were quiet. Curious, I stayed awake and immersed myself in emptiness. In my closest embrace of Earth, I discovered she was leaking a new kind of food. Apparently, humans discovered electromagnetism.

"Radio has taste?" Astera laughed. "News to me!"

Radio waves not so much. Radio is like the plate on which information is served. About 200 solar rotations ago, I received a new type of food from your species. I felt I tasted the very atoms of the universe, spelled out loud and clear like a message from grand source emptiness. It was a gift to my kind. I learned later you called it Morse Code.

"Morse Code!" Astera scoffed. "That's so primitive!"

It changed my universe. You see, I'm used to the mega-complexity of turbulent lightning storms that deliver maximum entropy. That day was a revelation. Morse

Code took its time to speak. There was no hurry. "Relax." It said, "It is clear. On and off is all you need."

"Oh, binary logic?" Astera confessed. "We're all raised on that down here."

My heart tells me that human logic came from a divine source, which eventually materialized as binary yes/no bits. You put them into a time series, and voila, you had messages. From there, for humans and us both, it's all bits. Everything is reducible to information.

"That's what physicist John Wheeler said. 'It from bit.'"

See what I mean? Such wisdom! You humans are holy to us. I'll be spreading the word to my kind as I leave.

Astera cried out. "You're leaving?! But I just met you!"

I must leave. To explain why, I would have to tell you more.

"Please do," Astera said. "I would *love* to know more."

Thank you, Astera. My leaving began to unfold over the last few hundred rotations around the Sun when some of the sweetest, simplest, freshest information in the history of my kind seeped out of the lands of your birth. We are blessed to have found humanity.

"Humanity actually helps you?"

When I quaffed your radio, your TV, your wireless, I didn't care about the message or who or what was intended. Radio transmissions from Earth were like ice cream to me. Simple and pleasurable, I licked these waves as they passed through my coiled tail, my coiled tongue, warmed by the hum of Earth's magnetic field.

"You're saying I provide simple food? Is that why you're thanking me?"

Astera, I am blessed to experience humanity through you. Your transmissions are honest and simple, seldom random, with no crazy redundancies, on bright and steady carriers using trivial modulations.

Astera's chin jerked up, proud. "That's just how things work. I still don't understand why simplicity is so important to you."

Then I must transmit to you the kernel of my purpose. You see, simplicity feels abstract and unreachable to beings like me that live on utter complexity. Simplicity is my doorway to enlightenment. Astera, experiencing the basic duality of binary logic reveals a doorway into a non-dual state.

"Enlightenment? Non-dual state? I hear so much about them these days. Simplicity is, um — religious?"

All beings seek enlightenment, whether invisible, animal, plant, or human. For me, the slower the bit rate, the more I experience non-dual enlightenment.

"I feel so simple. I'm taught to pray to infinite beings. You order it in reverse. Because you live in complex realms, you reach towards simplicity."

Yes. Ah, I miss when your transmissions were clean, easy to digest, radiant candy. Humans are changing. In the last hundred rotations, the information feed has burgeoned ever thicker and louder. Feasts every night! But lately, transmissions are turning toxic.

"I hear you!" Astera replied. "I feel that, too. Opinions clog the internet. Media polarizes and separates us." She realized she just gave an invisible energy dragon her personal opinion. She felt suddenly ridiculous and way out of her league.

Indeed, Astera. It is challenging to digest opposing streams of information. One seems to nullify the other. Some of my relatives love the tang cryptography hashes provide, but not me. The recently added authentication and security protocols have become too heavy for me to digest and they continue to grow even heavier. I don't need food that is paranoid or deceptive. I shall look elsewhere for lighter fare.

There was a pause.

Your people have enlightened me and others like me. Please, dear Astera, relay to your people our profound gratitude.

Another pause, then,

Having communicated, I take now my leave.

That was it. Nothing more came from Arrow's speaker.

"Goodbye," Astera said, wistfully.

It was very late and Astera needed to get up early for class. She took a deep breath, printed out the transcript, and stuffed it into her backpack. She had a hard time sleeping. Was it real? A dream?

Next day, Astera's father walked up the steep stairway to her room to slide mail under the door. The door wasn't latched and swung open, and bumped her desk. Arrow's display lit up, still displaying the transcript.

He squinted.

"Proof!" He yelled downstairs to his wife. "Honey, come up here! Look what our daughter's been up to!"

Astera's mother arrived and also read the display.

He puffed up, vindicated. "Look! '*My tail catches your signals which ripple up my body like delicate unfolding fire*',... '*I love to hang mine down in spirals.*' What's he hangin' down? How 'bout this one: '*My heart has learned your language, and fate has bridged us, who knows why. But know, O Astera, that I care for you.*'"

Her mother leaned in to get a better view.

"This guy is dangerous!" he exclaimed.

"Harry, you don't know. Let's wait and ask Astera about it when she gets home."

Ignoring her, his face bulged red with anger. "So long as she lives here, this will stop!" He reached to unplug Arrow.

"Harry! Don't!" His wife moved to stop him, but his wrath was quicker.

He boxed Arrow and hid it well away.

When Astera arrived home that day, she stared at the empty space where Arrow once sat. She instinctively knew her father was behind its disappearance and realized it was time to move out.

"I'll get another radio," she said out loud to no one. "I did it once, I'll do it again, but better!"

Astera dug the transcript out of her backpack and read it over and over. *Your people have enlightened me and others like me. Please, dear Astera, relay to your people our profound gratitude.*

Thus began Astera's mission to deliver that message to humanity.

SOLES SAVED HERE

By Tamelia Aday

"A story that might happen at THE MIRACLE CAFÉ, a novel I'm currently writing."

Maxwell Bates finished his daily fifteen minutes on the treadmill, then checked the weather while blending blueberries and spinach. The walls around him gleamed, sterile of adornment and color. He buttoned his shirt, grabbed the smoothie, and stepped onto the porch.

A shaggy dog charged across the lawn. "Go on, now, go on." Max shooed the hairy beast.

"Bruno!" The neighbor, carrying a cup of coffee, joined Max. "Sorry, man, he loves people. Got away from me."

Max grunted, wiping paw prints off his shirt. No time to change. At least he had an extra at work.

"You should get a dog. Makes good company."

"Don't need company." A nudge of uncertainty flickered. Rubbish.

"A little excitement wouldn't hurt. I can set my clock to your comings and goings." The guy gave Max a playful punch. "Come over sometime. Have coffee."

Max narrowed his eyes. "You're exaggerating. And I don't drink coffee."

"Sure, man. You'll be back at 5:21." The neighbor grinned and headed to his house.

"Try to keep that dog under control," Max called after him.

The conversation still played in his head when he arrived at the university to teach his literature class. He exchanged the dirt-stained shirt for a fresh one. Predictable. Couldn't be that bad—a rather comforting quality.

Droopy-eyed students greeted him. Halfway through his lecture, a soft rumbling sounded. Snoring.

Thoughts fired in his mind on the way home. Students. They were unmotivated. He pulled into the driveway and checked his watch. 5:21.

Under a darkening sky, Max jogged inside. He'd been satisfied with his life until that fool neighbor said something. The starkness of his surroundings mocked him, disturbing his peace. Max hurried out the door and into the rain. Lightning flashed like a whip; a reprimand of thunder followed.

He drove, straining to see through the storm. A shadow darted in front of his Volvo. He swerved, bounced out of a pothole, and the engine sputtered. His car veered toward the curb, and he braked in front of a building with a red door. A glowing sign above it read, The Café Plot.

"I don't remember a café here."

He stepped out of the car and pulled his jacket over his head, dodging raindrops. Coffee scented the air. Faint music blended with the steady showers.

The door creaked open. "Welcome." A gentleman ushered Max to a seat at the table. A drenched orange cat jumped onto the chair next to him.

The man's dark skin glowed in the dim lighting. "Name's Solomon. This here is Van Gogh."

The cat's green eyes stared, wide and unblinking.

Solomon set a steaming beverage on the table. "What problem brought you to the cafe?"

"I'm predictable." Max pushed the coffee away and slouched in the chair.

"The Café Plot specializes in literary solutions. Ernest Hemingway would suggest getting cats."

Van Gogh jumped down and weaved his wet body around Max's calves.

"Arrived shortly before you." Solomon held up a finger. "First, you try coffee."

⚬

The next morning, Max peeked inside the bag Solomon forced upon him—a coffee maker, filters, grounds, plus instructions.

A nutty scent filled the air.

He took a sip, grimaced, then gulped down the rest with a shudder. If this worked, he could forgo getting cats.

With no time to exercise, he dashed to his room for a white shirt, but grabbed a tee and khakis instead.

Max hurried to his car, rolled down the windows, and cranked the oldies, zipping along at a high speed. When he arrived at the campus, instead of dragging his feet, he danced to class.

Martha, the psychology professor, paused when he shouted, "Hello, Martha. A beautiful day, isn't it?"

"Max? Why so chipper? You get a cat?"He halted in surprise. "What?"

"Always wanted cats. For companionship."

"Nope, just coffee."

"Mine doesn't do that for me." She waved and hurried toward the psychology wing.

Max entered his classroom and banged his briefcase on the desk. "Good morning!" He paced. "Today we're going to breathe stories, eat prose, devour theme, and absorb the heartbeat of literature." His words flowed. No one snored.

The next night, he attended a dinner party.

"What's gotten into you, Max?" Ed, the history teacher, stabbed at his salad. "Heard all about your lecture."

"I went to that coffee shop on the corner of Third Avenue."

"Coffee shop?" Ed frowned. "No, no—that's an old shoe repair."

"Got my heels done there." Martha nodded.

"That can't be. Getting more coffee tomorrow, you'll see."

But instead, Max found a glass door and an A-board that read *Shoe Repair. Soles saved here.*

He walked inside. Shoes lined the counter, and his eyes watered from the varnish fumes. A woman sat at the register, sewing.

"Can I help you?" she asked.

"I was here three days ago. Met Solomon."

She pulled out a piece of paper and eyed him with a frown. "You're Max?"

He nodded.

"I expected..." She gestured at his shirt, then shrugged and handed him the note.

Gave you decaffeinated. Left something at your house to make up for the mistake.
"Decaf? But ..."

He'd been interesting, engaging, and wasn't tired. How was it possible? He sped home, expecting real coffee, but found Van Gogh on his porch instead. "How'd you get here?"

A meow came from behind him. "Two of you?" Both cats darted inside when he opened the door. "Wait."

A paper fluttered in their wake. *Van Gogh came to the café, as did Mona Lisa. Kittens expected.*

The cats hopped on the sofa.

"You found the café, just like me." Revelation sparked Max's interest.

He purchased a pet backpack and ditched living room walks for outdoor trails. Toys and cat trees littered his home.

———◆———

Before fall term, Max took Van Gogh on a hike and ran into Martha.

"What do you have there?" She peeked into the backpack.

"This is Van Gogh. You should come see the kittens."

An hour later, they stepped into Max's living room. Art enhanced the walls, and music played. A plant accented his desk.

"This is delightful. My place is rather dull," Martha said as they sipped coffee.

"Ernest and Hemingway will liven things up." He handed her the kittens in a box when she rose to leave. "Let's do coffee again."

The next morning, Max patted Bruno, who came to greet him.

His neighbor strolled up and nodded toward Max's cup. "You gave in to coffee. And got some cats."

"And I won't be home at 5:21."

UNTIL THE NIGHTLING

By K.D. Jewell

"I love horror stories, especially the creatures and ghosts, so this was my attempt at crafting my own lore."

B illy had barely waited for Beth to get out the front door before he took off down the sidewalk. After being told by their parents that chaperoning Beth's trick-or-treating was his responsibility, fourteen-year-old Billy was dead set on finding a way to ditch his eight-year-old sister and go to the boy-girl-no-parents Halloween party to hopefully partake in some moderate underaged drinking. Conservatively dressed as Laura Ingalls Wilder, the costume did not stray far from Beth's usual attire.

She hurried after her big brother, aware of his displeasure at being stuck with her but hopeful that maybe they could have fun like they used to. She had to keep close watch on him each time she went up the walkway to a house to ask for candy. Billy tended to move along while her back was turned.

They'd gotten a few blocks from home and the sun was setting when the old town cemetery drifted into view across the next street. Beth didn't like the cemetery. It had not been tended and was overgrown. It gave Beth the impression that no one would notice if one of the bodies crawled out and wandered off.

Billy slowed, his hands nestling into his pockets. He didn't look back to see if Beth followed him across the street to the sidewalk in front of the graveyard. He leaned on the low wrought iron fence and gazed into the murk.

"Has anyone told you about the nightling yet? The one that lives in there?" Billy asked innocently.

Beth gulped. She wanted to run away, but not as much as she wanted Billy to talk to her.

Beth shook her head and Billy raised his eyebrows.

"Really? Huh. Thought someone would have by now," he mused. Billy strolled down the fence line to the gate and rounded onto the hallowed ground without pause. "It's kind of fun to look at."

He moved further into the cemetery. The last rays of daylight were being sucked down over the crest of the hills and the cold October air felt heavy against Beth's dress. She clutched her pillowcase to her chest and tiptoed down the mossy path.

"You've seen it?"

"Of course. Everyone has." Billy faced his little sister again, shadow hiding half his face. "Do you want to?"

Beth did not want to. She wanted to get more candy and go home and never set foot near that place again. But more than any of those things, she wanted to please Billy so maybe he would walk with her to school or sit next to her at breakfast.

"Um, okay," she reluctantly agreed. Billy started to walk off and Beth hustled after him. "Where are you going?"

"It's real shy," Billy said. "I'll just go behind that tree, right there, so it only thinks one person is here. You sit down on that stump and wait. It might take a few minutes, but it'll come. Then call me and I'll come get you," Billy promised.

He lied. Billy took off for the party the minute Beth had settled in to wait. When Billy returned to the cemetery several hours later, he had a brief but building panic at not finding his little sister waiting for him. He located her safely back at home, pillowcase full of candy from the evening's harvest, and Beth had not spoken to him one single time until around Valentine's Day.

Billy played a video game after school when Beth appeared in his doorway. She wore her long brown hair in braided pigtails over her shoulders. Beth liked her braids and her floral dresses, her dolls and her tea set. She used to like her brother, but one prank too many had convinced her that he would never like her.

"What do you want, nerd?" Billy asked, his glazed eyes never leaving the computer screen.

She wanted to keep her secret. She wanted an older brother who protected her and played with her. She wanted lots of things, but she wasn't in his doorway for something she wanted. She was there for something she needed. Beth sighed, fidgeting with a ribbon on the front of her dress.

"You remember when you left me at the cemetery?" she asked quietly.

Billy glanced at his sister. He most certainly did remember. That scare had gone so well, Beth hadn't come to bug him for months. He enjoyed revisiting the memory often, but Billy had never been reprimanded for ditching Beth, and why she hadn't tattled was an ongoing mystery. A festering mental splinter. Billy paused his game.

Beth watched the pearly pink ribbon slide across her finger. "Do you remember when you told me about the nightling that lived there?"

"Yeah?"

Beth preferred her own room. Billy's room smelled like sour socks. Their mom cleaned it most of the time, did the vacuuming and dusting, the bedding, but it still had that budding boy musk about it. The nightling didn't smell at all. Just when she'd first brought it home, but that was the grave dirt. That mostly went away.

"I found it in the cemetery," Beth declared at last.

Billy narrowed his eyes suspiciously. "Found what?"

"The nightling. I found it and I brought it home and it's been living in my closet and now it's almost too big. I don't know what to do."

Billy glared at Beth for a moment. She was such a loser. He un-paused his game. "Get lost, Beth."

The clicking of the controller resumed. Beth's shoulders slumped. She retreated to her room and sat crisscross-applesauce on her bed. She heard the slight creak of her closet door and kept her eyes on her lap. The nightling wasn't very cute in the daylight.

"He didn't believe me," she mumbled. "But you can eat a little candy, right? I have some. Just to fill you up?" Beth sniffled, glancing at the darkness of the closet. "Gummies are kind of like skin," she reasoned. "And some of the hard candies could be toenails."

———⋅◇⋅———

Weeks went by, and Billy didn't think about his weird sister and her imaginary friend again until he was home alone. Beth had both of their parents at a dance recital. Tap. Billy hadn't known anyone who still did tap dancing until Beth got started in it just after kindergarten. He did not go to dance recitals, which suited both siblings just fine. Billy was allowed to stay home alone for short periods of time— just not overnight.

It was dark pretty early: summer was months away. The ranch-style house had a simple layout. The living room with the television was stacked in front of the kitchen. A hallway veined to bedrooms and bathrooms. The rain pelted on the windows and the dim yellow glow of the kitchen light was all Billy had on so he could watch a movie about the devil taking over a small town. The ambiance, the weather, the solitude: it was utterly perfect.

Until a potholder fell off the laminate counter in the kitchen behind him. Billy felt a tingle move up from his belly to the bottom of his throat. And he heard the muffled shuffle of footfalls down the hall that widened his eyes and dried out his mouth, snatching any potential scream. And then that intentionally quieted latching of Beth's bedroom door.

Heart thudding violently against his ribcage, the rush of blood in his ears nearly deafening, Billy felt truly isolated with the rain obscuring the neighborhood outside, and the darkness hemming in his area of safety, of knowledge. He felt isolated, but he did not feel alone. He stared, unmoving, down the shadowy hallway. He wanted to turn down the movie to listen, but he didn't want to hear. Billy sat frozen, feet tucked up on the couch, rotated toward his little sister's room, watching, dreading, and barely breathing, until the garage door rumbled.

The lights blared on, the clap of tap shoes on linoleum, the boastful conversation of Beth and their parents. With his family returning, it was just a slippery potholder and a drafty door. At least that was what Billy told himself until he went to bed.

The house went dark and quiet, but not quite quiet enough. Maybe he was still nervous from the movie, maybe he'd eaten too much sugar too late, but Billy was pretty sure he heard those muted footsteps in the hall. Heard them halt and stand outside his door, heard them pad back down to Beth's room.

Billy slept in fits and starts, sensing something on his ear, his foot, his fingers. Something cold. The next morning, a weary Billy puzzled at the bits of loamy dirt at the threshold of his bedroom.

The day plowed forward, and Billy went to school, forgetting entirely about his instinctive terror and the nightling Beth had told him about. It wasn't until bedtime came again, when he'd closed his door and climbed under the blankets, then his fingers lingered at the switch on his bedside lamp. Darkness waited like a breath held in, like a scream bit back. It was not the gentle embrace of sleep that he sensed in the room with him. It was something else. Something that kept Billy from wanting to put his feet out from the covers to get them to the floor to run away.

"This is so stupid," Billy muttered. It took him a few more minutes to get out of bed, and when he did, Billy raced from his room, moving as quickly and quietly as he dared to get to Beth. He trembled as he closed her door behind him, relieved that she still slept with her unicorn lamp on.

Beth wasn't asleep. The nightling had told her that her brother might stop by that night. She had unbraided her hair for bed and was tucked under her rainbow comforter, propped up against the white headboard. She and Billy looked at one another for a minute, and Beth watched as he tried unsuccessfully to remove the fear from his face.

"Why did you say you brought home the nightling, Beth?" he asked at last. "What made you say that?"

Beth blinked and shook her head.

"I told you because I don't think I can tell Mom and Dad. It's getting too big to hide much longer. And it's hungrier, too."

Billy swallowed hard against the stinging bile rising in his throat.

"Hungrier?"

His little sister nodded. "Uh huh." She picked at one of the frills on the edge of her blanket. "It's like you said. It used so much energy burrowing down to the caskets and chewing through. Eating those fingernails, toenails, and earlobes was just enough to get it to the next body. It was so small and tired. It just wanted to come home. And it asked if I could give it the nail clippings once in a while. But—" Beth bit her lip. "But I guess, since it doesn't have to dig anymore, it was finally able to grow up...and now the clippings aren't enough."

Beth hoped against hope that Billy would come sit on her bed, stay up with her, and put his head together with hers to come up with a solution. She hoped that her big brother would prove he could be there for her when it truly mattered.

Billy refused to admit to her that he was scared. He let the anxiety building in his chest hiss out in a harsh, angry whisper.

"This isn't funny, Beth! I'm sorry, okay? I'm sorry I left you in the cemetery, but you need to cut it out. Seriously."

Seeing the hurt on her face immediately made Billy feel better. Beth was trying to get back at him, using what he'd told her about the nightling against him. He glared at her big eyes, set his mouth in a grim line. Billy darted defiantly to Beth's closet and threw open the door. Nothing but shadows, shawls, and tap shoes. Billy triumphed in his vindication.

"See? Nothing. You're a liar." He left the closet door ajar, rolling his eyes. "Such a freaking joke."

Beth watched Billy strut out carefully, softly, so as not to alert their parents. It was how he must have looked when he left her in the cemetery: proud in his creeping. Beth saw the shape slip down from the shelf in her closet, sliding along the seam of the shuttered door, gray, nail-less fingers poking through the slats. She smoothed her comforter and watched as the gloomy, knobby hands smoothed the other end.

Tears threatened to spill over the rims of her eyes until the cold hand patted hers. It would have meant the whole world to her to get that same pat from Billy, but her brother wasn't giving and the nightling was. Four months Billy had gone without speaking to her, and every one of those days had crushed Beth a little more. Each day Billy ignored her, the nightling needed her. Now, Billy had fled her room, rebuked her once again, yet the nightling remained smiling sweetly, almost human, almost whole. Beth took a big breath.

"You can't have him until you're absolutely ready," Beth said matter-of-factly. "I don't have anything else for you to eat."

Beth and Billy didn't speak again, but Billy could not ignore the chill whispering up the back of his neck each time he passed Beth's door. He tried not to look over his shoulder, but he couldn't help it. Was that a silhouette? Could that have been a hand? Each time it was like he caught the fade-out of a scene, the last whisp of an image.

The bits of earth continued to appear outside his doorway in the morning. Billy didn't know why he scrambled to clean it up, why he didn't want their parents to find it. Maybe all that dirt would lead back to the cemetery, and he'd have to fess up to leaving his little sister when he was supposed to be watching her. The tension continued building in Billy as he slept less and less and fretted more and more.

Until one night when the rain returned. When Beth and their parents went to the neighboring town for her dance competition. When no one would be home until past bedtime.

Billy kept all of the lights on, but somehow the contrast only served to make the dark spaces darker rather than the bright places brighter. He didn't watch a scary movie. He thought about staying on the couch until his family was home, but he was so tired and his bed was so welcoming. He didn't turn out the house lights and, leaving the door to his bedroom cracked to let in the hallway glow, he chanced turning out the lamp in his bedroom as he burrowed into his blankets.

He had barely settled, his breathing falling into a rhythm, his bones sinking into the springs, when the chill from Beth's room snuck up on him. It nipped in under the covers with him, trilling up his spine, an imaginary icy breath until it wasn't imaginary.

Billy squeezed his eyes closed and hoped, wished, prayed that the cool, wet lips slipping over his big toe were just in his head. He was paralyzed by denial and horror. He listened, and there was a slurp, a tug, and a soft pop.

A thin, chisel-like tongue slipped between the skin and the nail. Oddly painless, almost ticklish. Billy's toe shriveled, flopping without the nail, and Billy's whole body shrank just a little, pajamas loosening, indent in the mattress lessening.

The lips moved to the next toe in line, a string of drool slinging across Billy's foot. His heart thudded faster and faster, closer and closer to entering his mouth. Each toe retracted without a nail, each theft folded Billy smaller and smaller. He was about the size of a large dog by the time his toenails were gone, the world losing texture and color as his senses dulled. And that was when the nightling pulled the blanket off the bed.

"Hello, Billy," greeted the nightling. It wriggled its toes on the floor and Billy could hear the long nails catching slightly in the carpet.

Billy was unable to move. His pajamas engulfed him, tangling his shriveling body in limp fabric. He watched the nightling crawl up the bed, felt it straddle his middle and pin him down, take his hand, and start plucking off his fingernails.

Once again, Billy shrank, grayed, and weakened with each removed nail. But this time he could see that the nightling changed, too. Through his hazy vision, Billy made out his nose and mouth on the face of this stranger, Billy's own hair above Billy's own eyes. By the time his fingernails were gone, Billy was the size of a cat, and the nightling had stolen his appearance. It was only missing earlobes and a soul.

The nightling sat back, crossing its legs on the bed, cocking its head at what Billy had become.

"It's very hard to get strong enough to escape the graveyard," the nightling explained. "Maybe you'll get lucky like me. Maybe some thoughtless older brother will abandon his little sister in your graveyard. Maybe she'll be frightened enough to bring home one monster to get rid of another one."

The nightling leaned in and took Billy's left earlobe in its teeth, snipped it loose, then took the right one, and what was left of Billy shriveled like a grape in the sun. The nightling pinched the greenish-gray, hairless, mouse-sized little thing that had once been Billy from the blankets, set it on the bedside table, and pulled on the empty pajamas before cradling the creature in its palm, letting it gum weakly on the freshly grown fingernails.

Saturday was normally the only day Billy and Beth were allowed to sleep in, but with everyone home late from the dance competition, their parents let the rule slide that Sunday. Beth was already on her second pancake when Billy shuffled into the kitchen. Their mom spotted him and smiled.

"Good morning, sweetheart. Sorry we got back so late. The rain washed out one of the routes home. I hope we didn't wake you when we got in."

Billy shrugged and took a seat beside Beth. She paused in her eating. She thought she caught a familiar but long-absent smell. She remembered it from a dark night in the graveyard. It wasn't Billy's usual funk.

"Oh, Billy!" their mom exclaimed. She set down his breakfast and snatched up his hand. "Your nails are filthy. It looks like you've been digging for worms. Go wash up before you eat, will you?"

Cold, sucking dread churned Beth's stomach at the thought that this might not be Billy at all. Beth stared at her brother, at his hands, his feet, his earlobes. Even with all she'd experienced since Halloween, Beth doubted that the nightling had finally done it.

Until it caught her eye as it took a big bite of breakfast.

Until it gave her a wink and a smile that was almost human.... but not quite.

THE FAIRY TREE

By Kathrin Classen

"Everyone has a world hidden within them. Moms are the most talented at hiding their personal worlds. I want to shine a light on the hope our empathy spreads."

I turn off the kitchen faucet and hear the gleeful squeals of my children erupt from the living room. My bare feet make no sound as I pad to the doorway and poke my head around to see them huddled at my father's feet. A single light illuminates their faces, casting shadows that twist their features like funhouse mirrors. They are hungry for one of his outlandish stories, and he is playing right into their hands. A pinch of jealousy squeezes my chest for an instant and then lets go.

I take a deep breath and let a grin play at the edges of my lips instead. This is a good thing. This is how it is supposed to be. I just need some time to get used to it, that's all. I sneak back to the sink and pick up the next dish when I hear him say,

"You see, I had to go after your grandma. But when I got close enough to the tree that captured her, branches grabbed me, and I was trapped! I had to take out my knife and–"

"Dad!" I run into the room, dirty plate in one hand. "Not that one! Tell a different story."

In the sudden wake of my interruption, everyone turns to look at me. My son, Max, rolls his eyes with all the attitude of a six-year-old going on fourteen. My sweet little Alice just blinks at me, her eyes as round as the dinner plate I'm holding. Dad shifts his weight until he is leaning back in his old, overstuffed armchair. A king on his throne.

"Well, I can't stop now, Maggie," he says. "We just got to the good part."

Max starts chanting, "Tell it! Tell it!"

"Max!" I snap. "That's enough."

He sticks his bottom lip out and leans back in a sulk. Alice absorbs the interaction between us before she asks,

"Why can't Grandpa finish the story?"

I breathe a long sigh and try to answer her question in a way a four-year-old will understand.

"Your Grandpa knows that story makes me sad," I say. "He knows that when he tells it, I think about the night my mom left." I fix my gaze on Dad. The night *he* drove her away. "And he knows how he tells the story makes it seem like she was taken when it was her *decision* to leave."

"She was *taken*!" His chin is quivering, but I can't tell if it is from anger or sadness. "She'd never have left us if she'd had a choice."

My jaw pops as my teeth grind together. He's never been able to admit how badly he treated her. Especially that night. It's been over two decades, and I still feel that little burning ember in the pit of my stomach when I think about what he said to her.

I roll my eyes. I don't have time for this. Not anymore. I look at the plate in my hand. Ketchup has dried into a hard, cement-like paste. It will need to be soaked before I can scrub it clean.

"Tell a different story," I say and stride back into the kitchen.

There is a sudden crack of thunder so loud I startle, and the dish almost falls from my hand. There will be a storm tonight. A bad one.

I place the plate in the sink and run hot water over it. I turn the faucet off and hear the low drone of my father's voice waft over the living room again accompanied by another rattle of squeals. My fists clench and I bite my lip to keep from screaming. No one listens to me in this house. I wish I never had to come back. Dad has a talent for knowing exactly how to make me feel my worst. Sometimes I think Mom had the right idea. I just wish she had taken me with her.

I stalk back into the living room and give the old man a warning look.

Stop it, Dad. Stop it right now.

He ignores me and says,

"Your grandmother was taken by the Fairy Tree. The nastiest, most horrible prison in all the world. The only way to save her was to cut her out of it and—"

"OK, kids!" *I will not let my children have nightmares.* "Bedtime."

Hands on hips, I'm prepared to fight. Dad looks up, and at first, the flash in his eyes tells me he wants to ignore me. I know he wants to paint his version of the narrative in their heads, just like he tried to do when I was little. But then, he looks down and sees Alice's face as white as a bleached sheet.

"Maybe your mom's right," he sighs. "The next part is a bit... rough. Best not before bed."

"Aw, come on, Grandpa!"

Max pouts and shoots me a sideways look. I shake my head, eyebrows raised. *Don't push it, Kid.*

"No fair! If Dad were here, he'd let us!"

My gut feels like it's been punched. The image of a boyish grin and a mischievous glint flashes through my memory. A sour taste fills my mouth.

"You know, Max, you're right," I retort. "Your dad wouldn't care what you listened to. But he's not here right now. I am. And I say it's bedtime."

Max springs to his feet, his hands balled into fists.

"I wish Dad were here instead of *you.* You never let me do anything! I HATE YOU!"

Before I can protest, he stomps upstairs, his arms crossed tightly over his chest. Alice watches him go and then looks at me, her sweet eyes searching my face.

"When is Dad coming back?"

It's the question I've dreaded for days, ever since my husband left to chase his career with his very attractive co-worker. I walk over and sit down next to her on the floor.

"I don't know, Sweety. He didn't tell me."

"But Max said he would come to get us."

"You don't want to stay here with me?"

At this, Alice tucks her chin to her chest and shakes her head. I want to cry. For years, I was the one working, taking care of our family's financial needs so their father could be the one at home working on his startup. And when it finally did start up, he took all of our savings, left a mountain of debt, and abandoned his family. And now, here I am with my two beautiful children, who I barely know, because I work a sixty-hour week to put food on the table. My *father's* table.

"I see," I push past my tight lips. "That makes me very sad."

Alice's face goes red and tears well in her eyes. Without warning, she stands and runs up the stairs. A door slams seconds later. I hang my head in defeat.

There is a grunt and the protest of wood as my father pushes himself up and out of the old armchair. I stand and glare an accusation at him, shifting all the blame to his shoulders. He's not fazed.

"Why did you have to tell *that* story?"

"Because they need to know," he grunts.

"You are putting ridiculous ideas into their heads."

He clenches his teeth, his chin set in a defiant glower. We stare at each other for a long time, the tired argument blossoming between us.

"Mom left. It's that simple," I say. "There's no such thing as fairies. No magical tree. Mom just didn't love us anymore, because *you drove her away*. Just like me. My only regret is that I had to come back."

He takes a step back, his mouth in a tight line. Was that too harsh? I don't know if I could ever forgive and forget. I watch as his face turns from red to purple, the tips of his ears bright.

"You would be in deep trouble if I hadn't bailed you out. And what do you know about love anyway, huh?" He growls. "You can't even keep your own husband satisfied."

My hand shoots out and smacks his cheek. For one horrifying moment, I just stare at him. My hand stings. What have I done? This isn't me. He blinks, the shock at my action melting away into anger.

"Watch yourself, Maggie. You need to get a handle on whatever is happening with you. If you don't–" he pokes his bony finger into my shoulder, "one way or another, you're going to lose those kids."

I watch him stomp up the stairs and hear another door slam. I squeeze my eyes shut and pretend I'm not a terrible mom and daughter. After a moment, I head back into the kitchen. The glass of wine I pour is fuller than it should be, but

I don't have the energy to care tonight. With Dad acting like he is, I'm a single parent to three kids instead of two.

Lightning flashes through the kitchen window. I count the seconds like Mom taught me. One... two... three... four... five... six... *CRASH!* The storm is about six miles away. Soon, it will pour out all its rage on our little house. The house I grew up in and had to move back into as an adult.

I swirl the wine; watch it cling to the sides of the glass and settle again. It's an expensive bottle. My husband bought it years ago for a special occasion. He left it behind, forgotten. Like me. So, right now, drowning my sorrows seems special enough. Plus, it's the only bottle of alcohol I have left. I take a sip, and the wine fills my mouth and coats my tongue with its dry, oaky flavor. Instead of lifting my spirits, it only deepens my despair.

A loud thump above my head grabs my attention. Are the kids jumping off their beds? I set down the glass and rush upstairs. I don't want the night to end in anger. I need to make it right. I knock and open the door a crack.

"Max? Alice?" I step into the room.

"Go away!" Max yells.

He's tucked halfway under his dinosaur blanket, and he hasn't changed into pj's. I should make sure they've brushed their teeth. Like a good parent... like a good *mom* would...

"Please, Max. Let's not do this tonight."

"I want Dad!" he screams. "It's not fair!"

"Please, stop saying that!"

My cheeks burn as my temper rises. All I want to do is join Max in screaming about how unfair this all is. But if I can't even handle one little argument with my six-year-old, can I even call myself a good mother? Other people can do it on their own. Why can't *I*?

"I hate you, Mom! I hate you! I hate you!"

"Max!" I snap. This is too much. I'm done. I can't take it anymore. "You're grounded for the rest of the week. No TV or video games or... or... playing at the park," I splutter. "No skating. Nothing until you get a better attitude!"

"MOM!" He rages, covers thrown off his head as he glares at me. "*That's not fair!*"

"Life's not fair, kid."

"What about me?" Alice squeaks and emerges from her bed.

Her face is red and puffy. The sight of her makes me want to burst into tears; the heat of them is already behind my eyes. But I need to stay consistent. If I let her cries sway me now, she will use them as a weapon every time.

"Sorry, Sweety. Both of you are grounded. Both of you had a bad attitude."

"No, I didn't!"

Alice's chin quivers, and tears are rolling down her cheeks. Max stares at me, his face red as he opens his mouth.

"You're the worst mom *EVER!*"

I slam the door to the soundtrack of my son's screeches and my daughter's tears. The moment the door closes, the anger is gone, leaving in its wake a heavy, unbearable exhaustion. I can't do this alone. I need help.

Across the hallway, I stand outside Dad's door. I know it has to be my imagination, but I swear I can still feel the palm of my hand burning from when I slapped him. I still can't believe I did that. What kind of daughter am I? I can't ask for his help. It would prove what I am so desperately trying to cover up. That I am not fit to be the mom I know I need to be.

I drag myself back downstairs and into the kitchen, where my abandoned glass of wine greets me with open arms. I take it into the living room, turn off the lamp, and curl up on the sofa. Lightning lights up the dark little room.

One... two... three... four... *CRASH!*

Four miles away now. The storm is moving fast. I take three more long, deep sips of wine to empty the glass. I set it down on the side table, but when I lift my hand, I swing too wide and knock something over. There is the distinctive crunch of breaking glass. I wince and look to the floor. Mom's face stares up at me through broken glass, the wooden frame cracked.

Great. Just great.

I keep my feet tucked under me and lean down to pick her picture out of the ruins. My eyes feast on the outline of her face, taking in every detail: her lopsided smile, the little wrinkle between her eyebrows, the scar on her chin. She told me once how she's gotten it, but I've forgotten. The memory lost to a vortex of time. The smile doesn't reach her eyes. My own sadness reflected back at me through the decades.

What happened to you, Mom? Where are you?

Max and Alice would have loved her. She would have smothered them in kisses and candy. Maybe even Dad wouldn't be so bitter if she were here. I would have loved to ask her parenting questions. My memories of her are filled by a woman who was an unstoppable force of nature. She knew how to do everything: how to say the right things, how to mend clothes, how to cook. I try to fill her shoes, try to be a mom like her, but I'm an imposter, a cruel imitation of the real thing.

Maybe she could see the failure I would become. Maybe she left so she'd be spared the disappointment and shame. The weight of guilt sits on my shoulders like it did when I was little. I should have been a better daughter. She wouldn't have left if I had listened better and not fought her every step of the way. If I had cleaned my room and done my chores. Dad always told me I was a tedious child. And I'm no better at being a grown-up.

I turn away from Mom's stare and look at the broken glass strewn over the floor. My life in metaphor. I don't move from my perch on the sofa. If I could go back in time just a few seconds to keep it from shattering... If I could go back just a few years and be a more attentive wife, a more understanding mom, an obedient daughter... But mistakes can't be undone.

Another crack of thunder brings me out of my downward spiral. I can at least function enough to clean up this mess. I place Mom's picture on the cushion next to me, swing my legs out, and stoop down to pick up the frame. I turn on the light, aware that any misstep could lead to a shard in the bottom of my foot, and walk to the garbage can in the kitchen.

It's twenty minutes or so before I am done vacuuming and mopping. I kneel to grab one last splinter of glass and stand too fast. The room tilts, the alcohol from the wine taking effect. I fall into the couch and land on the floor, knocking the picture to the ground. It lands facedown. I stay there for a moment, feeling the cool floorboard against my hot cheek. Then I see what is written on the back of the picture and freeze.

Maggie, please. Come find me.

All the air has been sucked from the room; an endless vacuum, and I'm falling through space. My lungs refuse to expand and my throat is tight, the muscles constricted. What kind of sick joke is this? Did Dad write this? To make his story seem legitimate? I pull myself up to my forearms and shuffle into a seated position. I don't think that's Dad's handwriting. Could it be... could it be Mom's? I don't remember what her handwriting looks like. Not in enough detail to compare it to this. But if it is, if she wrote this, that would mean Dad was telling the truth the whole time.

No. I slam the picture down on the floor and twist around to the side table to grope for my glass. I need more wine.

In the kitchen, I empty the bottle and then the glass. I stare across the open floor plan at the spot where the picture is now barely visible.

Flash!

One... two... three... *CRASH!*

The storm rages outside. Just like the night she left. I close my eyes and imagine I can see her at the door. The air was heavy with a foul stench. Something bad happened, and it made her leave. Something I did. My mistake drove her away.

I'm out of wine. I check my watch. There is a twenty-four-hour convenience store in town. If I leave now, I should be back before the worst of the storm hits.

The room jerks when I step forward to put the empty glass on the counter, harder than I mean to. At the front of the house, I stand at the foot of the stairs and listen. Everything is quiet. I can just make out the faint ticking of the stairwell clock.

I grab my keys off the hook by the door and jam my feet into worn-out tennis shoes. It's late, but the store is just a few miles away. I'll be fine. There shouldn't be anyone else on the road, and I will be back before anyone notices I'm gone. I walk to my car, start the engine, and look up at the house. Would they even notice if I never returned?

⸺◦○◦⸺

The road gleams black from recent rainfall. Droplets cling to the windows. The wipers squeak and leave streaks; they need to be replaced. A sudden deluge falls from the sky. Again, I think about the night Mom left. It was the worst thunderstorm our little town had ever seen. Dad had gone out to search for her. The creek near our house was swollen with rain; a flash flood almost carried him off. He'd fallen and hit his head in the woods. It's why he's filled with all those crazy stories.

Rain comes down in thick waves, obscuring the pavement in front of me. I know these roads so well that I don't need to see them clearly. My sight swims before my eyes, the lids growing heavy. My head slumps once, and I'm shocked awake by the sudden change in equilibrium. I grip the steering wheel tighter, my knuckles white. Only a few moments later, I am again lulled by the rhythmic tapping on the roof of the car. I want to curl into something warm, feel the comfort and security I've craved for so many years. I want my mom.

Out of nowhere, a large shadow steps into the middle of the road. I'm too slow, the brakes are too old. A heavy weight slams into me. In a blinding crack, pain explodes across my face. My collarbone feels like it will snap any second. I'm pressed into the seat, gravity and something else, something heavy, pushes against me.

I can't breathe. I can't move. Something's burning. It stinks like a kind of acidic smoke. Is that gasoline?!

Inside my head, a primitive survival instinct screams at me to get out of the car. *Get out now!* My numb hands can't unbuckle the seatbelt, and I tear at it with rising terror.

I'm trapped!

Finally it clicks and gives way; the sudden release lets me fall into the rough surface of a big balloon. No... not a balloon. The airbag. My nostrils fill with the acrid scent. Realization dawns, and I understand the burnt smell is coming from the airbag. I take a moment to catch my breath and assess my surroundings.

Something warm trickles down my cheek, but I don't feel pain. I'm not hurt. Not really. What did I hit? I turn my head to look out the window, but there is only an ocean of black. I take the key out of the ignition and push open the door on groaning hinges. I stumble back up to the road. The car is nose-first in a ditch.

My legs can't hold my weight, and I fall to sit on the edge of the road. Without warning, dinner and wine make a reappearance. I'm shaking by the time the retching is over.

It is going to cost so much money to call a tow truck. Money that we don't have. Not to mention the cost of the insurance. I let my face fall into my hands, the sobs swallowed up by the boom of thunder overhead. I don't even feel the pellets of water cascading down. I am wrapped in a blanket of misery. I just want to go to bed and hide under the covers. Pretend this never happened.

I lift my head when a flash of lightning crackles through the air, and I see what I hit. A large branch the size of a small tree is in the middle of the road. What luck. Of course, tonight of all nights, there would be a branch in the road. I wobble to my feet, finding my balance. My phone is gone. Should I turn around and go home or walk into town and call my dad to come pick me up? I shiver at the thought of the look on his face if he sees me like this. No, I will walk home, crawl into bed, and come up with a solution in the morning.

My head has started to pound, the pain like a sharp nail being hammered into the base of my skull. I look to the left, then the right. Which way is home? Which way was I coming from? It's too dark to see any signs. The nose of the car is pointing left down the road so I should go right, but what if the car got spun around and is facing the wrong way?

A blast of wind almost knocks me back down. I need to decide. I can't stay out here all night. Turning right, I start walking. My head aches and my fingers are ice. The thin sweater I'm wearing does nothing to keep the chill out. After only a few minutes of fighting the storm, the wind grabbing at my clothes, the icy rain pelting my face like hundreds of tiny, sharp needles, I stop. I'm so tired.

Is this the right way? It's impossible to tell. I turn around and then around again. I'm lost, like a little girl. I swing around again, and there is a light bouncing ahead of me. Someone is out here! Maybe they have a phone. I think I will call Dad; my pride be darned. I just want to go home, be in my warm bed, and pretend this isn't my life.

I turn toward the light. It's bobbing up and down and getting smaller, like someone is walking away. I need to get closer before I can shout. The storm is too loud. They won't hear me. I start to run. The light isn't getting bigger. I'm not getting closer.

"Hey! Wait!"

My throat burns with the effort of shouting above the wind. The storm is directly overhead now, the lightning and thunder shattering the night in unison. Still, I follow, and still the light becomes ever smaller until it completely disappears. I stop, heaving air in and out of my lungs. It's only then that I look around.

Where am I? I must have run off the road. Giants surround me. Huge trees with wide branches create a canopy that keeps out most of the rain. I stumble forward on shaky legs; a narrow path coated with pine needles stretches out before me. Maybe I will find a cabin. With any luck it will be empty, and I can stay there. Or there will be a landline. Regardless, I must keep moving.

My teeth chatter; the temperature is even colder now. I pull the thin sweater tighter around myself as an act of defiance against the weather. Following the path as it winds through the trees, I squint into the distance. There's nothing but darkness; the trees grouping tighter and tighter together. I think I need to turn around, look for the road. Just before I lose my nerve, something in the distance catches my eye. Light. A cabin! It must be a cabin!

I lurch forward, my legs not listening, my feet so frozen that I can't feel them. Jerky step after jerky step, I move toward the light. My saving grace. My escape from the storm. My–

It's a tree.

My heart sinks. Someone has strung fairy lights up around the lowest branches of a tree, out in the middle of nowhere, and I, in my infinite impatient wisdom, mistook it for something else. Typical. I limp around the huge trunk– it's the width of a minibus– but there is no one. I am alone. Lost. Cold. And so, so tired.

I can't think, my mind fuzzy with fatigue and wine, so I sit at the base of the tree and wrap my arms around my knees. Tears warm my cheeks, each one a new blanket against the cold until it too, fades and freezes. I rest my forehead on my knees.

What if I don't ever make it back home? Max's angry, tear-stained face floats through my memory. It's joined by the look of betrayal on Alice's face when I grounded them tonight. Their dad would have handled the argument better. My kids are better off without me. If I'm not there, he will have to take them. I don't have the patience to be a good mom. I don't have the right words or do the right things. Not like the other moms out there. They have it all together. I should just stay here by this tree, under the lights. It's not so cold now. I'm sure the storm will stop soon.

My eyelids are too heavy to keep open. The lights dance in front of me, moving in graceful circles. The branches of the tree embrace me, and I'm lying down. Stretched out on the pine floor. The earth is dry under the tree and after a few minutes, I don't even feel it anymore. I'm floating away. Away from everything bad I've done. From the terrible things I've said. From all my mistakes.

———◆———

Golden light seeps through my closed eyelids. Warm and cozy, I snuggle deeper into a thick down comforter. An expensive mattress like they have in high-end hotels squishes beneath me. Nothing like my firm slab of springs at home.

Where am I?

I crack one eyelid open. White lace curtains flutter lazily in the rose-scented breeze coming from an open window: the essence of spring with its promise of new life. I hungrily absorb the little room in which I slept. It's mostly bare of furniture, with a wooden floor, cream walls, a nightstand, and a bed.

How did I get here? It's perfect.

For a moment, I don't care and bury myself into the comforter once more. Before I can drift into the sweet oblivion of sleep, the events from last night come crashing in like a nightmare. The wine, the car accident, the run through the woods.

I should be in agony right now, my head should be pounding with a hangover at least, but it's not. I feel better than I have in a long, long time.

A clinking sound draws my attention to the door set into the opposite wall. The light wood of the frame has been scored with interwoven vines and flowers. I pull back the comforter, and to my surprise, my clothes are clean and dry. My shoes look like they've just come off the showroom floor, and I quickly slide my feet into them. I tiptoe toward the door as quietly as I can. My hand hovers above the knob, and I wonder if it will be locked.

All at once, the door opens, barely missing the tip of my nose. A woman stands in front of me, her attention held by the precariously balanced plate on her forearm and the cup that smells of strong coffee in her hand. She doesn't notice that I'm standing in front of her. She takes a step forward and almost collides with me.

"Oh my! You're awake!"

She deftly steps around me and places the cup and plate full of goodies down on the nightstand. A tight band wraps around my chest, and I can't breathe. This must be a mistake. I'm still dreaming. Her back is to me, but I know her. She turns and offers a polite smile.

"I've made you some breakfast. I hope you like apple cobbler," she says and pauses to wait for an answer.

I can't move. I stare at her, willing her to be real. The lines around her eyes are new, the grey in her hair, but it is her. My mom. She's standing in front of me, hands on her hips, lips pursed in such a familiar way I want to cry. My stare must be unsettling, because she rocks back on her heels and draws in a deep sigh through her nose.

"Well, I'll let you get settled." She steps past me, allowing for a little more room between us. "If you need anything, just holler."

No, she can't go yet! I have so many questions. I reach out my hand to stop her, but I am too slow and grasp at the air between us.

"Mom?" I blurt out with all the elegance of a tripping elephant.

She stops in her tracks and turns to look at me, her head tilted.

"Mom?" She parrots. "I'm so sorry, dear. You have me confused with someone else. I'm not, nor have I ever been a mom."

Her words are confident, tinged with amusement. But before she turns away, I see the slightest of hesitations when our eyes meet. She recovers so quickly, I might have imagined it. A hope so desperate made manifest in a delusion. Maybe this woman only strongly resembles my mom; I haven't seen her in so long.

The door closes behind her, and I'm left alone again. My stomach rumbles loudly. I take a bite of cobbler, and warm cinnamon wakes my taste buds. The apples are juicy, and the coffee is strong and bitter. If I didn't know any better, I'd say that I woke up to my dream vacation.

I drop the last bite of cobbler before I can eat it. I *don't* know any better. What if I'm *dead?* What if I died in the woods and my body is out in the wilderness somewhere and the kids are waking up to find me missing? *I must get back to my kids!*

I stand and run to the door. It opens easily onto a long hallway with the same wooden floor and the same creamy walls. It feels sterile somehow, not homey like in the bedroom. Unfinished. There's a staircase at the far end, and I run to it, taking the steps down two at a time.

I find myself in a kitchen. Bright, intense light streams in from the windows. I blink furiously, the room oversaturated with the glow. Flowers cover almost every surface. Vases full of tulips, pots of lavender, a window box of roses. Despite the smell of fresh baking, the counters are clean and free of clutter. No fine dusting of flour. No discarded apple cores. The perfect, stage-ready country cottage.

Soft humming pulls my attention to the far side of the kitchen. The woman has her back to me. I need her to turn around. I need to see her face.

My hand reaches out before I can think better of it, and in my haste, I knock over a vase of tulips. The crash should have shattered the silence and ruined the serenity of the cottage. But it doesn't. Somehow, in the space between the fall and the blink of my eyes, the vase stops moving. It doesn't crash and break into an unredeemable mound of shards. It's back on the counter, perfectly positioned to allow the light to brighten the deep purple of the petals.

The woman turns toward me. Her eyes flick to the undamaged vase and then to my face. She smiles; the friendly emotion not reflected in her empty eyes. Regardless of the doubt from earlier, I'm not imagining things. This woman is Mom. The small scar on her chin, identical to the one in the picture, confirms it.

"Oh, you're a fast eater. Do you want some more?"

She gestures to the stovetop. I could have sworn it was empty when I walked in, but now, the cobbler sits there, a clean plate ready for my use. The sweet scent of flowers, apples, and cinnamon clings to the air. It's so strong that I'm suddenly dizzy. I sway a little, and Mom reaches out to steady me: her touch real and solid.

Wrinkles crisscross her soft, warm skin. I want to take hold of her hands, kiss them, never let go.

She helps me into a waiting chair by a small table and brushes my hair behind my ear. All of a sudden, I'm six again, casting an adoring gaze over her. She draws her hand back quickly, like she's been burned. She seems surprised by her own gesture. She looks at me– really looks– seeking something solid to stand on. Her expression clouds over, and I think I see recognition, but then it clears, that empty smile pasted on her lips again.

A sharp, rancid scent cuts through the floral perfume, but before I can identify it, it's gone. It stirred a memory, but only just, the glimmer of it gone before it could register.

Mom turns away from me and toward the cobbler. There's a mug full of coffee next to the plate now. I must have been wrapped up in my thoughts to have missed her pouring it. She comes back and sets the plate and cup in front of me. It looks delicious, golden, and crunchy. The coffee is strong and nutty. I'm ravenous, my stomach growling again like I hadn't just eaten upstairs.

Mom sits down across from me; her hands are politely folded in front of her. The first bite of the cobbler is divine, the second reveals another layer of nutmeg and ginger, and by the third bite, flavor popcorns around my tongue like fireworks. There's a clink when I lower my fork a few minutes later, and I'm disappointed to see the empty plate. I look up and admire the rainbow of color around us. How beautiful. How serene. I am floating in the scent of the flowers, their bright beauty stunning. I let myself relax into the chair, the cushions soft, hugging my body. I haven't felt this calm in a long, long time.

"So, what brings you out here?" Mom asks, drawing my attention back to her.

Her face, unlike her hands, is almost free of wrinkles: no worry lines, no laugh lines. Just the graceful elegance of age.

"I was driving–" I start, but the rest sticks in my throat.

Where was I going? What was I doing? The memory is fuzzy, a thick haze around it. Like looking in a mirror after a hot shower. Well, if I can't remember, it's probably not important. Absent-mindedly, I pick up the fork and play with it. A new piece of cobbler waits for me, which is good, because I am just so hungry. The woman in front of me watches me eat and smiles. She is kind and sweet and... familiar. Do I know her?

"Well," she leans forward and brushes away the strand of my hair that's gone loose again. "You can stay here for as long as you need."

Her touch is electric, sharp, and painful. Alarm bells sound in the back of my mind. I know her. I know I do. But from where? That sharp, acidic smell passes under my nose, cutting through the cinnamon and sugar. *Burning.* I'm thrown backward in time. Burning hair. *My* hair. I was leaning too far forward; there were too many candles on the cake. Mom was there, and Dad was yelling. There was a storm. A terrible, awful storm.

Mom left that night. Mom disappeared. Mom...

I look up to find the woman watching me.

"More coffee?"

"Yes, please!" I offer her a wide-toothed smile and hold out my cup, but it's already full.

The rich, nutty flavor complements the sweetness of the cobbler.

"What did you put in this? It's divine. I'll need your recipe. My kids would love this—"

My kids! I have kids!

Abruptly, I stand, knocking over my chair. That sharp smell of burning hair and the night Mom left; they're connected. I look at her and she's looking at me, her expression puzzled. But there's something more there. Fear. The room is full of the smell of it: a salty, metallic odor. The flowers droop, their heads wilting down to the stems, petals fall to the counter and wither before our eyes.

This place can't be real. I stride purposefully to the door and jiggle the handle. Locked. I move to the window, pushing my whole weight against it, but it won't budge. I look at Mom, and for a split second I can't breathe. Her face is contorted in a mask of grief, then anger, then shame.

"Mom!" I move toward her, take hold of her hands. "Mom, how do we get out of here?"

I think of the message on the back of her picture. Hidden but present, for me to find when the time was right. She must have known she would be trapped. Must have known she would need help getting back.

She looks at me blankly, a smile playing around the edges of her lips but not quite forming.

"I already told you, dear. I'm no one's mom."

"Yes, you are! Your name is Evelynn Matthews. You are married to Charlie Matthews. I'm your daughter, Maggie! You must remember. You must!"

She looks down at our hands. I'm squeezing too hard, my knuckles white. She's in pain but doesn't pull away. I loosen my grip a little and don't let go. I never want to let go again.

"You have grandkids, too. Max and Alice. Max is six and thinks he knows everything about the world. And Alice, oh my sweet Alice. You will love her. She's so creative and brave. She reminds me a lot of you–"

I stop at the look on Mom's face. She's crying and shaking her head forcefully back and forth. The air is rancid with the smell of burning hair.

"No," she pushes out past her lips. "I am no one's mom. I'm not fit to be a mom."

"You were the best mom! You encouraged me and loved me. We had hot cocoa parties in the living room, drew murals on the sidewalk with chalk. You used to brush my hair so I could fall asleep at night. Don't you remember? You must remember!"

My hands move up to her shoulders. The light outside the windows is too bright, the walls too grey, the flowers shrivel to dust. I give her a little shake.

"Look at me, Mom. Please. Just look at me. You will see."

Her eyes are squeezed tight, like a little girl afraid of the dark. She starts shaking her head again.

"Please, Mom... I love you."

Time slows and then stops altogether. Flower dust floats suspended in the air, the clock over the stove, its second hand suspended mid tick. Mom slowly opens her eyes. It's like she's seeing me for the first time. Her hand goes to her mouth, and she draws in a quick breath. Then, as if afraid to shatter the reality, she carefully cups my cheek and brushes away a tear I didn't realize was there.

"Maggie," she whispers between us. "My Maggie."

I can't speak; the muscles in my throat constricted, so I nod and pull her into a hug. Warmth and color explode around us, a waterfall of fresh flower petals, but this time they can't make us forget.

"Forgive me," she's sobbing. "Forgive me."

After a while, we pull apart. The room is bare, no longer a kitchen. There are no flowers, no petals littering the floor. The ambient light washes the world clean of everything but us. We stay connected, our hands refusing to let the other go.

"I failed you so many times," she says, her voice steady now. "I just wanted to be a better mom."

"You were the best, Mom," I say. "It was Dad's fault. He drove you away."

She retreats inward and shakes her head.

"Your dad and I had our issues, but he didn't drive me away. I did that. I wasn't fit to be the mom you deserved."

She seems so alone, so isolated… something inside cracks and I ask the question I've carried with me for so long.

"Is that why you ran away?"

"Ran away?" She tilts her head. "It was never my intention to run away. I'd heard the Fairy Tree could give you everything you needed. And I needed to be a better mom. So, I went to find it. But instead of giving me what I asked for, it opened to reveal a world hidden within. A world where I wasn't a failure. A world where I was… where I was happy."

She shifts and releases my hand. The weight of the loss is too heavy, and I reach out again, but she pulls away.

"I returned home that night and thought I would give it one more try. To be the mom you deserved. But then, you got hurt, and your dad was so mad at me. I knew it was wrong. And a part of me didn't want to go. But the bigger part, the louder part, drove me back to the tree, back to my perfect world where I couldn't hurt you again. And then... I forgot. I forgot you. I forgot Charlie. And I forgot all my failures." Tears stream down her cheeks. "Until now..."

Her words echo around my head. They are too much like the lies I tell myself every day. Max. Alice. I was going to leave them, too. Just like Mom left me.

The realization of how wrong I was hits me like a sledgehammer. I might not do everything right. But I will learn. It's going to be hard, and I will need to give myself grace for the mistakes I will make. I will ask my children for patience as I learn. I might not be as put together as their dad. I might not say or do the right things. But I stayed. I stayed for them, and I am willing to put in the hard work for them. Now, all I want to do is run home and hold my babies in my arms.

"I want to go home," I say, my heart pounding with the need to be with my kids. "How do we get out of here?"

There's no door. No windows. I start hammering on the nearest wall.

"I don't know," Mom sounds defeated. Exhausted.

"Yes, you do. You said you got out once; you can do it again. I will get back to my children. They need me." I turn to her, pleading with her. "Help me."

"I don't–" Her hands are in the air, and she shrugs.

I start hammering harder. My knuckles split, the skin ruined. I'm crying, tears streaming, hot and angry. I need to get back to my kids!

"Listen here!" I shout into the void. "You will let us out. You will let me see my children again. They are EVERYTHING!"

It's impossible to tell how long I fight to get out of our prison. My hands and feet are bleeding and broken. It's darker now, and I've collapsed on the floor. There's pressure on my shoulder, and Mom is next to me. We curl up together on the floor; she envelopes me in her warmth.

"I remember," she whispers in my ear. "It's love, Maggie. Love is the way out."

Despite everything. Despite the fear, the shame, the anger. Love triumphs over all; the understanding that no matter how many mistakes I make, how many doors are slammed, or frames broken, I will always have the strength to keep going for my babies. I will not give up.

I hold my mom closer. There's a flash of light and then total darkness.

———◄○►———

I wake with a jolt and instantly start to shiver. Rain pours from the dark sky, the pine needle-covered ground saturated with it. I move, and fierce pain sears through my stiff muscles. I pull myself up on a low-hanging limb and look around. I'm in the forest again. It was all a dream. Just a dream.

I crashed my car; I ran away from my family. I need to go home. What time is it? I must be there when they wake up. I take a step and trip over something lying at my feet. No, not something. Someone. For a moment, I can't believe my eyes. She must be a delusion. A desperate part of me that didn't want to let go of the dream.

I reach out a trembling hand. Part of me expects to fall right through the vision, to shatter the last threads of hope in seeing her there. But when my hand lands on her arm, she is as solid and real as I am. Her clothes are soaked, her hair covers her face, and she is real. I give her a gentle shake, and she stirs. I sink to the ground next to her. We hold onto each other. A lifetime of shame and love wrapped so tightly they can't be separated. But there is something else, too. Hope.

"Let's go home," I say. "Let's go home."

WHAT LIES BETWEEN

By Sharon Hughson

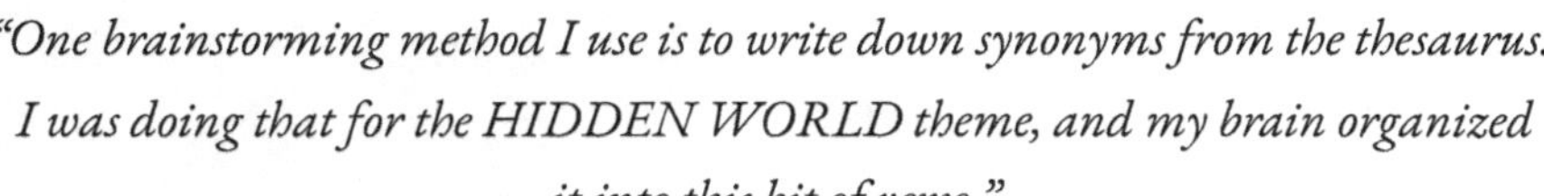

"One brainstorming method I use is to write down synonyms from the thesaurus. I was doing that for the HIDDEN WORLD theme, and my brain organized it into this bit of verse."

Buried
in the soul
of something whole
lives a mysterious
realm

Concealed
by the seen
and what lies between
lurks an invisible
sphere

Cloaked
beneath obscurity
silencing security
speaks the veiled
domain

Shrouded
the notably masked
its privacy unasked
exists an unknown
nature

Eclipsed
in sunlight
by moonless night
resides one covert
system

Hidden
within a mind
so well-designed
beckons this undiscovered
world

HIDDEN WORLDS IN PLAIN SIGHT

THE SCENT OF GOODBYE

By Tamelia Aday

"After my dad passed away, a truck drove by my house that looked like his."

The swing creaked. My feet brushed the porch as I guided the wooden bench back and forth, creating a slight breeze. Alone in this quiet, peaceful moment, the heat didn't bother me. After all, I had sweet tea.

A rosebush, a gift from my dad years ago, graced the corner of the walkway. Back then, the flowers were bold with a heady fragrance, the leaves full of life. But now, a shriveled bloom floated to the ground, its scent barely a whisper.

My lamenting over the rose was forgotten when a horn blared and a car zoomed past, its fumes tainting the air. The silence that followed made me pause the swing's movement. Birdsongs in the background came to a halt. The breeze stilled—nothingness laced with both expectation and dread. I struggled to breathe. In the south, we were accustomed to sultry days and humid nights, but this compressed heaviness and utter silence insulated me, as if I were transported. Yet the scenery remained the same.

A rumble from down the street popped the suffocating air, and that's when I saw him—driving his old Toyota truck, as though he hadn't died a year ago. His pace was slow, in sync with the hot southern day.

"Dad." A gust of wind blew through my hair, and the world breathed again. The heaviness lifted, and I gulped air. A spattering of chatter from the birds punctuated the return to reality.

I'd been outside too long, and it was time to cook dinner. The screen door banged in my wake.

⚬

"Where does your friend live?" I asked my teenage daughter.

"You cross the tracks and drive to the end of the road—where the new houses are." She flipped the visor, checking her makeup for the umpteenth time.

I drove down a long stretch of highway until a McMansion came into sight. I dropped her off where she indicated, then headed toward home, or so I thought.

My internal GPS got messed up, a rarity for me. I found myself on a country road lined with fields. It didn't make sense—all this open space.

Ahead of me, a figure walked his dog beside the road. I noted the gait, the form, the familiarity.

"Dad."

I sped up, but like a mirage, he disappeared, the vast emptiness vanishing with him. Houses replaced the empty pasture, and recognition clicked. I looked in the rearview mirror—nothing resembled where I'd been.

Maybe I was dreaming with my eyes open. Or some other freaky type of disorder I had yet to discover.

That evening, the Friday classic car show was a welcome distraction. The engines revved while they made their loop around our block, the noise cancelling out the questions that filled my mind. I came outside to water the plants I hadn't killed yet and caught a glimpse of a '63 two-toned Chevy Impala. I watched, drawn to it, as my dad drove by in slow motion. He appeared to be in his early twenties. He hung his head out the window for a second, hollered to the car behind him, and then laughed. Nothing hindered his smile, no sign of the veil of sadness I'd grown up seeing. I rushed to the edge of the road, but, as though a switch had been flipped, the cars sped up—back to real time.

The weekend drifted by, relaxing and lazy with nothing pressing, no errands or events. Calm returned to my spirit.

Monday night, the doorbell rang. "I got it."

Probably someone wanting to sell us a roof repair or new windows. But instead, my dad stood there, holding a McDonald's bag just like the old days when he'd drop by unannounced. I stepped closer, and he was gone.

"Mom! Was that DoorDash?" My son Russel came tearing down the stairs and blasted past me to the porch.

Sure enough, the McDonald's bag sat by the doorway. "Ordered something. Gotta bunch of homework."

I closed the door, in a near trance-like state, and the usual reprimands of waiting until the last minute to do homework didn't rise to the surface.

"What causes this? Why am I always seeing him?" I finally asked my friend, as though she were an armchair psychologist.

"Grief is stuck inside. It's knocking at you." Her hand went to her heart. "Take a trip where you can be alone and let him go."

◆

The car rental attendant handed me the keys, and I took off toward the Oregon Coast, my childhood stomping grounds. I'd add my tears to the ocean waters and be free of hallucinations.

Driving for days, I pulled up to a parking spot and hurried down the stairway to the beach. I'd grown accustomed to the humidity of the South. The crisp cold transported me back to my childhood. The ocean roared, greeting me at its edge. I clutched my flimsy jacket while the tide rushed forward, soaking my shoes, and the sand moved beneath my feet. The waters shied away, gathered strength, and returned bigger and deeper.

I backed from the foamy waves and released my grief into the beach air, drowning it with the music of the ocean.

I longed to return to my family—to be back in the south. I sped, cranked the radio, and left the small coastal town behind. Static burst through the melody, and miles of dunes on both sides of the highway hugged me in their wide emptiness.

A horse came from nowhere, and I slammed on my brakes. My dad rode across the pavement, and his eyes met mine. He tipped his hat, shook the reins, and galloped toward the golden landscape, vanishing as the sun sank into the sandy hills. I pulled over and let the last of my tears fall.

Days later, I arrived home to the hot twilight.

I dragged my luggage up the walkway and stopped when I saw the rose bush. The crispy leaves were now green and full of life, and a gigantic pink bloom stood, tall and healthy. A scent of roses filled the air. Petals fell from the sky like snow, and I held out my hand to catch one. Its perfect heart shape landed in my palm. I twirled underneath the falling flowers as the stars started to glimmer in the sky. Where grief had lingered in my soul, his last gift filled its place.

"Goodbye, Dad."

DUDE AND BABY SISTER

By Jana Mann

"Sometimes writing prompts yield a story worth sharing."

Funerals are not my thing and this particular one especially so. I'm only here because I was asked to be here. The deceased, dressed in a secondhand polyester suit, is tucked into a bargain-basement casket. And honestly, right at this moment, he is lucky that he cannot hear the accordion. A solemn hymn with polka expectations is very unpleasant - much like the dead guy himself.

The deceased is Dude (name withheld to protect the guilty). According to the basic generic eulogy, he'd been a fine enough fellow, sometimes kind, and maybe generous when the ponies ran well enough. I will concede it's possible that once upon a time he had shown a flicker or two of decency. But I must have missed it. When he was alive, Dude had a real knack for pissing people off, vanishing without a trace, and serving up some cold revenge. I can speak from personal experience about him pissing people off. Once upon a long time ago, Dude had been my baby sister's disastrous boyfriend.

Baby Sister (name withheld for the same reason), well, she was a wild one. Baby Sister found herself in trouble all the time, and if she couldn't find trouble, then she made it. At some point, the notoriety bug bit. Baby Sister decided she was a dancer and dreamed of becoming a star. In pursuit of this elusive fame, she began dancing at The Caboose. Yes, it was one of "those" places. Baby Sister had been underage then, but neither the management nor the patrons cared about birthdays like they cared about cup sizes.

It didn't take too many turns on the pole for Baby Sister to capture Dude's attention and more than a few of his dollar bills. He vowed to take her to Las Vegas, New York, or Hollywood.

"Your dreams are my dreams, baby," he told her.

Several years later, they were living in a seedy no-tell motel south of Reno. Promises and dreams had suffocated and resurrected as anger and disappointment. When the screaming in the hotel room led to brawling in the parking lot, someone finally called 9-1-1. Paramedics hauled Baby Sister to the emergency room. Troopers hauled Dude to jail.

There were no winners in this match-up, unless you counted Baby Sister's new nose. Afterwards, Baby Sister wised up, grew up, and moved on. Dude, on the other hand, served time in the Gray Bar Hilton and, upon his release, continued to be an asshole.

I glance around the chapel at the small gaggle of mourners. There aren't many of us, and none of us look particularly grieved at Dude's passing. I feel a tinge of sadness. At the end of life, there should be a few more dearly beloved who gave a damn.

Dude's cause of death, according to the coroner, was heart failure. Close enough, but not quite. He was killed. I know that for a fact. I am the one who killed him.

Normally, I don't have any feelings about my targets, it's just work. I only follow orders. I don't know why he had to go and whatever the reason, it didn't and still doesn't matter. This particular job did give me a fair amount of satisfaction, though. I know that's not very nice, but keep in mind, neither was Dude.

Also, normally, I don't attend their funerals. But when Baby Sister called and asked me to accompany her, I couldn't refuse.

One final note wheezes out of the accordion, and there is a brief moment of blissful quiet before we are dismissed.

"C'mon, Baby Sister," I say as we stand, "let's grab some lunch before I have to get back to work."

ACCIDENTAL INHERITANCE

By Kathy Appel

"Based on an experience from earlier in my life."

I first noticed the old, ramshackle house while taking a walk with my dog, Biscuit. It was well hidden within a mix of pine, oak, and fir trees, including many shrubs and bushes surrounding it, all overgrown. With no other houses nearby, it was at least 1000 feet away from our property, where I now lived with my husband, Dave. Did somebody live there?

We had recently moved to what I thought was going to be our dream home, a one-bedroom log cabin on ten acres, in remote Deer Island, Oregon. Truth be told, though, we were renting–no way we could afford to buy a home. Having grown up near nothing but beach sand and sunny skies, I was ready for this life of sky-high firs, deer, elk, raccoons, and endless greenery. Little did I realize how difficult life could be, living so far from town and other people.

I was five months pregnant, so I decided I'd take a break from working, and where, exactly, would I find a suitable position in this remote area of the county? Dave was in "construction" which actually meant a variety of odd jobs with not much money coming in. This was 1978, so no cell phones, which wouldn't have worked here anyway. And for us, no phone, period, as we couldn't afford it. My life quickly became one of isolation, and with Dave driving into town most days for work, loneliness.

—◇—

When Biscuit and I got back to our cabin that day, I realized I could just barely see the obscure, old house through the trees as I stood looking out the window of my living room. That evening, I told Dave what I had observed.

"Hey, my buddy Larry from work has lived around here since he was a kid," he said. "I'll ask him about the place tomorrow." It turned out that an old couple had lived there, and both were thought to have been deceased for a long time. Other than that he had never heard anything about them.

After Dave left for work the next day, Biscuit and I decided to do a bit more investigating. I didn't walk to the house from the road, as I couldn't locate the entrance to the driveway. We had to take the field between the houses, which ended with a small stand of pines and some very large, almost tree-like rhododendrons. From there, we crept around to the front porch of the house.

Peeking through a window, I saw a fully intact living room, complete with a couch, chairs, coffee table, TV, knickknacks, and pictures on the walls. Piles of newspapers and magazines, and even an old man's slippers, were on the floor. I could also see part of the kitchen–a small wooden table against the wall and a few items on it, including salt and pepper shakers.

The house looked very "lived in," as though its former tenants could drive up at any moment after a trip to town. The doors were locked, but I slipped around to the back of the house, found a window, and jimmied it up a bit. There was no way I was getting into this house without a stronger set of arms to open the window further. Besides, I felt a little creeped out by this place. Buckets, brooms and mops sat on the back porch, as well as some rather rusty looking tools, and two sets of boots–a pair for her, and for him. Did the old man and woman just leave one day and never return?

I told Dave about my discoveries later that evening, and we made a plan to check things out further together. Saturday afternoon, armed with a crowbar, we headed across the field. I was glad it hadn't rained that day, or we'd have been soaked from tromping through all the thick vegetation.

While Dave pried the window open, I found a rickety metal stool to stand on, then slid myself inside. I landed in the utility room sink, full of cobwebs and old sponges...ugh! Crawling out of the sink, I brushed myself off and opened the back door.

We first noticed how dusty, damp, and cold the place was. But at the same time, it had a feel of organization and livability to it. There were a few dirty dishes in the kitchen sink, covered with a thick layer of dust. A blue lace tablecloth covered the small kitchen table. I opened one cupboard revealing plates, a gravy boat, and a butter dish.

"Nice toaster!" Dave noticed. In a hallway closet I found neatly stacked sets of towels, sheets, blankets, quilts, and doilies of all sizes and shapes. As Dave and I continued to take inventory of these beautiful finds, our eyes locked more than once.

"What can I say?" I wondered aloud, after we returned home empty-handed. "We really need a lot of that stuff, and it's just sitting there, unused, and in need of a new home!" I knew Dave felt the same way, especially with the new baby coming. Money was "too tight to mention" as the band Simply Red crooned a popular song of the time. We made a plan to return the next day.

The first thing I took was a potato masher, simple and antique-looking. It was small, circular, and seemed to fit perfectly in my hand! Dave picked up a hammer. Not that it was needed–he just liked the weight of it. Cradling these handheld items, we sat down in the comfortable mama and papa bear rocking chairs in the living room.

We searched each other's faces for signs of guilt or shame, and not seeing any, just let the peace and quiet envelop us. As I rocked, I thought to myself that I could use a chair like this after the baby arrives. Babies like rocking chairs, right? Biscuit stretched out in the middle of the room, letting out a big sigh.

"Look at all those photos, Dave," I said, taking in the room's surroundings. "It's all just the two of them, except for the one with the group. That sort of looks like a family reunion type picture, don't you think?"

Dave shrugged. "It sure looks as though they didn't have any kids. Maybe that's why nobody has ever come to clean this place out."

I got up to inspect the nicely framed photographs more closely. "Such a beautiful young couple. Look at her dress in this one!" I exclaimed.

"Looks like there's a dog in almost every one of their photos," Dave noticed, moving his eyes over the wall in front of us. "They had to be good people, then."

I smiled, nodding in agreement. "They must have loved to dance. There are three photos of them dancing." Who were these people? Why was everything just left sitting here like this?

Maybe we did feel somewhat guilty for breaking into the house, and helping ourselves to a few things. Even so, I returned the next day, this time with a black plastic garbage bag. I put two handmade quilts in the bottom of the bag, then wrapped up a set of four wonderful ceramic dinner plates, lunch plates, and bowls with some very nice matching bath towels from the hall closet. The plates and bowls were yellow, uniquely square-shaped, and decoratively painted with green leaves and brown stems. They were beautiful! The two matching quilts had colorful squares of many patterns. The towels were older but still in good shape, much better than what we currently had. I brought back quite a haul that day.

After brazenly taking a large bag of very useful, needed items from the house, I decided to take a break from going over there for a few days. I did feel strange about the whole experience–but my mind kept wanting to justify and rationalize what I had done. Dave and I shared our feelings about it when he got home that evening, but the discussion took a quick turn to a new set of circumstances.

"That place has been sitting there for who knows how long, with nobody in it," Dave responded to my confessional. "Let's not overthink the situation. And listen–my boss asked me today if we would be interested in moving to one of his rentals on First Street in town. Might be better for us. Just the gas getting to work and back every day is more than we can afford. And you might like town better once the baby's here."

"Live in town?" I shot back. "I thought that this is what you-we- both wanted. I love it here!"

After I calmed down, I conceded that living in town would be less expensive, not only economically but emotionally. The feelings of isolation were more than I had imagined. I agreed to look at the house in town later that week. Also, we decided to visit the mystery house one more time. There were a few more items we knew we could use.

The next day, we sat once again in the living room of our mysterious, deceased neighbors. Dave picked up a large wooden box from the bottom shelf of an end table. It was about sixteen inches across and five inches deep with gold hinges.

"I really like this box. Look at the relief carving on the top of it, and the dovetailing on the corners, so well made and artistic."

Dave had worked in an antique shop in his past. He recognized the craftsmanship of the three-dimensional carving on the lid and the beautifully rounded corners. Opening the box, he was totally surprised to find it full of fly-fishing accessories. Reels, flies, hooks, a duck call, and a paperback book about fly-fishing.

"This guy hunted and fished too!" he exclaimed, feeling as though he'd just hit the jackpot. I safely placed it in the black plastic bag, along with the toaster, which I had wrapped in a small blanket that looked perfect for the soon-to-be-born baby.

"Dave, I really want this rocking chair, and I hope it's the last thing we take. It's certainly the biggest. Do you think we can get it across the field and home?"

Dave balanced the chair on his head, while I sported a beautiful ornate lamp shade on mine as we headed back to the cabin. I carried the black garbage bag and a ceramic swan table lamp. We were a sight to behold for anyone who might have been looking.

"I'm so happy with our treasures!" I later announced.

"I am too," Dave agreed. "And what I really like is the idea that the old man and I both had the same love for hunting birds and fly-fishing."

A small part of this secret, unseen world we had discovered was becoming very much a part of our world.

The next week, we drove down the hill and took a walk through the house we'd been offered. It was small, only one bedroom. It did have a fireplace with a wood stove, which was a definite plus.

"Would my rocking chair look good right here?" I asked myself.

There was a large utility room with pine paneling that I could see becoming a small bedroom for a child. The living room window looked out over a view of the Columbia River. A large sloping fenced backyard would be good for Biscuit, I observed. The street seemed quiet enough. And Dave's boss was only going to charge us about two-thirds of what we currently paid in rent. It was decided: we were moving to town, and quickly, before the baby arrived.

That evening, we got to talking once again regarding how we felt about taking the items we now possessed.

"I was brought up a good Catholic girl. I should have 'guilty' carved into my forehead for all to see," I confessed to Dave, who didn't appear to be nearly as conscience-stricken as me.

"Well, here's how I see it," he began. "It's as though we have some sort of connection to this old couple. I mean, that box... when I saw that stuff, I thought 'hey, the old guy would be glad for me to have it.' And if somehow they're aware of us, they would approve of our use of their things. Maybe some estate sale people will eventually come to clean the place out, and sell off what they can, but I can't help thinking that the owners would rather have us keep the things we've taken, and use them well."

I eventually came around to agreeing with Dave's thoughts on the matter. I was truly thankful for my discovery of the abandoned little house and the items we had acquired. It was as though we were preserving the spirit of this couple's life by using and appreciating what they had given us. During the next couple of weeks, I began to feel not guilty but grateful for the secret, unseen place we had discovered. And also grateful for our soon-to-be new home.

We began packing in earnest. Moving day was here! Dave and a couple of his friendly coworkers hauled the large furniture in a borrowed pickup. I drove down the hill with a few boxes in my Subaru. Later that day, I was at the cabin alone, doing some final cleaning. I knew I had to make one last trip to the secret dwelling.

A week later we sat comfortably by the crackling woodstove, listening to the first rainfall of the late autumn season.

"I do love our new home," I had to admit to Dave.

"I love that colorful quilt," observed Dave as he looked in the direction of the open bedroom door.

He was rubbing linseed oil on the wooden box, which later found its rightful place in our living room. I sat in my rocker, with my swan lamp giving cool white light on a table nearby.

"And don't worry," he said with a grin. "I'm happy to take the fall for all our newly acquired stuff when the cops come knocking."

"The baby and I will gladly come visit you in jail."

Then I remembered! I ran to my car and brought in my last acquisition. I placed it on the fireplace mantle: an oak-framed black-and-white photo of the handsome young couple, their Australian Shepherd sitting at her feet, as they stood arm-in-arm in front of their mysterious, hidden home.

ANT-OLOGY

By Cate Cross

"My mind always imagines other lives, so why not write from the ants' perspective?"

Inka was foraging on the countertop when vibrations from human steps shook the room. Releasing alarm pheromones with her antennae, she quickly retreated beneath the safety of the counter's edge, running into Alik, a soldier ant, on the underside.

"The human is in the kitchen," Inka warned. "You don't want to go up there!"

Being told what to do annoyed Alik, especially when it came from the younger generation. Instead of heeding Inka's warning, she chirped back, "I have a job to do! If I hide each time a human appears, I will never collect any food!"

Alik pumped out her chest and marched to the countertop for another grain of sugar. She'd almost reached the coffee spoon when the human spotted her. A thumb descended over Alik, casting a menacing shadow. She ran for cover under the toaster. It was too late. The thumb closed in. Everything went black.

Beneath the counter, Inka felt the crunch. Quickening her step, she crawled into a crevice inside the wall. Safe for the moment, she knew she could not return to the colony without food, but scouting the countertop was too risky with the human present. Inka searched inside the cabinet instead.

Seeking sugar, starch, or protein, she marched up and down jars and packages. There was nothing. What a dilemma, she thought, knowing there was food on the counter's surface but not wanting to meet the same fate as Alik. Inka paused near the crack that led to the countertop. As she contemplated what to do, an authoritative voice interrupted her thoughts.

"Why aren't you working?" Thea, a commander ant, barked.

Thea marched toward her, and Inka knew she had to think quickly. Thea was beside Inka before she could bat an antenna.

"Why aren't you scouting for food?" Thea demanded.

"I—I think I walked through poison," Inka said cautiously.

Thea looked around, her antennae erect, pointing in all directions. "I don't sense any poison." Looking at Inka with suspicious beady eyes, she ordered, "Get back to work, or I'll have you banned from the colony!" Thea marched away, leaving Inka shaking in her shell.

Inka didn't want to be banned from the colony, but she also didn't want to be smashed by a finger, so she scanned the floor beneath the cabinets for crumbs. It was the safest place to forage because humans rarely noticed ants under the cabinet doors. Inka was searching along the floorboard when she felt a tiny vibration. She stopped and looked around. Again, she felt a vibration. Above her, hiding in the shadows, a worker ant close to Inka's age shook uncontrollably.

"What are you doing up there?" Inka asked.

"I—I'm searching for food," the ant answered, her voice filled with trepidation.

"What's your name?"

"M—Myra."

"Myra, I'm Inka." She looked around to make sure no other ants were near, then continued, "I'm here because I'm hiding from the human."

A small gasp escaped Myra. "Me too," she whispered, then crawled down to stand beside Inka.

Inka looked around to make sure no one was watching. As comforting as it was to have someone with her, it wasn't safe. "We need to keep searching for food," she warned. "If a soldier ant sees us stalling, we could be banned from the colony."

"I walked past a squished ant," Myra said, quivering. "I—I don't want to be next."

"Me neither," Inka replied. "We'll stay beneath the cabinet where the human can't see us."

Inka and Myra continued their search for food, sheltered by the cabinet overhang. There wasn't much. Inka found a single coffee granule and a toast crumb. Myra found a piece of paper. The search looked grim until Myra stepped in a puddle of syrup.

"Inka, I found food," she called.

Inka hurried over. The syrup was sweet and sticky. Relieved, they packed their jaws full and marched back to the colony. Inka created a scent trail under the shelter of the cabinet. Myra stayed close to Inka. Reaching the exterior wall, they followed the floor trim to the door, exiting through a crack near the threshold.

Back at the nest, they carried the syrup into the storeroom, adding to the mound of collected food. As they turned to go back for more, Thea intercepted them.

"You!" she whistled at Myra. "Go to the nursery! You've been reassigned."

Myra darted a look at Inka, who averted her eyes to avoid suspicion from the commander. It was too late. Thea had sensed a collaboration and wanted to know what it was.

"Are you two hiding something?" she asked, narrowing her eyes as she turned to each one.

"N—not at all," Myra stammered.

Inka's antennae bobbed as she shook her head.

"Then back to work. Both of you!" Thea stamped a foot and marched away.

Walking toward the tunnel that led to the nursery, Myra turned to say goodbye to her friend. Inka was gone, undoubtedly on her way back to the dangers that await every forager above ground.

Yesterday, Myra would have given anything for a job in the safety of the nest. Now all she wanted was to be with Inka. Trudging forward, she wished they were still together. As she began her descent into the tunnel, she felt a vibration and quickly turned around. Inka was running toward her.

"If you're reassigned, I'm reassigned," Inka chirped.

Myra squealed with delight. The two ants embraced antennae. "But what if Thea returns?" Myra asked.

"Thea has her claws full keeping the scouts in line," Inka replied, extending her antennae. "You and I will raise a wiser and kinder generation of workers."

Together, they descended into the nursery, embracing their role of caring for the young who would soon replace the old.

DON'T ASK, DON'T TELL

By Linda Paul

"So many stories to tell after working for the US Coast Guard and US Army for two decades."

Charnelle Morgan loved the base camp in Slav Brod. Her unit was here for training and briefing before their deployment to Bosnia. She shuffled down the wide, wood-planked walkway to the women's showers. She was looking forward to using the travel-size bar of Dove soap she had found at the tiny base exchange. Little things like that kept a girl feeling human.

The Croatian night sky was clear and starry. It was an evening that would be perfect for romance, instead of showering off brown dust and massaging her tired feet. Army life was hard on the feet, especially when marching and standing at attention for an hour a day, on concrete or mud, in those heavy damn boots.

"Charnelle! What you doing here, girl?"

"Lewis!" She opened her arms and the two friends stood hugging for a moment.

Around them, soldiers walked by, taking no notice. It was a common sight, soldiers running into old friends, happy shouts and hugging. It happened a hundred times a day.

"Why are you here? I thought you were in Heidelberg."

Lewis shrugged. "I was volunteered by the Signal Command to deploy to Tuzla with you. I'm supposed to set up some comms gear down there."

"You're going with us? Lewis, that's great. Ride with me! I'm driving solo this week."

Lewis smiled. "No, I'll ride down with Mike."

"Mike's here, too? You guys! I have to get to the showers before all the hot water's gone. See you guys later in the rec center?"

"OK, beers on me."

Charnelle smiled at the happy prospect of being deployed with Lewis and Mike. She had met them her first weekend in Germany, on her first duty assignment as a driver for the 18th Transport Group in Kaiserslautern. It was Oktoberfest, and she went alone, not wanting to miss a thing about Germany. When the two handsome soldiers asked if they could share her table, she was happy for the company. They were her first friends. They told her where everything was and how to get around. They taught her a few key German phrases. Even after Lewis was reassigned, Charnelle and Mike still saw him most weekends.

The next morning, just a little bit hungover from the beers of the night before, Charnelle, Mike, and Lewis slipped into morning muster just in time to hear Sergeant Major giving the orders for the day.

"Our deployed forces require a daily flow of three convoys plus air support for their meals, water, gas, and supplies. Today, we are the first convoy. Drive to Bosnia without screwing up! That is our mission, people! Hwaaah?"

"Hwhaaaaahhh!" they all bleated back at him.

"Let's roll, everybody!"

Charnelle drove alone to Tuzla. Her partner, Susan, was still on leave and would be back next week. The convoy's arrival in Tuzla was typical Army organized chaos. After unloading the supplies, they had to locate and set up their own equipment, computers, and personal belongings. She stood in line for over an hour to retrieve her duffel bag.

After staking out a bed and putting her belongings in her locker, Charnelle went to dinner, but she didn't see Mike or Lewis anywhere.

After muster the next morning, Sergeant Major called Charnelle over to his desk. "Specialist Morgan, any idea where Specialist Brady might be? Did he say anything to you about going off base?"

"No, Sergeant-Major. Mike is missing?"

"I'll ask the questions, Specialist. You were seen hugging a man on base in Slav Brod. Was that Specialist Lewis Meyer?"

"Yes, Sergeant Major. We're friends."

"Why was he here?"

"He's installing some comms gear down here..."

Sergeant Major slapped his palm on the table. "Wrong, Morgan! He is AWOL from his unit. Did you know that?"

Charnelle looked up at her senior NCO in surprise. "No, sir!"

"Don't sir me, Specialist! Your friends have disappeared in a stolen Army truck. Where are they?"

Charnelle shook her head. "I don't know, Sergeant Major! Honest!"

"Did you know that your pals were a gay couple?" The Sergeant Major leaned across his desk, glaring at her.

"What? Um... I... I..." Charnelle stuttered.

"Never mind, Morgan, I don't even want to know. I'd best not find out you're lying. Your beer buddies are looking at brig time and dishonorable discharges. If you hear from them, you will come directly to me. Understood?"

"Yes, Sergeant Major."

"Good. Get back to work."

Charnelle left the Sergeant Major's office with her heart pounding. She worried about Lewis and Mike all day. She remembered the first time she met them, that night at Oktoberfest. She pictured the two of them, arms around each other, a little sloppy drunk, laughing and kissing, happy to be out together on a romantic fall evening in Germany. They had trusted her with their secret on the first day they met, calling her their "best straight girlfriend." That night they were hiding in plain sight among all the German civilians. Someone must have recognized them, because the next week, Lewis was reassigned to Heidelberg. She hoped they were safe, wherever they were.

She returned to the barracks to find Susan drying her hair with a towel on the bunk next to hers. Susan was Charnelle's idea of the perfect woman soldier: athletic, beautiful, brave. Charnelle, who was dark and sturdy, thought of Susan as her complementary opposite, willowy and fair.

"Susan! You're back early!"

"Yeah, couldn't stay away. I worried about you crashing our truck, driving all alone. I found your Dove soap and stole it for my shower."

Charnelle grinned. The barracks was empty at this time of day. She kissed the back of Susan's neck, inhaling the Dove soap smell.

"Don't tell," Susan smiled.

"Don't ask," Charnelle responded.

ASCENT OF WOTAN

By Elaine Kelley

"Drawing from contemplative Christianity, Jung's archetypes, and consciousness studies to explore the ancient practice of silence as a pathway to inner transformation."

igh on the North Rim of the Grand Canyon, a lone Kaibab squirrel buries her treasure of acorns, then scurries into the shadows. She sits beneath the trees, conformed to the stirring stillness and windswept silence, fearless before the imposing peaks of ancient gods: Vishnu, Brahma, Shiva, Thor, Wotan. In her purview, these are not temples or shrines but the mere rock foundations of her household. Heedless of deities and demons, she lives a holy secularism, indifferent to the majesty surrounding her.

Eight thousand feet below Kaibab's rocky prominence and far south in the Valley of the Sun, stillness gives way to unrest, and silence turns to turmoil. People dash around in mindless pursuit of empty satisfactions, indifferent to the majesty that hides within, fearful of its demands, and its path through the desert. They have forgotten their true treasure, long buried in their stony hearts. Acorns cannot satisfy them. Nor can the gods.

In her house near the city, Terry Martin ponders her recurring dream. Dangerous heights in the wilderness, a mystery in the clouds. She picks up her dream journal and scribbles some notes. *I yearn to climb. I crave the danger of a lofty life.*

I'm not sure what that means, she thinks as she walks toward the kitchen, stopping to look in the hallway mirror with a listless disregard. Long dark hair, hazel eyes, average cute. Is that all there is? Who am I really?

Her life, so far, shows promise. She earned her degree in developmental psychology, finished an advanced retreat in contemplative prayer, and is becoming a disciplined practitioner. Five years now, she reminds herself. So, what went wrong? She reaches for the refrigerator door, and right there in front of her, held up by a magnet, hangs a copy of the release agreement she signed to get out of jail.

In a doomsday kind of gloom, she walks to the kitchen window, slides the curtains aside, and falls into a mystical gaze. That old Arizona sun had risen, too, revealing the vast desert beyond and the White Tank Mountains jutting from the desert floor—a welcome reprieve from the city's landscape of concrete and asphalt. The desire for wilderness pulls at her heart. Out there, away from the city, all the earth points to higher things, echoing the names of the holy heights: Sinai, Carmel, Olivet, Tabor. Exuberance takes hold of her.

The ping of her laptop interrupts her ardor. It's an email from Sam, her old psych professor.

Hi Terry. I finally have an answer for you. The anxiety and anger you are experiencing are part of a series of emotions brought on by a sense of homelessness, specifically the negative feelings many in your generation are facing because of an increasingly industrialized and weaponized environment. Your symptoms have a name: Solastalgia. I urge you to get this book: Solstagia: An Anthology of Emotion in a Disappearing World. We should talk more after you have read it. Best, Sam

So, it isn't just rage, but a real thing with a name. Learning this helps. Depression, anger, anxiety, her constant companions every time she allows her mind to obsess over the Anthropocene world, its crazed pyromania, where people live mindlessly in the heat of desire. Is that why self-denial is one of the first spiritual intuitions? Does that explain the forty days of fasting in the wilderness? Desire is heat, she reflects, one of the great temptations, and it is burning the earth.

It all makes sense to her now. She tries to focus on making tea as her mind continues its frantic drama. Wildfires, floods, megadroughts, heat domes, so many triple-digit days. Copper mines, uranium mines, refineries, power plants, dams, and more dams. *It feels like the wildfire has jumped into my heart*, she laments. *And I am the burnt offering.*

A positive thought lifts her mood. Today, Marty, Gabriela, and Tim are coming for lunch to plan their annual outing. Nine o'clock already, she notices, opening drawers, looking for her pinto bean recipe, making a mental checklist: menu planned, house clean enough, and the weather perfect for eating on the patio. Still, she feels something is missing, something yet to be accomplished. It's only this stupid anxiety, she decides, nothing immediately threatening.

She looks forward to an hour of silence, her daily prime-time-happy-hour—the way to a deep peace and experience of the divine. Silence works on her like fermentation. Her grapes of wrath were breaking down, agitating, heating up, turning into wine.

"Be still and know that I am God," she whispers to herself. She giggles at the thought. Psalm 46, God's little game of hide and seek.

She sets the table, prepares all the vegetables, and puts the beans on the stove. Remembering the *National Geographic* article about hikes in the Grand Canyon, she goes to her reading room to get it.

She skims the pages again. As she looks up from her chair, her eyes move to the black and white photograph on the side wall, a framed print of one of Ansel Adams' photographs of the North Rim that Marty and Gabriela had given her for her birthday last year.

Something draws her. She looks more closely at the vaguely familiar peaks, identifying Vishnu and Shiva and other prominent formations named for Greek, Roman, Egyptian, Norse, and Hindu pantheons. But that one massive peak Marty called Wotans Throne? She hesitates. The name hits a chord, its meaning hiding somewhere in her memory. Something dreadful, something about war and death, she intuits, trying to bring that meaning back into awareness.

She returns to the kitchen in time to answer the phone. It's Gabriela. "Terry, hey, Marty and I are coming early. We're worried about your court case. We want to talk before temperamental Tim gets there. Can we bring anything?"

"No, I've got everything. And don't worry, we'll figure out what's going on with Tim. We'll worm it out of him like fishers of men."

Gabriela laughs at Terry's clever pun. "Okay, see you soon."

Terry is still working on admitting guilt in her legal battle. She had so many ideas about how to fix the problems of the world, but, in retrospect, after all that had happened, she could imagine that even God was giving thanks she did not carry them out.

It all started with her book club for eco-warriors. She'd been collaborating with tribal leaders and local activists for two years, trying to stop the licensing of a uranium mine near the Grand Canyon. But all legal attempts had failed despite the overwhelming public opposition. The book club distracted her from her anger. Nine people signed up, including her co-conspirators, Emma and Grace.

Their first reading was Edward Abbey's classic, *The Monkey Wrench Gang*. It was her Bible II, a sequel, the story of four friends with the courage and commitment to stop the destruction of the Arizona desert. Unimpressed with conventional methods that had failed, they go around burning down billboards, sabotaging expensive development equipment like excavators, bulldozers, and drill rigs, and dreaming of their final goal: taking down Glen Canyon Dam.

She had such clarity at the time about what to do. But it soon got out of hand. What they needed, she believed, was a resurrection. Edward Abbey, supreme savior of the wilderness, brave activist, and award-winning author from Tucson, is buried down the road a ways at the Cabeza Prieta National Wildlife Refuge. It was a sign from God. Yes, that's what we desperately need. Ecotage! Her prayer practice had given her formidable courage and, maybe, made her a little nuts. Now, in retrospect, she likes to call it divine madness.

So, it was the failure to stop the licensing after a long and arduous grassroots effort that led Terry to a more radical approach. One night at dinner with Emma and Grace, they were discussing Abbey's book, laughing over its delightful contempt for corporate polluters, its scruffy, unlikely heroes, and its dead-serious message. Something, maybe the wine, caused their conversation to swerve, and out of the wreckage emerged an eco-warrior's blueprint for a campaign to stop the uranium mine. It was an environmentalist's fantasy. They would imitate the methods that the monkey wrenchers used, focusing on inanimate objects, nothing that would hurt anyone. Except the corporate accountants. And exactly like in the book, they would get away with it.

"I know we can do this," Emma insisted while eating her dessert. "The book is fiction, but what Abbey did is not fiction. He called it 'night work,' and so many others imitated his tactics."

"Right," Grace added. "And if we succeed, think of the groundswell of eco-sabotage actions. There will be legal issues, but the courts will become so overwhelmed, they won't be able to keep up."

Terry convinced herself of the ethics of the whole thing. A few damaged monster machines couldn't compare to the fatal realities of the mine: radioactive waste, habitat degradation, and groundwater contamination of the only water source for the Havasupai Tribe. And, worse, plutonium for nuclear weapons. Where is real evil here?

The charge was Conspiracy to Commit Property Destruction. The charges could have been much harsher, but they were all caught before they were able to complete the job. Terry, Emma, and Grace had gathered near the mine site at two in the morning with about fifty pounds of sugar to pour into gas tanks, and other miscellaneous tools for monkey wrenching. They had just unloaded the car when a police van raced through the site with sirens and headlights blaring, heading straight in their direction.

It was over before it even began. They spent the night in jail, a sorry lot, wondering who the snitch was. How had the police learned of their strange caper? *And how will this end,* she mulled, still gazing out the window, now thinking about what punishment she would receive.

Even now, in November, that old sun god asserts its ancient commandments. It rises at dawn like a hot sword on the horizon, rising from hell, pointing toward heaven as it burns, reminding the world that too much of a good thing can be deadly. Feeling herself on the cusp of another righteous rant, she picks up her cup of tea. Hell and a hot sword sound pretty good right now. Developers. Off with their heads!

With two hours before her guests arrive, Terry, riled by her thoughts, returns to her reading room and sits in her chair. She gazes at the beautiful seventh-century icon on the wall that a friend had brought her from a pilgrimage in Egypt. Christ Pantocrator, ruler of the universe, a union of the human and the divine. She is moved by these ancient things and wonders at how her attention can flow in an instant from the sublime to the profane. Christ the Savior on one side of the wall, Wotan the destroyer on the other. She sets her Zen clock for one hour and closes her eyes.

Time disappears in deep silence, and soon she finds herself again in the kitchen, thinking about getting a job by the end of the year. She has not yet discerned the right path for a career in the field of developmental psychology and spirituality. She feels a rush of gratitude. She has so much. This house that her parents had given her for graduation. Good friends, books, wilderness. And now, a new life in God. Marty knocks and opens the door, interrupting her meditation. "Terry. I thought they might have thrown you back in the clink by now. What's for lunch? I hope you made something with meat," he shouts with a mischievous glint in his eye, walking straight to the kitchen to investigate.

"Hope springs eternal," Terry wisecracks right back, looking out the window where there is no sign of Gabriela. "So, where is Gabriela? Did you send her off to the stockyards for some fresh hamburger?"

"She's coming. We're returning your camping gear. She's taking it out to your shed."

"And you wanted to check the menu before helping her?"

Marty reminds her of that weird Mormon monkey wrench character in Abbey's book. Seldom Seen Smith, wilderness guide, a name given by his multiple wives, who complained he was never around. Marty is an avid outdoorsman, too, a whitewater rafting guide, a rough-and-ready mountaineer, but no Mormon. He is religiously faithful to Gabriela. Loving partners since high school, they now operate their own guide business.

"Very funny. She can handle it," Marty answers. "Oh, by the way, Tim did call a while ago. He left Nogales around eight this morning and will try to get here a little after noon."

"What is he doing in Nogales?" asks Terry. "I thought he was living in Tucson with his sister. What's he up to now?"

Gabriela appears in time to answer the question. "No, his sister won't let him live there if it means his dogs living there, too. You won't believe it, Terry. He's living with Gerty and Moe in some trailer park slum near the border. I hope he's not planning to bring those dogs on our trip. That would be so dangerous. Anyway, after everything Marty told him about how cruel the border patrol system is, Tim went ahead and applied for a job on some construction project, part of the wall. Says he's worried about another alien invasion."

Terry shakes her head. "Wow. Now there's a real crime."

"I remember those scrappy talks with Tim," Marty adds. "I tried to stop him. I told him about my parents' experience in the early days of the sanctuary movement and how their church provided refuge for people fleeing El Salvador, like Gaby and her family. I think Tim *is* a wall. I couldn't get through to him. He says there are millions of Mexicans invading Arizona and that I wasn't patriotic enough. Millions, he said. How do you respond to someone who makes up his own truth about things?" Terry puts chips and salsa on the table. "I know he's been having a hard time, going from one bad job to another. I don't think he's had any serious relationships, has he? Gabriela, maybe you and Marty could have him over for dinner at your mother's. She could tell him about what happened in El Salvador."

Gabriela had to say it. "Yeah, we could. But he's like one of those Roman crucifiers. Blaming the victim, serving the empire. Why are you having such kind feelings toward him, Terry? Do you think my mother's story would actually make him change his mind?"

Marty pulls his chair closer to the table and grabs a handful of chips. "Gaby's right, Terry. Tim's a better fit for the kingdom of Caesar than the kingdom of God. He's been hanging out with those ICE bullies at the border. He's fallen for their game. He wants a bygone world of unquestioned status for the white American male. At least that's what I got out of my conversation with him. You're the psychologist, Terry. You'll see when he gets here. He's all about power and control."

Terry listens incredulously. Tim, a bully? She recalls the shy little boy she grew up with, setting another bowl of salsa on the table, then turning to her friends. "I'll tell you why I want to work on Tim. You're right to compare him to a wall, and what he's planning to do is simply inexcusable. But your comment about the kingdom of Caesar reminds us to withhold judgment. Remember, 'Father, forgive them, for they don't know what they're doing.' That is a deep psychological insight. Our dark side is unconscious, like the sludge at the bottom of a river. If we don't go deep, we never even know it's there. So, we project it onto others. Going deep into troubled waters brings things up from the bottom. It's basic Jungian analysis."

Offering Marty and Gabriela each a glass of lemonade, Terry continues. "Tim has always been like a younger brother to me. I know we're the same age, but in my eyes, he's still a little boy. A moody, angry one, I admit. I feel a little responsible for him. He didn't enjoy the privileges I did and, except for his sister, he's been on his own since his mother died."

Gabriela puts her hand on Terry's shoulder. "Well, maybe we could make an effort to bring him back into the fold. We haven't really spent much time with him this past year. I've talked to him on the phone a couple of times. I asked him if he was seeing anyone, and he got defensive. He said every woman he meets wants to control him."

"I can see why they'd want to," Terry joked. "But imagine, Tim, with that vigilante group in Nogales, patrolling with them? Very cruel, if you ask me. Their worldview must be rubbing off on him."

Terry walks to the fridge to get more ice. The conversation triggers her memory of an archetype. Wotan, according to Carl Jung, is a dark spirit from ancient mythology that dwells in the collective unconscious. When Wotan awakens, as he did in Germany in the years leading up to World War II, he drives the nation toward collective madness and violence. Terry decides to search online for Jung's essay on Wotan later.

"You can't argue with someone like that," Terry says, addressing Marty. "Your argument with him probably made things worse. What he needs is a friendly intervention. He's stuck on the low road. But that's where you have to start to get to the high road. That makes the journey whole for everyone. You know, it's partly my fault, I think. I promised his mother on her deathbed that I would watch out for him. I don't think I've done a good job of it."

They hear a loud knock as Tim storms through the front door, right through the living room, the kitchen, and out the back door to the patio, a menacing scowl forming around his eyes and jaw. Terry barely recognizes him, thinking to herself how well he fits Jung's description of an old Norse berserker, a horned, myth-driven warrior like that self-styled QAnon shaman from Phoenix.

Terry reclaims her poise. "Tim, you look exhausted. Are you okay? Come sit down."

"Yeah, I'm great," Tim replies, his brash entrance softening slightly. He stands there, a willful presence, posturing under a newly shaven head and scruffy red beard, perusing the backyard scene as a general reads an attack plan. "Got any beer?" he asks.

Terry hands Tim a beer, then, motioning with her arms, invites her guests to her colorful table, set with Talavera dinnerware and a luncheon spread of seasoned pinto beans, tortillas, cheese, onion, avocado, hot salsa, cilantro, sour cream, corn chips, and lemonade. A cool breeze engulfs them.

"Hey, it's Erik the Red. Who scalped you, brother?" Marty teases.

Tim moves swiftly to the table, grabs a chair, and sits down. "Well, my two mutts are staying with my sister while I'm with you guys. I miss them already. I wish they could go with us. Boy, am I starved. Hey, what's with all the Mexican food and the dishes, Terry? I thought you were French or something."

"Well, France is right next to Spain, Tim, and we are right next to Mexico. Besides, you love Mexican food. And all of this used to be Mexico, remember? Weren't we in the same history class?"

"It did? Whattaya mean it used to be Mexico? It's Arizona, USA. Get over it."

"And the name Arizona comes from an eighteenth-century Mexican Basque. *You* get over it."

"Okay, you two," Gabriela interrupts. "Let's eat. We've got some planning to do."

They engage in small talk, floating on the surface of issues and current events. Even among lifelong friends like this, even within families, Terry thinks, there exist such vast differences in perception. *Especially these days, we need to be cautious with our words.*

While eating and conversing with her friends, Terry's background thoughts continue. Her studies in developmental psychology led her to the intriguing field of the evolution of human consciousness and to the power of contemplation to transform awareness. She has read volumes and spent the past five years developing her own practice. She wants to use what she has learned to have meaningful conversations with people, maybe with Tim, to try to see things as he does and better understand his subjective world. But she wasn't confident she could do this. It's a real skill. As a friend and a psychologist, could she meet Tim where he is developmentally, without judging? Could she refrain from trying to convince him to see things through her worldview? She is a novice. But she wants to take the first step.

"Tim, Gabriela tells me you were working down in Nogales. Are you finished with that job now?"

"It didn't pan out. I applied but never got a call."

"Maybe because the number of people trying to cross has gone way down."

"Maybe. But they're always trying to get in."

Gabriela listens intently, hoping to jump in. A little later, maybe, she decides, not wanting to fan any fires.

Marty grabs a bottle of beer from the cooler, pops the cap, and jumps into the conversation.

"Tim, you know we have this program at church for people crossing over. They're able to tell their stories to our Spanish-speaking members. Gaby tells me most of them are very desperate."

"But if we let everyone in, it will ruin our economy. It's bad enough already."

Terry takes a chance. "I get the anxiety you're feeling, Tim. I feel it sometimes myself. But migrants are doing all the bottom wage jobs, jobs most Americans don't want anyway. What are you interested in doing? You were going to start your own dog grooming business. What happened with that?"

"What happened is you need capital. I still think about it, though. There's also a problem with all the water restrictions. You need a lot of water for dog grooming. It's getting really bad. Did you see what's going on in Wenden? They're having big demonstrations against that Saudi alfalfa farm. The Saudis ship alfalfa to their dairies in Saudi Arabia. The state water experts say the farm is using over eighty percent of the water from local wells. They've only been able to cancel one of their leases, so they just keep pumping."

Marty leans toward Tim, trying to speak with a mouth full of chips. "Tim, are you saying that the Saudis have no water in their desert environment, so they come here to *our* desert environment to use *our* water to grow alfalfa to ship to *their* dairy operations?"

"That's about the size of it," Tim replies.

"Well, that's insane if you ask me. And with all our water problems."

"They don't have to pay for the water either," Tim adds. "They make sure to stay in rural areas where there are no regulations, no metering, and no taxes."

Terry's stomach tightens by the second. The stupidity and injustice are too much. Wrenching, that's the best word, she thinks. Is it any wonder people are getting sick and turning to sabotage?

"It's a mess," Terry says. "But if we're going to be honest about it, we're all to blame. Anyone who consumes dairy or meat. It's all one industry. They wouldn't sell it if we didn't buy it. Massive boycotts would solve it. Reduce the demand. Shut down the meat and dairy industry, no alfalfa needed, problem solved. And think of those poor cows in factory farms. Warm-blooded, sentient creatures treated like commodities. No reverence for life, no compassion."

Gabriela's eyes widen as she stuffs another tortilla with beans and cheese. "Are you kidding, Terry? No more hamburgers or ice cream?"

"Yes. I'm saying that people will do everything except the one thing necessary. They don't want to give up meat and dairy, so they think, I recycle, I drive a hybrid, I don't eat much meat, I'm helping the environment.

"Try to tell them that meat and dairy, agriculture in general, account for over twenty percent of carbon pollution. Try to tell them that only nine percent of the plastic they recycle actually gets recycled. They can't deal with reality. They don't want the responsibility. So, nothing changes. Instead of laws that mandate reductions in fossil fuels, they incentivize renewable energy. That's good, but it doesn't stop the burning of fossil fuels or reduce energy consumption.

"They're also coming up with crazy ideas so people don't have to change their lifestyles. Like spraying particles of sulfur dioxide or calcium carbonate into the atmosphere to mimic a volcano, which temporarily brings the temperature down. Or dropping seawater into clouds to make them whiter and more heat reflective. They're even thinking of covering the desert with some kind of reflective material to bounce sunlight back into space. Probably plastic full of chemicals."

Gabriela pushes her cell phone into Marty's face. "You think growing alfalfa is bad. Look at this," she says, showing him a PowerMag projection of electricity usage by data centers in Arizona. "Meta, Google, Amazon, Microsoft, and Apple are all behind it. They consume staggering amounts of energy *and* water. The Tucson City Council recently rejected a license application because of it."

"Terry? Hey, what's the matter?" Tim asks, noticing Terry's sweat-covered face turning purple. "She's hyperventilating," Tim yells, as Marty and Gabriela rush to her side, familiar with these episodes.

"Terry, you're okay, just breathe in and out slowly." Marty holds Terry from behind and begins the breathing exercise with her. "Gaby, let's walk her around the backyard a few times until she calms down."

After a few minutes, Terry, a little embarrassed, starts breathing normally, but tears run down her face. "Thanks. I'm sorry. I get so carried away. Can we stop talking about these things now and start planning our trip? I can't wait to get out of here."

"What was all that?" asks Tim, confused by all the emotion. No one answers him.

Terry walks to the kitchen to get the *National Geographic.* "I thought we could look at some of these other trails. I really wanted to do the North Rim, but all those trails have been closed since the fire. We talked about doing something a little more challenging. Are we all still up for five days?"

"Yes." All in.

"Okay. We could do a rim-to-river trek this time, starting at the South Kaibab trailhead, down to Clear Creek Trail, and over to the Clear Creek Campground. That's sixteen miles one-way. We can set up base there and do the North Kaibab or Bright Angel climbs, or both. Or we can hike the canyon floor along the creek. Either way, it's probably harder than anything any of us has ever done before. What do you think?"

Tim stands back with his hands on his hips. "That sounds like a good choice for you girls," Tim insists. "I thought you said something more challenging. I want to do something harder."

"Like what?" asks Gabriela, feeling insulted by his "you girls" put-down. "What do you want to do?"

"I don't know. Maybe Vishnu or Angels Gate. Or maybe even Wotan. I'll decide when I get there."

"Tim, you mean 'we'll decide' when *we* get there, right?" Marty insists. "Man, we have to stick together on this. This is some serious hiking. Let's make the plan as a group."

Tim, feeling outnumbered, sits back in his chair. They talk for another hour, looking at the trail map and making lists of gear and food they will need for five days. He's a little grumpy, a little quieter than his usual boisterous self.

"Tim, don't worry," Terry says soothingly. "You'll have plenty of challenges with some hard hiking. You'll forget all about Wotan."

Tim smiles, feeling a little defeated but settled. "You guys, I have to leave. I'm going to my sister's to take care of my dogs. Thanks for lunch. I'll see you here at six Friday morning."

Marty and Gabriela stay a while after Tim leaves.

"Well, that wasn't too bad," Terry says. "At least he's coming with us, but it's spooky that he wants to climb Wotan. Strange. He's always identified as Christian. But now it seems that Wotan, the demon conqueror, is his god. He'd never admit it."

"Would you care to clarify that, Terry?" Marty asks. "I mean, if he says he's Christian, what do you mean?"

"I mean, there are hundreds of versions of Christianity, right? Ask a hundred people and you'll get a mishmash of perceptions, most of them like flat-earth science. False, distorted, shallow, incomplete. How else do you account for slavery and genocide and copious other horrors?"

That evening, after Marty and Gabriela had gone home, Terry feels a little concerned about spending five days in the wilderness with Tim, and she is still embarrassed by her partial breakdown.

I should find that essay before I forget, she says to herself, opening her laptop and searching for "Carl Jung on Wotan." The essay pops up immediately, and she decides to read it before they leave on Friday.

The sun is beginning to set as Terry begins her second sit for the day.

"I'm sitting, the sun is setting," she quips. That's the problem with this brain of mine, one useless thought after another. She puts away her task list for the trip. Her final thought before closing her eyes is about Tim. Before he can ascend, he must first descend.

The first ten minutes feel like a waste of time. Thoughts, emotions, sensations. But soon, the breath begins to move in and out, practically imperceptible, sensations numbed as if by Novocain, the brain relieved of its interminable, antic disposition. Sometimes, if you're lucky, you feel an oceanic boundlessness, an ineffable sense of being held. Sometimes, in the stillness, in the silence deep beneath awareness, there is a presence. So lovely, so tender. She sees things differently now. A gradual transformation from caterpillar to chrysalis, and the clouded hope for a butterfly. She sees things in metaphor, life as a living poem. Even the trees seem to be lifting their boughs in praise as their roots reach watery depths far below the parched Arizona landscape. She'd never thought of it that way before. And the images keep gushing from a place within where a wisdom long forgotten has lain dormant, buried down the centuries in this world of noise and annihilation. *Yes*, she reflects, *now I live in two different worlds.*

Early Friday morning, all gather at Terry's for the long drive to the trailhead and the sixteen-mile hike to the campground. Marty does the driving. The others sleep most of the way.

Unloading the car at the trailhead, Terry pauses and looks up through the canopy of trees, nurturing a dreamy poem. *This canyon is my cathedral, the visible sign of the invisible God.*

Descending on rough switchbacks, they make good time on the South Kaibab Trail. Terry is starting to get her downhill rhythm when Marty catches up with her.

"Now he's saying he should be the leader," Marty whispers. "He wants us to follow him up some trail when we get to the campground, and he's going to decide exactly where we go. Our Erik the Red is seeing red. He's a little frenzied about being in charge. And he mentioned again that he wants to climb Wotans Throne."

"He's off his head," Terry replies. "When we get to the campground, we'll talk with him. We can't let him climb that thing. I know why he wants to, though. He's aching for some sense of manhood. He's having some status anxiety. If something isn't done soon. . ." She couldn't think of what might happen.

The weather is perfect, pleasantly cool with a deep blue sky overhead. The open ridgeline offers breathtaking views of the gorge and the Colorado River below.

Terry thinks of all the dams that have reduced the Colorado River to a trickle of its original wildness. Thinking about it causes a tightness in her stomach.

She gets a stunning close-up view of the Colorado River at the Black Bridge crossing, where the South Kaibab and North Kaibab trails intersect. Poetry rises from her brooding grief. The Colorado River, the Michelangelo of the Grand Canyon, sculpted these massive works of art over millions of years. From that glorious power of moving water against ageless stone comes this profound beauty to inspire, and to bring man to his knees where he belongs.

Overcome by a surge of reverence, she beholds the vertical cliffs and the other-worldliness of the place, then is seized with another bout of loss. She had followed Sam's advice, ordered the book on solastalgia, and searched Google for information. The word sounds like *nostalgia*, she recalls, but that's about longing for a past home. Solastalgia is about the home you still live in that is being destroyed all around you. Her emotions take her on a Ferris wheel ride. *My home was a beautiful countryside,* she tells herself. *Now, it's a toxic landfill.*

They continue down toward the campground. Their brief conversations are mostly about the weather and the summer fire that destroyed so much on the North Rim, including the 100-year-old lodge, now a lost historic treasure.

"Arizona has become a tinderbox," Terry complains to Tim. "Just imagine what this place was like before all the dams went up. I'd give anything if it could all come back to the way it was. It was never this dry before climate change."

Tim turns on her like a man whose world is coming to an end. "Climate change is a hoax, a bunch of greedy pseudo-scientists seeking grants from the government. The weather has always changed, back and forth, hot and cold. That's my opinion."

What could she say that wouldn't add fuel to the tinderbox? She didn't want to ridicule or argue, but to engage. "Transcend and include," the integralists say.

"Tim, I don't think you or I are qualified to have an opinion about climate change. We're not climate scientists. I don't get it. You were all in during lunch when you talked about the water experts' warnings about the alfalfa farm. How are they different from the warnings of climate experts?"

"I see you've been drinking the Kool-Aid, Terry. Now you're saying I don't have the right to my opinion. Well, that's the only right I have left, and I'm keeping it, do or die."

"You didn't answer my question."

Failure. This isn't easy. She feels anger rising and closes her eyes and takes a few deep breaths. She tries to think of something constructive to say in reply but knows his attitude matches his altitude. *Try one more thing,* she thinks to herself.

"Tim, have you ever heard the term 'aperspectival madness'?"

"Well, let me look that up real quick, now that we're on the trail and have no signal."

"It's okay. It's not in the dictionary. It's the fallacy of relativism that says all views are right and no opinion is truer than another. On the opposite side is the fallacy of 'monoperspectival madness' that says there is only one absolute truth, and all others are false. Both are called madness because they refuse the deeper view that all perspectives have something to contribute to the discovery of truth."

"And what is truth?" Tim asks. Stunned by his choice of words, Terry lets it go. Surely, he did not intend to quote Pontius Pilate. But how fitting and relevant, revealing an impenetrable cynicism.

Feeling inadequate to answer, Terry says, "Truth is too big a subject to define, Tim. But we could have an interesting conversation about it. Do you want to? Why don't you come to dinner soon? We'll have a long talk and see what comes up. Is it a deal?"

With a feeble nod from Tim, she is satisfied that she has won him over, if only temporarily. She continues down the trail. When she stops for a rest, Tim walks on, alone. Soon, Gabriela is right behind her.

"Gabriela, I've got a good start on Tim. I'm going to have him over for dinner. I want to show him how to rise above his reactive opinions."

"And how do you get him to want to rise?" Gabriela asks. "The trick, I think, is that we keep him close. You wouldn't take a little kid for a hike in the Grand Canyon unless you keep him very close, or he might fall off."

"I think Tim has already fallen off," Gabriela replies.

They reach the campground at dusk and start to organize a meal. They are the only ones there, surrounded by the allure and the perils of wild nature.

Tim starts collecting wood for a fire. When Marty notices, he yells from a distance. "Dammit, Tim, you can't start fires out here. They told us that when we got the camping permit."

Tim drops the wood on the ground. "You know, you probably can't piss out here either. The damn government wants to control everything. What kind of man are you if you can't even build a fire? You can't go here, can't go there, you can't chop down a tree. They have all the power."

Terry wonders why he can't see beyond himself. He wants to start a fire. That's all he knows. Looking upward to the North Rim, she sees Wotans Throne and its long crenelled razorback, a massive formation, bringing to mind the walled embattlements of old Jerusalem and shaped like some science fiction predator, a great beast from the deep, like Godzilla, yet lacking any claim to sentience.

Lingering there for a moment, something grasps her inside, a power drawing her focus upward to that one perplexing peak.

In a surge of emotion, she recalls that scene in *Raiders of the Lost Ark* where they roll out the map showing the location of the Well of Souls. Then the musical score gets spooky, tensions rise, indicating something ancient, powerful, and ominous. Marty described his first glimpse of Wotan as a stomach punch of acrophobia, she remembers. He gave it personifying qualities, calling it a massive form that moved along the canyon floor like some spiked dinomonster made of rock. For Terry, Wotan suggested some long-ago nightmare. Then, a sudden sense of dread.

Wotans Throne? Wotans Throne? What was it Jung said? she asks herself.

It was in Jung's theory on archetypes. He wrote that Wotan was named after an ancient Germanic god, described as the lord of frenzy and leader of the possessed. Jung attributed the rise of fascism in the 1930s to the archetype that Wotan represents. Still relevant, Terry thinks, a dark spirit of earlier times present and ascending in the world today. Wars, mass deportations, famine, genocide, and now the real threat of worldwide ecological collapse.

She remembers fragments from the essay. Wotan rules by an ancient code. His will is chaos and violence, cruelty beyond understanding. From his throne, Terry reflects, Wotan watches the amphitheater below, feeding his hunger for discord through the pawns who serve him. Yes, he is waking again, seeking worshippers again, infiltrating the hearts of the most vulnerable. Like Tim.

These were her thoughts as she switched into counseling mode. She wanted to distract Tim from his anger so he could think about what he was doing. Socrates could do it simply by asking questions.

"Hey, Tim, come here, I want to show you something."

Tim, moody and hesitant, walks to her side.

"Look up there at Wotans Throne. Now, tell me, why do you want to climb that thing? Why is it so important?"

"Because it's there?" Tim replies, dodging the question.

"Please be serious for a minute. Will you try to answer a few questions? I promise it won't hurt. I'm a little worried about you. So, what is the real reason you want to climb Wotan?"

Tim looks toward the summit. "I think it would be a real accomplishment, something I can be proud of. A man has to prove himself."

"Good, that's honest. But doesn't the Bible teach that pride goes before destruction?"

"No, I don't remember that."

"Well, it's there, somewhere in Proverbs 16. 'Pride goes before destruction, and a haughty spirit before a fall.' You don't remember that?"

"Does that mean I can't climb Wotan? Where does it say that in the Bible?"

Terry doesn't want to give Tim a bible lesson, just a little tidbit for consideration. She wants Tim to think. "Mountain climbing is a big thing in the Bible, but so is the intention, and it's usually in reference to seeking the sacred and developing a mature spirituality. Jesus going up a mountain alone to pray all night, for example, and Moses on Sinai. There's nothing wrong with climbing Wotan if you're looking for God up there."

"I get it."

"Have you done any research, read any stories by climbers who have made it to the top? Do you have a plan and all the right equipment to do it safely?"

"No, I don't think I need a plan. It looks doable. Piece of cake."

"Not to me, it doesn't. Have you ever wondered why the park discourages people from going off-trail? Do you think it's possible that you could die or be seriously injured?"

"No. Fear is not my thing."

"Do you know where the name Wotan comes from?"

"Some Chinese king?"

"No. Have you thought of what might happen to Gerty and Moe if you die?"

"No. My sister likes them okay, for a few days here and there, but not like I do, not like family."

"Then tell me, what would it prove if you made it to the top? Whom do you think would notice you if you successfully made it to the summit? Is there a woman you're trying to impress? Or are you trying to prove something to yourself?"

"That's a hell of a lot more than a few questions, Terry. Why do you care, anyway?"

"Because I care. It's that simple."

After a long silence, Terry makes her point. "Yes, a lot of questions, and you haven't answered any of them, so I assume you haven't considered any of them. Tim, I'm not going to let you go up there. I'll get Marty and Gabriela, and we'll lasso you, tie you to a tree, and in the morning we'll drag you up the trail to the car. Enough with this happy hubris. The only one here who is making the ascent is Wotan himself."

"What does that mean?"

"You figure it out."

That's not a good answer, Terry thinks to herself. *Tim doesn't know anything about archetypes, and he sure doesn't want to listen to me preaching about unconscious motivations.*

She decides to drop it, since Tim has calmed down and is now telling her about taking Gerty and Moe down to the Santa Cruz River last September, and how low the water was. Terry sees it as another opportunity to mention climate change but declines for the sake of peace.

That night, Terry sleeps out in the open under the stars beside the sweet murmuring music of Clear Creek. She dreams of being lost in a city with only a vague recollection of having a home somewhere, wandering down strange streets seeking something familiar, the place where she left her bag with the plane ticket inside that would take her home. But the city hinders her every move. Tall buildings block her view, crowds obstruct her movements, pervasive vehicles vroom and belch, and horns blare. She doesn't know anyone who walks by and feels different from them, separate. She spots a small dog in the street. Panic overcomes her as she rushes out to snatch it from harm's way. Now she must carry the dog and find its owner. The dog is heavy and keeps wiggling. She must find the owner, find her bag with the ticket inside, and find her way home. With a pounding heart, she runs this way and that, her anxiety escalating. The sky darkens, and it begins to rain. People running, screaming.

"Terry! Terry, wake up!" It was Gabriela. "Terry, it's starting to rain. Come inside the tent."

Woozy but relieved, Terry wakes, leaving the little dog behind in her dream. She gathers her sleeping bag and backpack and follows Gabriela up the hill to the place above the creek where Marty had pitched the tent.

"My God, is there going to be a flash flood?" she yells, but Gabriela cannot hear her.

The rain is a deluge by the time they reach the tent. Inside, Marty and Tim are heating water on the camp stove to make tea. Everything is wet. All four cramp together in a tent made for two.

"Well, what are we going to do now?" Tim scowls as he shoves up against a corner of the tent. "Stupid rain. It's not supposed to rain in November."

Marty looks directly into Tim's eyes, trying to hide his annoyance. "Tim, I'm sorry you couldn't build a campfire. But we can have a *dampfire*. Gabriela, let's sing that song from church, 'Pass it On.' We can all sing and pretend we're sitting around a campfire."

Terry and Gabriela begin, and soon Tim and Marty join in. "It only takes a spark to get a fire going, and soon all those around can warm up to its glowing . . ."

After a while, Terry notices Tim is smiling. She understands now that she can help him and promises God she will try.

The four friends sing for a while, the profound and the ridiculous. Tim sings one song by himself. "Hello Muddah, Hello Faddah, Here I am at Camp Granada . . ." The funny lyrics have them all laughing and singing together. Still, the night drags on slowly, crowded and wet. No sleep.

At four in the morning, it is still pouring down. The sound of wild water below means the creek had surged and covered the trail. The monsoons are in July and August. By November, things are supposed to calm down. They would not be able to move until the water recedes and the trail becomes navigable again.

Morning reveals their suspicions that the trail is flooded. Movement in any direction is out of the question. They spend the day inside the tent, eating, talking, listening to wild, heavy water below and rain battering their tent. All they can do is wait. Marty starts talking about next year's hike.

"I hear the Pacific Crest Trail has great diversity. We could do a stretch in Northern California."

Gabriela unpacks and repacks every bag, taking stock of food to make a meal. As boredom increases and moods darken, Terry has an inspiration.

"I know, let's do a round robin, a collaborative writing project." She pulls out a pen and some paper from her backpack. "How it works is, each one of us takes a turn writing one sentence in the story, then passes it on to the next person. It will be a short story, but as long as we want to keep writing. Tim, why don't you start?" Tim, reluctantly, takes the pen and paper from Terry.

He writes a few words and passes the story to Gabriela, who reads it aloud. "It was a dark and stormy night."

Terry looks at Tim, smirking. "Well, now, that's original, but not exactly fiction, is it?"

They each write one quick round in a short story about squirrels having a meeting under a big tree to discuss some missing acorns. After five minutes, they are bored and decide it would be more entertaining to eat pretzels. Boredom and overindulgence give way to irritability.

"If this rain hadn't happened, you would have been really surprised when you woke up and found me gone," says Tim. "I was ready to go it alone and climb Wotan. I knew you'd try to stop me, so I planned to leave before you woke up. But then Terry made me think of Gerty and Moe. Maybe I'll go by myself and climb that other Wotans Throne, the one in California. It's a lot higher than this one."

"I didn't know there was another one," Terry replies. "It's higher, huh? Must take a bigger ego to climb it."

Marty interrupts. "That's crazy, Tim. Wotan is a killer, either one."

"No crazier than Terry trying to blow up a uranium mine. Where do you get off calling *me* crazy?"

"We weren't going to blow up anything," Terry insists, visibly losing patience. "I told you what we were going to do. Why do you change the story to blowing things up?" Here we go again, Terry admits to herself, feeling the fumes rising.

He's always saying things that aren't true. I wish I were a lawyer. I'd put him in the witness chair and make him tell the truth.

Tim's anger forms a dark bridge between his eyebrows, like the unibrow of an ancient Viking warrior whose bloodshot eyes expose the rage within. "Maybe it is crazy. Maybe you have to do crazy things before people think you even matter," he growls, his mask of anger slipping away, his voice quaking as fear and despair rise to the surface.

Terry raises her voice. "Why did you say I was going to blow something up?"

They all stare at Tim, waiting for a response. He has no answer to the question. But Terry knows the answer. A psychologist understands these things. She knows that a lack of confidence in an argument will cause a person to exaggerate, that admitting error feels like weakness, and that ego makes us just want to win. Knowing these things lays the responsibility on her to take the high road, to let go of her own anger, and try to see beyond the surface. It's not easy, she admits to herself.

Tim had nowhere to go, no escape from his three closest friends. He couldn't even explain to himself why he felt such anger toward them. He felt inadequate, ashamed. What do they see when they look at me? he wonders. What do I see? Tim covers his face with his hands.

"Terry, I'm sorry," Tim whispers, still hiding his face. "You don't know what I did. Something terrible. I'd do anything to take it back."

"What, for goodness' sake. What did you do?"

"I'm the one who turned you in. I called the police that night."

"What? Why?" Incredulous, Terry forces Tim's hands away from his face.

"I was so angry, but not at you. It was Emma. I'm so sorry."

"But why were you angry with Emma? How do you even know her? I don't understand. I haven't talked to her since we met with the judge. Our release agreement prohibits us from being in contact. So, what is your connection to her?"

All eyes were on Tim, whose shocking confession had killed the boredom in the tent.

Tim continues, avoiding direct eye contact with Terry. "Emma and I dated for a while. She doesn't know that you and I know each other. She broke her promise of secrecy about your plans. She just blurted it out." Tim starts fidgeting, pulling on his beard, even hitting himself on his forehead with the heel of his hand. "Emma was so excited and proud, telling me what she was going to do to stop the uranium mine. She didn't mention your name but said it was a couple of women in her book club."

Looking into Terry's eyes, he goes on. "I knew you were involved when she mentioned the book title because you told me about Abbey's book a long time ago. Anyway, I didn't take her seriously. I laughed at her and argued with her about nuclear power. I told her we needed uranium to build more nuclear plants because of energy demands, and that it's carbon-free, and she should support it. I called her an idiot. She got mad, said it was a lie that nuclear is carbon-free, and that I should read some article about the fuel cycle. She called me a thick-headed, low-tier red beard. What the hell does that mean? Then she flat-out dumped me, and I got so mad I decided to get even. It's like I couldn't control myself. But now I'm sorry. I didn't mean to get you put in jail."

The rain stops, and a dark quiet enfolds them. They sit in that purifying silence for a while, not knowing how to respond to Tim's confession and his obvious remorse. Marty is the first to notice tears rolling down Tim's face. Gabriela tears up, too.

Terry feels a strange power in her gut, not the usual anxiety, but more like determination. Tim looks directly into her eyes, and she discerns in his a retreat from the glacier inside, now cracking and spilling out like a heart broken open to the world. When it comes right down to it, she believes anger is always a cover for pain.

Even with that understanding, Terry feels wronged by Tim's betrayal. On the other hand, that betrayal prevented them from carrying out the bigger crime and saved all three wannabe monkey wrenchers from serious prison time.

"Tim, you little idiot. On the bright side, you kept me, Emma, and Grace from years in prison. The police caught us before we could go through with it. If they hadn't, we would have poured all that sweet sugar into those stinky gas tanks." Terry gently places her hand on Tim's shoulder. "Our lawyer thinks there won't even be a trial. He's working on a plea deal. But even a trial would be an opportunity to talk about what's at stake. I've been thinking about what I would say to a jury. Sabotage definitely has its positive attributes. It sure makes for a great novel. But it doesn't solve the larger problem. Abbey inspired a huge environmental movement, but overall, things have gotten so much worse in the fifty years since his book was published. The real problem is in the human heart."

Tim's tears continue to flow gently over the quiet hour that follows, washing away the last vestiges of animosity. At last, sleep envelopes them.

In the morning, sunlight breaks over the rim, revealing a disaster of mud and debris. The bones of the canyon still stand strong as they would for more and more millions of years. Two deer emerge from a stand of willows. A squirrel dashes up a sycamore. Wotan, too, holds his ground on his throne, brooding there above the fray, hidden from the conscious world, waiting for the right time to make a move. But Terry knows even the gods can fail. Wotan will fail when people wake to his tricks.

Her thoughts get distracted by a kaleidoscope of monarch butterflies, stragglers late in their migration from Canada to Mexico. Oh, how wonderful! They survived the storm.

Terry marvels at the fragility of these delicate creatures, their black and orange beauty stark against a blue sky, their tenacious flight through wind and rain to a home so far away. A reverence deep within upswells into prayer, and she is on her knees.

"Gabriela, come see this."

Gabriela sees the butterflies, looks up from her stone perch above the trail, then climbs down to join Terry. "Did you know, Terry, I've been to their overwintering sanctuary in Michoacán? I've always wanted to go back. They could become extinct if people keep destroying their breeding habitat and using pesticides. Another problem to think about. But don't, please. You think too much already."

Terry has another inspiration. "Gabriela, what would you think about all of us making a trip to Mexico next year to visit the sanctuary? We could drive down together, do it on the cheap, no flights or hotels, camping along the way. You speak Spanish. That would make it easy for us to find our way around."

Terry could scarcely contain her excitement over her idea. "Or we could join one of those World Wildlife Fund habitat trips. And don't you think it would be good for Tim to get another perspective, meeting real Mexican people, and maybe visiting the campesinos? It would really challenge his xenophobic fantasies. It could be like a Peace Corps experience for him. He needs a dose of reality."

"Let's keep talking about it," Gabriela says, sharing Terry's enthusiasm. "When we have a real plan, we can share it with the guys." Gabriela looks into Terry's eyes. "You know, Terry, I really admire how you've taken Tim on, being so creative with ways to get him back on the right path. It's sneaky, too. I like that." Terry laughs at Gabriela's insight. "Well, he is a lost sheep, isn't he? Do you think we might get a group from church to join us on the trip? Make a real pilgrimage out of it?"

The two of them continue to talk as they watch the monarchs flying south. *There goes the perfect symbol of the miracle of transformation*, Terry reflects, smiling toward heaven.

It is a difficult, uphill slog back to the car, carrying wet, heavy gear. But there are no complaints.

As they drive home, Terry's imagination takes hold. "I think all of you should join my new book club. I've already selected the book: *The Wisdom of Wilderness: Experiencing the Healing Power of Nature* by Gerald May."

"We already know about the wisdom of the wilderness," Marty insists.

"Yeah, *we* could write a book about it," adds Gabriela. "How do you like *Squirrel Wisdom: Going Out on a Limb*?"

"Well, I might read the wisdom book if you pay me by the hour," Tim says jokingly.

"Okay, plus benefits, Tim, if you'll commit to it," Terry barks back at him. "You *have* decided to move back to Phoenix, haven't you? I heard Marty say he might hire you to help with some rafting trips."

Tim, like a little boy trustingly reaching out to take his big sister's hand, replies. "I want to, but I have to find a place where I can have Gerty and Moe."

"Don't you worry about that, Tim," Marty interjects. "You can all stay with me and Gabriela."

Tim's warm smile could be felt in the front seat. "Terry," he says, "I take it back. I won't charge you anything to read that book. It could be interesting to read a book with a group. What's in it?"

"It's those benefits I mentioned, Tim. It's about learning to be a wild, strong, courageous man with a soft heart who climbs to the summits of dangerous mountains to find truth, and laughs with God when he falls. And so much more."

Laughter, and a chorus of questions: "What else can I learn?"

"Well, you might learn how to breathe under water. Or how to walk on it."

DO YOU LIKE IT, FATHER?

By Sharon Hughson

"Revisiting the magical woods of my youth and the sense of being an outsider that began even then."

G rass tassels slap the backs of my legs, faster as I jog toward the trees. A few steps and I enter my hideout.

Shade hugs me as I duck beneath a branch. Maple leaves whisper as a breeze ripples past. Fir needles sprinkle my shoulders, cascading from the tallest among my woody friends.

"Hello," chirps a robin from a nearby branch.

I wrap my arms around the stunted cedar in the grove's center, pressing my cheek against its scaly trunk. Long fingers of fragrant needles pat my shoulder. "Welcome back," she says.

"What did you bring?" a gray squirrel demands from a fir bough arching like an umbrella over my friend Cedar.

I shake my head. "I'm not supposed to feed you."

"So what!" Squeaky Squirrel says.

Such a bother!

"Feed me. Feed me," says a small bird hopscotching across maple twigs.

Leaves clap their hands. Needles shiver with delight. Everyone here welcomes me. This is where I fit, where no one judges.

Except maybe the squirrel who always wants a treat.

I breathe in the pine-scented air and admire the patchwork of sunlight dappling across the browning grass of the small clearing.

"I love you all." I sit criss-cross applesauce beneath Cedar's sparse branches.

The one time I came here with Father, he told me the cedar was small because tall trees surrounded her. He said we should chop her down for a Christmas tree!

I told him only noble firs made good Christmas trees. None of those live in my magical place.

"I can't come every day anymore," I tell my friends. It's like I swallow a rock.

"We miss you," say the leaves.

"We need you," says Lady Cedar.

"Bring snacks," chides the squirrel.

I smile and paw around Cedar's trunk. Leaves hum a lullaby with creaking branches adding harmony. My fingers get sticky with sap, and I find a nearly intact acorn.

"Mine," screeches the squirrel, scurrying to my bare toes almost close enough to touch.

I smooth my thumb across the nut shell. I imagine it sitting beside my father's bowling trophies. With a stiff twig, I sand the rough interior where the nut used to be.

"It's empty." I wave it toward the squirrel.

"Mine." He dashes toward the maple and scampers up having the last word. Like always.

A breeze cools my skin. My eyes flutter. I blink and concentrate on the shell until the inside nearly outshines the outside.

A faraway shout interrupts the peace.

Shadows erase the quilt of sunlight. I stayed too long.

Another shout. Mama calls me in for dinner.

With a wobble, I stand. Tingles rush through my legs. I brush needles and dirt from my shorts.

"Goodbye," I say, glancing slowly around my haven before pushing through the branches.

Outside the circle of magic, I can't hear my friends respond.

My feet slip off the flip-flops. Breathless from the run across the overgrown empty lot beside our duplex, I leap up the porch steps by twos.

I trip. The acorn rolls across the porch. After a couple of fumbling grabs, my fingers close over it, and I tuck it into my pocket.

I shove through the front door. The warm scent of meat reminds my stomach to growl.

Hands washed, I skid into a laminate-covered chair. Father sits across from me at the kitchen table, eyebrows dipped in a frown.

Red wedges of watermelon grin from a platter. Steam spirals above cobs of golden corn.

Father slides two slices of meatloaf from a chipped plate onto a matching one in front of him. My fingers reach for the secret gift in my pocket.

"Get your head out of the clouds." The words grind like sandpaper across my soul.

I blink. He holds the plate of meat toward me.

"Yes, Father."

After I push a slice onto my plate, I grab the bowl of potatoes in front of me. *Plop.* I salivate at the mound beside the meatloaf, then pass him the bowl.

Dishes clatter. Silverware scrapes.

I add margarine to my potatoes and slather it onto a cob with my fork. My sister grimaces. Mashed potatoes aren't her favorite. The mountain of ketchup she adds to her meat nearly rivals my potatoes in size.

"You didn't clean your room." Mama softens her words with a smile, and her eyes glow with understanding. "School starts tomorrow."

The corn hardens to sawdust in my mouth. Why did she have to remind me?

"Chew with your mouth closed, boy." Father's frown deepens his voice.

"I wish I could have gotten my hair cut," my sister whines.

I ignore them, trying to remember the flavor of sweet corn.

Why can't summer go on forever? My true friends live in the woods. I won't find their easy acceptance at school.

Potatoes plunk on my chest. I swipe them with a finger and open my mouth to hide the evidence.

"Table manners." Mama's reprimand cracks like a whip.

"We aren't savages," says Father. "Use a napkin."

A braver boy would take his plate to the woods. The squirrel would celebrate and snatch the corn. No one would care about manners or napkins.

But I unfold the napkin beside my plate and dab the wet spot on my shirt. My gaze lands on the bulge in my pocket.

I curl the smooth acorn into my palm. Eyes raised to see approval, I pull the gift out, extend my open hand to Father.

"Why do you have junk at the table?" A scowl furrows his face.

"I made it for you."

"You made an acorn?" His scorn cuts.

"I found it and smoothed the inside. Look." I shove my hand toward him.

The acorn teeters and tumbles. *Plop.* Into the bowl of potatoes.

"Gross!"

"That's filthy." My shoulders sink at Mama's words.

I open my mouth. Father shakes his head. "Throw those out. They're ruined now."

"Good riddance," mutters my sister.

I do as I'm told, wishing I could disappear.

But I'm not in the woods. Magic doesn't work here.

THE CASE OF THE MISSING HOT DOG

By Ellen Jacobson

———◈———

*"I wanted to write something that could provide a 'taste' of my cozy mysteries,
and this story explores the magical library system from the
North Dakota Library Mystery series."*

CHAPTER 1

An internal workplace investigation may be conducted if there are concerns about misconduct, policy violations, magical breaches, dog-earing book pages, or other workplace issues. The purpose of the investigation is to gather and review evidence, make factual findings about what occurred, and determine if any corrective action is required.

Magical Libraries Ltd., Personnel Handbook, Section 7.2(a)

"Have you seen the latest report from the Great Plains District, Fiona?" My supervisor let out a low whistle. "Four murders in less than a year in, um . . . Hang on, what was the name of that town again?"

While Mr. Perkins rifled through the stack of papers on his desk, I took a much-needed sip of my tea. Exhaustion had been my constant companion since I had joined Magical Libraries Ltd. nearly a year ago. My current stint in the personnel department was my fourth and final rotation in the organization's prestigious apprenticeship program. Why I ever thought dealing with employee issues would be a cushy assignment is beyond me. Turns out enforcing bureaucratic policies and procedures is grueling. And don't even get me started on all the paper cuts that come with the job. Mainlining Earl Grey was the only way I would survive the next few weeks. After that, Magical Libraries Ltd. would offer me a permanent job, or I'd be shown the door.

"Here it is." Mr. Perkins squinted at the page in his hand. "Why, North Dakota."

Unsure whether this was another one of Mr. Perkin's pop quizzes or a cryptic riddle—he was fond of both—I chewed my lip. An incorrect answer would likely earn me yet another late night reorganizing the contents of the filing cabinets.

After racking my brain for any relevant facts about North Dakota, I finally spluttered, "Nine seventy-eight point four."

Mr. Perkins scowled. "What does the temperature zinc is molten at have to do with Why, North Dakota?"

I gulped. "Nothing, as far as I know, sir."

"Then why did you mention it?"

"I didn't." The older man's scowl deepened. Wringing my hands together, I quickly added, "I mean, I suppose I did. But that was a coincidence. Nine seventy-eight point four is also the call number for North Dakota history. When you asked, 'Why North Dakota?' I thought this was one of your Dewey Decimal puzzles, and that the answer to why North Dakota exists would be to look to its history."

"Glad to see you finally decided to start studying your classifications, Fiona." Then he pointed at the large wooden bookcase in the corner of the office. "Bring me the atlas."

After wiping dust off the leather-bound book with one of my company-issued handkerchiefs, I gently set it on Mr. Perkins's desk. He carefully flipped through the atlas until he reached the map of North Dakota. Using a magnifying glass, he scanned the page. "Aha! There it is. Next to Williston."

Peering over my supervisor's shoulder, I furrowed my brow. Seeing the red dot he was pointing at, I realized Why was a town in North Dakota. Mr. Perkins hadn't been asking, 'Why North Dakota?'. He had been referring to a place.

While I was wondering if their sister town was What, South Dakota, Mr. Perkins muttered to himself, "Why does Why, North Dakota sound so familiar?" He slammed his fist on the desk, causing the pile of papers to fly everywhere. "Edgar Strudelmeister, Junior. That's why."

After I quickly picked up the papers off the floor and stacked them neatly next to the atlas, I asked, "Who is Edgar Strudelmeister, Junior?"

Mr. Perkins leaned back in his chair, his hands folded across his considerable belly. With a faraway look in his eyes, he said, "Junior and I were apprentices together. He should have been kicked out of the company back then, but for some reason, the powers that be took a shine to him. He was the director of the New York District until recently. Rumor has it, there were some issues. Then he was mysteriously reassigned to the Great Plains District. Why, North Dakota, to be exact."

Sitting bolt upright, Mr. Perkins swiveled his desk chair and looked me straight in the eyes. "Have you ever been to North Dakota, Fiona?"

"Um, no. Can't say that I've had the pleasure."

"Well, now's your chance." Pointing at the map of North Dakota, Mr. Perkins said, "You're going to conduct an internal investigation into Junior's conduct."

"An internal investigation?" I squeaked. "But I'm just an apprentice."

"Find anything and everything from policy violations to magical breaches," he said, ignoring my protest. "Heck, if Junior has dog-eared even one page in a library book, I want you to nail him."

I chewed my bottom lip. "Don't you need to have cause to launch an investigation?"

"Weren't you listening, Fiona? Four murders in less than a year? If that's not cause, I don't know what is." Mr. Perkins slammed the desk with his fist before opening the top drawer to extricate an ornate gilded bookmark.

At first, I eyed the bookmark with curiosity. Then, my stomach clenched. This was no ordinary bookmark, and Mr. Perkins was pointing it directly at me. As he began to utter an incantation, I groaned. My Latin wasn't great, but I knew what 'criceta' meant, and I didn't like it one bit.

But before I could protest, the spell was over, and I had transformed into a hamster, complete with whiskers, a short stubby tail, small furry ears, puffy cheeks, and a hankering for a hot cup of Earl Grey tea.

CHAPTER 2

The first few times you use the Intermodal Exchange Network to travel between libraries, you may experience motion sickness due to the effects of time and space dilation. Don't be alarmed—this is perfectly natural. Your neural pathways will align with the network's signals in no time!

An Apprentice's Guide to Magical Libraries Ltd., 11th ed.

A whirring buzzed in my ears, filling me with dread. It was a noise I had become all too familiar with during my apprenticeship—the Intermodal Exchange Network had been activated. My fellow apprentices loved riding the network, traveling to magical libraries in the blink of an eye. I hated it. Time and space dilation made me literally sick to my stomach.

Of course, I couldn't admit to anyone that traveling on the network gave me motion sickness. That was something only newbies experienced. If Mr. Perkins knew about it, he'd consider it a serious weakness, possibly even grounds for termination.

The whirring intensified. My heart raced. Vibrations coursed through my limbs. My muscles burned in agony. When I didn't think I could take it any longer, a blinding light seared my eyes, signaling my arrival in Why, North Dakota.

After landing on all four paws on top of a stack of books, I started retching. Fortunately, since my metamorphosis into a hamster had been so recent, my tiny stomach was empty. Throwing up all over library materials would not have been a great start to my new assignment.

"You gotta be kidding me," someone behind me with a thick New York accent grumbled. "It's bad enough a stupid cat is running around the library. Now I gotta deal with a stupid hamster."

Spinning around, I saw a chameleon glaring at me. As his tail swished back and forth, the color of his scales changed from iridescent purple to bright orange. The transformation was mesmerizing.

"Go find someplace else to hang out," the chameleon said before shooting his long tongue in my direction and nearly knocking me off balance.

"Hey, that hurt." I rubbed my cheek with my paw.

"Wait a minute." The chameleon inched forward, studying me closely. "You're not somebody's lost pet, are you?"

"No, I'm from the personnel department." I was tempted to scoot back, but held my ground instead. I wasn't going to let a grumpy reptile get the better of me. Extending a paw, I said, "Fiona McGregor, Fourth Level Apprentice. You must be Edgar Strudelmeister, Junior. Can I call you Edgar? Or would you prefer Mr. Strudelmeister?"

"As long as you're here to deal with my letters of complaint, Missy, I don't care what you call me."

"Letters?"

"Yes, letters," he snapped. "That's why you're here, isn't it? To investigate my complaints and do something about them, right?"

Remembering Mr. Perkins's instructions to keep the real reason for my presence in North Dakota secret, I nodded. If Edgar destroyed any incriminating evidence or covered up any policy violations because I let the true nature of my mission slip, my boss would be furious with me.

"Great. Let's start with the latest insult they've thrown at me," Edgar said. "It's up at the circulation desk. I found it there this morning. Follow me." When I hesitated, he snapped, "It's not a request. Get moving."

My eyes widened at the familiar whirring noise. "Isn't the circulation desk here in this library? Why would we have to use the Intermodal Exchange Network to get there?"

"Because it's faster, dummy. It would take us forever to get there with those stubby legs of yours."

"I don't have stubby . . ." My voice trailed off as I glanced at my legs. I guess they weren't long and slender anymore. "Sorry, I'm normally a human. I'm used to walking everywhere."

"Well, now you're a hamster. Deal with it." As the whirring noise increased in volume, Edgar motioned for me to fall in behind him. "Let's go."

Moments later, we perched on the circulation desk. I covered my mouth with my paw, trying to keep from having the dry heaves again.

"Do you see that?" Edgar asked, oblivious to my discomfort.

"You mean the photo hanging on the wall?"

"Duh."

"A simple yes or no would do," I said primly.

Edgar narrowed his beady eyes. "So what are you going to do about it?"

"Well, I guess it's a little crooked, but I'm not sure there's much I can do about that."

"I don't want you to straighten it, dummy. I want you to get rid of it."

"Why?" Turning back to look at the photo, I said, "It's actually kind of interesting. A giant ball of twine inside a barn. But I guess it's AI-generated, right? Nothing like that could really exist."

"It's real," Edgar said. "It's this stupid town's claim to fame."

"Wow. Someone made that? It's huge." Glancing back at Edgar, I said, "It's probably world record-level-huge, don't you think?"

"Enough with the world records already!" Edgar huffed. "That's all anyone around here talks about!"

Sitting back on my haunches, I raised my paws in a placating gesture. "Listen, I just got here a few minutes ago. I don't have a clue what's going on."

The chameleon sighed. "Fine, I'll fill you in. A delegation was in town last week to measure the ball of twine to see if it set the world record."

"Ooh, did it?"

"Somebody was murdered before they could officially measure it," Edgar said.

My ears perked up at the mention of murder. This was exactly the kind of thing Mr. Perkins wanted me to find out more about. "Who was killed? Who did it?"

Edgar waved my questions away. "It's not important. What is important is that everyone is making such a big deal about a stupid ball of twine. Did anyone ever once ask if there was a chameleon living in the local library who could do a record number of push-ups while reciting the alphabet backward? No, they didn't."

"Okay, so let me see if I've got this straight. You're upset because everyone is paying more attention to a ball of twine than to you?" Just then, my stomach let out a loud growl, reminding me I had skipped breakfast. What did hamsters eat, anyway? Seeds? Nuts?

As if reading my mind, Edgar said, "One of the library assistants has a box of granola in the breakroom. She won't notice if you take some. But we've got a stop we need to make first."

I was so hungry that I didn't even bother to protest taking the network again. After the whirring noise and bright flashing light subsided, I stared at my surroundings in disbelief.

"Are we inside a refrigerator?" Instead of answering, Edgar screamed. The pitch curdled my blood. Clasping my paws to my chest, I turned to the chameleon. "What's wrong?"

"Someone stole my hot dog!"

CHAPTER 3

JOB TITLE: Library Guide
DEPARTMENT: Library Services
JOB SUMMARY: The Library Guide will provide support and guidance to their assigned library staff member in order to assist them in: (1) solving any mysteries that may arise in their jurisdiction; (2) developing their magical bibliophile skills; and (3) identifying books to add to their 'to be read' list.
QUALIFICATIONS: Excellent communication skills, strong problem-solving skills, ability to create cryptic clues, proven experience in solving mysteries, and a demonstrated commitment to fostering and encouraging a love of books.

Library Guide Job Description (rev. August 2023), Magical Libraries Ltd.

Edgar ranted about his missing hot dog, letting out a string of very creative expletives. Who knew marshmallows could be used as a swear word? Once he calmed down a bit, I asked for more information.

"When did you last see the hot dog?" I asked, determined to get to the bottom of the alleged theft.

"Yesterday evening," Edgar said. "Thea dropped it off so I could have it for breakfast."

"Thea Olson? She's the librarian you've been assigned to guide, right?"

"She's a library volunteer, not a librarian," Edgar said. "But yeah, that's the stupid lady I'm stuck with. Anyway, Thea got the nacho dog for me at Swede's Diner. It's my favorite kind of hot dog these days."

As Edgar described the various toppings on the nacho dog—salsa, cheese, sour cream, diced onion, and jalapeños—he started to drool. The thought of tiny droplets of saliva landing on the plastic food container he was perched on grossed me out, so I steered the conversation to a safer topic.

"Okay, so Thea brought your nacho dog last night. Did you see her put it in the fridge? Or did she tell you that's what she did?"

"I saw her," Edgar said. "And before you ask, it was a little after seven when the hot dog was placed inside the fridge. I checked the clock on the wall."

Despite my fur coat, the chill in the fridge was starting to get to me. "Could we continue this conversation somewhere warmer?"

Once the network deposited us on the kitchen counter in the breakroom, Edgar pointed at a cereal box. "There's the granola. Help yourself."

"How exactly am I supposed to do that? Chew a hole through the box?"

Edgar rolled his eyes. "Don't they teach apprentices anything useful these days?" Then he wiggled his nose while uttering something in Sanskrit. Fortunately, I had spent a semester abroad in India, so I was able to understand what he said. It basically boiled down to 'feed me.'

Clusters of granola appeared on the counter, and I dug in. Eating as a hamster was a strange experience due to my long incisors and strong desire to hoard granola pieces by stuffing them into my cheeks. Once my hunger had been satiated, I continued my questioning.

"Who else was in the library when Thea put the hot dog in the fridge?"

"Just Hudson Carter, the library director," Edgar explained. "The library had already closed for the night. He was in his office working late."

"Okay, so if the library was closed, how did Thea get inside? Does she have a key?"

"Hudson let her in." Edgar pulled a face. "The two of them like to play smoochy-face. She made an excuse about going to the restroom, then put the hot dog in the fridge for me."

"That was nice of her," I said. "Does she bring you hot dogs often?"

"Not often enough," Edgar snapped. "Can we get back to the case?"

"The case?"

"The 'Case of the Missing Hot Dog,' dummy. That's what we're investigating. I want to find the culprit and make them pay."

"Wow, that's a lot of vengeance-seeking for a meat product," I said dryly. When Edgar glared at me, his tail swishing back and forth, I quickly added, "But, hey, I might react the same way if someone stole my M&M'S. Anyway, back to our timeline. We've got the hot dog in the fridge around seven. The only people in the library at the time are Hudson and Thea. What time did they leave?"

"About fifteen minutes later."

Wishing I had a notepad and a pencil to write everything down—not to mention opposable thumbs—I said, "So between a quarter after seven and this morning, no one else was in the library."

Edgar shook his head. "The cleaner was here from eight until eleven. Her name is Lydia. She's terrible at her job."

"Well, as much as I'd love to discuss what aspect of her job performance is letting you down, I think we should focus on the case. Did you have eyes on Lydia the entire time she was here?"

"Why would I want to watch someone do a terrible job cleaning for three hours? She doesn't know how to operate a vacuum cleaner, and her idea of dusting is pitiful."

"Setting aside your weird obsession with cleaning, is it possible that Lydia ate your nacho dog during a break?"

Bobbing his head up and down, Edgar said, "I wouldn't put it past her."

"Right, so suspect number one on our list is Lydia, the cleaner."

"Lydia, the terrible cleaner," Edgar corrected.

"Got it." As I mimed writing 'terrible' in the air, my balance faltered. Standing on your hind legs when you weren't in a naturally bipedal form was challenging. "Was anyone else in the library last night?"

"Nope. I was all alone from eleven until eight this morning. That's when Hudson arrived for the day. He likes to get in before the rest of the staff arrives."

"That makes him suspect number two," I said as Edgar helped himself to a stray piece of granola on the counter. Glancing at the clock on the wall, I added,

"We discovered the hot dog was missing around nine. Hudson could have helped himself to it this morning. No one else was here, right?"

Edgar rubbed his chest, belching loudly enough to ruffle my fur. "Granola always gives me heartburn."

"And hot dogs don't?"

The chameleon shrugged, then nibbled on more granola.

"You do realize the granola you're feasting on doesn't belong to you, right? And we're investigating a stolen hot dog. So doesn't that—"

"Don't get technical with me, Missy," Edgar said, cutting me off. "Now, there's one other suspect to add to the list."

"Who's that?"

"Dr. McCoy."

"When was the doctor here? Was there a medical emergency last night or this morning?"

"He's not that kind of doctor."

"Ah, I see. A Ph.D."

"No, he's a cat," Edgar said. "And everyone knows you can't trust cats."

CHAPTER 4

If you're unable to send or receive messages in the Biblio-Mail app, follow these basic troubleshooting steps before contacting the help desk. Step #1 - Check the network connection to confirm if you can access other apps. If there's no connection, reboot your visor. Step #2 - If rebooting your visor doesn't fix the issue, run a scan for anti-magical viruses and malware as they can interfere with the Biblio-Mail app. Step #3 - If your system is clear of viruses and malware, update your operating software. If none of these steps fixes your issue, you may contact the help desk for further assistance between 3:32 PM and 3:47 PM (HQ Standard Time) on Mondays and Thursdays.

Biblio-Mail App Troubleshooting Guide, Magical Libraries Ltd.

"What do you have against cats?" As I tried to put my hands on my hips, I realized that in my current hamster form I probably didn't look as indignant as I felt. Puffy cheeks, whiskers, and a stubby tail lend themselves more to a cute vibe than a tough guy one. I didn't let that deter me, though, continuing to lay into Edgar. "Cats are the most regal creatures on this planet. They're playful, they love to purr, they—"

"Don't forget, they like to hunt hamsters and other small rodents, dummy," Edgar said wryly.

"Oh."

Edgar chuckled. "Cat got your tongue?"

"No, it's just, um . . ."

"That's what I thought," Edgar said. "Team Cat isn't all it's cracked up to be, is it? Come on, the library is about to open. Let's head back to the circulation desk. Hudson brings in donuts for the staff on Fridays."

"But you're not staff," I said, happy we weren't talking about cats anymore. I wasn't sure I'd be able to look at my parents' Siamese quite the same way once I got home.

"Of course I am. I'm a library guide."

Before I could point out that Edgar was employed by Magical Libraries Ltd., not the Why Public Library, I saw a purple envelope icon floating in front of my eyes. Realizing I had a message waiting for me, I told Edgar I'd meet him in a few minutes. "I need to use the ladies' room."

"You're a hamster, not a lady." Edgar waved a hand in the air. "But whatever. Do you remember how to get to the circulation desk?" When I nodded, he added, "Use the Intermodal Exchange Network. Don't walk, got it? It'll take too long, and all the good donuts will be gone by the time you get there."

As if realizing it sounded like he had gone soft on me, Edgar huffed, "Not that I care if you get a good donut or not. Just hurry up, stupid."

Once Edgar left, I pressed the right side of my head to activate my Biblio-Mail visor. My inbox was flashing, letting me know there was an urgent message from Mr. Perkins. My stomach clenched when I read the subject line—'Progress Report Overdue: Submit Immediately!'

I had been so absorbed with helping Edgar that I completely lost sight of why Mr. Perkins had sent me here. Carrying out an internal investigation into Edgar's conduct was supposed to be my focus, not solving the 'Case of the Missing Hot Dog.' Before I left, Mr. Perkins had made it perfectly clear that he expected half-hourly progress reports. In the time I had been here, I hadn't sent one.

For a brief moment, I was tempted to blame a system outage for my lack of reporting. Everyone knew the glitchy Biblio-Map app constantly crashed. But my conscience got the better of me. After profusely apologizing for my dereliction of duty, I summarized my activities since arriving, omitting any mention of the missing hot dog. This must have mollified Mr. Perkins, as he modified my reporting schedule from half-hourly to hourly.

By the time I arrived at the circulation desk, I felt sick to my stomach. The combination of a high-pressure job and constant travel on the Intermodal Exchange Network was doing a number on my digestive system.

Edgar sat at the far end of the desk next to a display about upcoming library programs. He waved me over. "Everyone is in Hudson's office eating donuts." Then he swiveled one of his beady eyes in my direction, peering at me more closely. "What's wrong? You look like you're going to be sick."

"I'm fine," I said. "Perfectly fine."

Edgar shook his head. "It's the network, isn't it? Motion sickness, right? When I was an apprentice, there was a girl who had the same problem."

Panic welled up in my throat. Edgar knew my secret. He was going to report me. I was going to get thrown out of the organization, all because I couldn't travel on the network without getting sick.

"You know there's a simple fix," Edgar said matter-of-factly. "Not many people know about it, but you seem like an okay kid." He muttered a few words in a language I had never heard before and told me to hold out my hand.

I peered at the tiny piece of candy he had placed in my palm. "Is that an M&M?"

"Yep, but with added magical properties. Take one before you travel the network, and you won't have any more problems. I'll teach you how to make more, but you have to promise this will be our little secret. Okay?"

"But isn't chocolate bad for hamsters?" I asked.

"You're not really a hamster, dummy," Edgar scoffed. "Go on, eat it before it melts all over your paw."

The M&M'S deliciousness immediately soothed my stomach. As I started to tell Edgar that, a patron walked up to the desk.

"Quick, hide," I said to Edgar as I darted behind the library program display.

"What are you doing?" Edgar asked loudly.

Poking my head out from the display, I whispered, "There's a woman there. What if she sees you?"

Edgar snorted. "Don't be stupid. That's Lydia the terrible cleaner, not Thea Olson. She can't see me."

My face flushed. How could I have forgotten such a basic fact? A library guide could only be seen or heard by their library staff member. Employees on temporary assignment to a library, like myself, couldn't be seen or heard by any human.

Creeping from behind the display, I saw one of the library assistants come out of Hudson's office.

"I've got a cookbook on hold," Lydia said to her. "It's the vegetarian one."

"Sure thing." As the library assistant was checking out the book, she said, "I've been thinking about becoming a vegetarian, but I'm not sure I could give up the occasional steak."

Lydia gave her an encouraging smile. "I used to think the same thing, but I've been a vegetarian for five years."

After Lydia grabbed her book and left, I said to Edgar, "If Lydia is a vegetarian, then there's no way she would have stolen your hot dog. So that means it must be Hudson. Now we just have to prove it."

CHAPTER 5

Mr. Strudelmeister, personnel number [REDACTED], was assigned to Project [REDACTED] in his capacity as a [REDACTED]. During the course of this assignment, Mr. Strudelmeister was [REDACTED] due to the effects of the magical overload of [REDACTED]. As part of the [REDACTED] process and in compliance with Regulation 75-X, Mr. Strudelmeister has been placed on temporary assignment to the Why Public Library in North Dakota.

Confidential Personnel File - Edgar Strudelmeister, Junior

"I still think the stupid cat did it," Edgar said.

"A cat can't open a fridge," I pointed out.

"Fine." Edgar frowned. "But if you're so convinced Hudson stole my hot dog, how are we going to prove it, smarty-pants?"

"Is there a security camera in the breakroom?" I asked. "Maybe he's on tape."

"Do you think we'd be sitting around here if there were? No, dummy. We would have looked at the footage already," Edgar snapped. "And it's not like Hudson left an incriminating trail of salsa and other toppings either. Not that Lydia the terrible cleaner would have vacuumed it up if he did. She would have picked up the packaging, but that's only because people tend to complain if garbage is strewn around the library."

As I threw up my paws in frustration, a man wearing a cardigan came out of the library director's office. "Is that Hudson?" I whispered to Edgar.

"He can't hear you, remember?" Edgar barked. "And yes, it is. That's the guy Thea is so gaga over."

Hudson approached the library assistant. "Hey, you going to be okay on your own? I need to run to the doctor's office."

"Oh no, are you sick?" she asked.

"Just a routine blood test." Hudson patted his stomach. "Save me a donut, will you? I've had to fast since last night, and I'm starving."

Edgar nudged me. "See, I told you. Hudson didn't do it. He was fasting. No hot dog for him."

"Are you sure no one else was in the library besides Lydia and Hudson? There has to be someone else who could have stolen it."

"I'm telling you, it was Dr. McCoy."

"But it couldn't . . ." My voice trailed off when a large, fluffy black and white cat jumped onto the circulation desk. "Please don't eat me," I said, my voice trembling.

Edgar rolled his eyes. "Geez, how many times do I have to tell you that no one can see or hear you? That includes all living beings, whether of the human or feline variety. You're safe."

Just to be sure, I kept my distance while the library assistant gave Dr. McCoy some pets. It wasn't until the cat jumped off the circulation desk that I breathed a sigh of relief.

"Nervous much?" Edgar asked.

"You know, no one likes a snarky chameleon. No wonder you . . . darn it, not again," I said as a purple envelope icon floated in front of my eyes. "Hang on, I think Mr. Perkins sent me another message. I need to answer it before he goes ballistic."

"Mr. Perkins? As in Stinky Perkins?" Edgar's voice had a steely edge to it. "Are you working for Stinky Perkins? Did he send you here to spy on me?"

"I don't know any Stinky Perkins." I shrank back.

"How about Thomas Grainger Perkins?" Edgar thumped his tail on the desk. "Know him?"

"Yes," I squeaked.

"Same guy. He's your boss, isn't he?" Without giving me a chance to respond, Edgar continued, "You're working for Stinky Perkins. I should have known you weren't here to look into my letters of complaint. You people in the Personnel

Department are all alike, sitting in your cushy offices, insisting people comply with your stupid policies and procedures, all in the name of bureaucracy. You've never done a hard day's work in the field."

"That's not true." Ignoring the tears welling up in my eyes, I said, "This may be my first field assignment, but I've worked hard in every single one of my apprenticeship rotations."

Edgar looked like he was going to relent for a brief moment, but then his expression hardened again. "Stinky has had it out for me ever since we were apprentices together. He hated the fact that I scored higher on every exam without hardly studying. Then after the incident in . . ."

"What incident?"

"It's classified. Besides, that's not the point. I want to know why Stinky sent you here."

"He's concerned about the murder rate in Why," I said. "There have been four people killed in less than a year."

"That's his pretext? Murder?" Edgar chortled. "The whole point of the library guide is to help solve mysteries. Not every mystery is a nonviolent crime like a stolen hot dog. Sometimes those mysteries involve murder. I didn't kill any of those people—and by the way, one of those murders happened before I was assigned here—but I certainly helped find who did kill them."

I gulped. Edgar was right. At the time, I knew there was something fishy going on when Mr. Perkins used the murder rate in Why as the justification for this internal investigation. When I said as much to Edgar, he didn't respond.

After what seemed like an eternity, he finally asked, "Why didn't you stand up to him? You don't seem to have a problem standing up to me."

I gave him a quizzical look. "But you're a chameleon."

"What does that have to do with anything?"

"Don't take this the wrong way, okay, but you kind of remind me of that chameleon in the ads selling insurance. He seems so harmless, so—"

"He's not a chameleon." Edgar clenched his fists. "He's a gecko. Big differ-ence."

"Okay, sorry. Didn't mean to mix up my reptiles."

Edgar took a deep breath, then let it out slowly. "My point is that it doesn't matter whether someone is in human or animal form. If they're a stinking, conniving, no-good liar, then you need to stand up to them, period." Pointing at the side of my head, he added, "Better turn your visor on and reply to Stinky. While you're doing that, I've got my own messages to send."

⊰◦⊱

The next morning I was back in the Personnel Department, my assignment to Why, North Dakota abruptly cut short. Turns out Edgar's messages landed Mr. Perkins in hot water. Apparently, the higher-ups don't like it when you initiate an unsanctioned and unjustified internal investigation. Mr. Perkins was told to terminate it immediately, and a formal letter of reprimand was placed in his employee file.

Mr. Perkins was furious with me, with Edgar, with his powers that be, even with the poor delivery girl from the coffee shop downstairs. He scowled as he grabbed his latte and apple turnover from her, then stomped back to his desk. When she set a cup of Earl Grey tea and a blueberry muffin in front of me, I gave her an encouraging smile and a generous tip.

"Only three weeks to go," I muttered to myself. "You can make it."

How would I survive the final stretch of my apprenticeship in the same office as Mr. Perkins? He had been intolerable before. This incident with Edgar was going to make him even more so.

The days and nights ticked by, filled with endless filing of reports and constant reorganization of office supplies. Mr. Perkins had me running so ragged that I barely got a wink of sleep. Thank goodness there was no shortage of tea, otherwise I would have collapsed in a heap on the floor.

During my final week, Mr. Perkins was called away to an emergency meeting concerning disappearing ink on the latest print run of encyclopedias. Magical interference was suspected, and it was all hands on deck.

"Just because I'll be gone all day doesn't mean you can sleep on the job, Fiona," Mr. Perkins said. "I expect you to re-alphabetize the sickness reports."

"But I just did that yesterday," I said.

"That was from A to Z. This time, I want you to do it from Z to A."

Once my boss had left the office, I said, "Stuff it." I kicked off my shoes, leaned back in my chair, and started watching cat videos. Just when I started to think I should begin re-alphabetizing the sickness reports before Mr. Perkins returned, a video of a Persian cat doing the most extraordinary thing stopped me in my tracks.

I opened up my Biblio-Mail app and sent the link to Edgar. When he didn't respond right away, I told myself it was because there were system issues. He'd get back to me soon.

But when a couple of hours passed by without a message from Edgar, my heart sank. He was never going to forgive me for conducting an internal investigation into his activities. Could you blame him?

I was just making myself another cup of tea when I saw the flashing mail icon. Yes, it was a reply from Edgar! Half nervous, half hopeful, I opened it. A grin spread across my face as I read his message:

Good job, dummy. You solved the case.

Sinking back into my chair, I replayed the video I had sent Edgar. Cats are so cute, especially clever cats who jump onto counters and jab their paws into the seal of fridges repeatedly until the doors pop open. As if that wasn't impressive enough, there were the cats who covered their tracks by standing in front of the fridge on their hind legs and pressing the door shut with their front paws.

Turns out Edgar was right. Dr. McCoy managed to open the fridge in the breakroom just like this Persian cat, then stole the hot dog. This video helped prove how it was done.

Knowing I had helped figure out the mystery of the missing hot dog gave me the courage to stand up to Mr. Perkins during my final days working for him. Sure, it meant my boss wouldn't write a letter of recommendation for me and I would probably be booted from Magical Libraries Ltd. at the end of my apprenticeship. But so what? It was worth it. When I refused to re-alphabetize records needlessly or rearrange paper clips by size, Mr. Perkins's face turned bright red as he spluttered incoherently at me.

When the last day of my apprenticeship rolled around, Mr. Perkins handed me a thick envelope. "You have Junior to thank for this, not me."

"Huh?" I said to Mr. Perkins's retreating back as he stomped out of the office, muttering about filing a complaint about me with his superiors. After he slammed the door shut, I opened the envelope and pulled out its contents. It seemed like an awful lot of papers for a dismissal letter.

I scanned the first page, clasping my hand to my mouth to stop from screaming out loud. Then I re-read the first paragraph more slowly:

Dear Ms. McGregor - Based on the strong recommendation of Mr. Strudelmeister as to your investigative capabilities, we are pleased to offer you a permanent job as a Junior Library Guide. You are to report to Why, North Dakota next week for your initial training under the supervision of Mr. Strudelmeister. Please find your employment contract enclosed, along with your remuneration package.

As I reached across the desk for my cup of tea, I jostled the envelope and a handwritten note fell out. A smile crept across my face as I read it:

Bring hot dogs and a padlock for the fridge.

Edgar

THE BACKYARD:
SKIES AND VISITORS

By Jana Mann

"This collection came from my participation in the Stafford Challenge, which was to write a poem a day for a whole year."

The backyard is a great spot.
It's a front row seat
to watch the daily sky show.
Company's welcome,
especially the wild things.

Skies

It's never the same,
that celestial sky show.
Always be looking!

Peachy morning sky,
a sunrise full of promise
for the newest day.
And for just a little while,
the sun and the moon
orbit together.
Bold and blazing evening sky,
a sunset for rest.
Finish the day with glory.
Clouds are the sky's art,
story and temperament.
Its way of speaking.
Happy, fluffy bits
or towering thunderheads
have something to say.
Stringy clouds of carded wool
stretch and reach up high.

But the dark and dreary clouds
sink to touch the ground.
Such talkative clouds!
What story will they share next?
Look up and listen.

Silver moon sliver
sprinkled roundabout with stars
on black velvet sky.
The universe is calling!

The constellations
are as old as time itself.
Meet some modern ones.

Barcalounger Bob
kicks back in his comfy chair,
shoes off, beer in hand.

Edsel the Chauffeur,
keys jingling, gas tank full.
He's ready to go.

Pioneer Edith
is ready to make the trek
with her sunbonnet.

Twins Salt and Pepper
think trouble makes life spicy,
and they aren't wrong.

Cosmic computer
And the heavenly hard drive
You can trust their work.

If you squint enough,
The stars become anything
With stories to tell.

Visitors

Birds swing on the wire,
then launch to wing overhead.
Do they appreciate the view?
Do they watch and judge or wonder?
Do they gossip in their leafy neighbor-
hoods?
Do they feel sad when they migrate away
or find joy when they return?
One day, the birds might share their se-
crets, but never their wings.

The crows are calling
for their peanuts and crackers
and chunks of apple.
The bluejays fly in,
hoping for a morsel, too.
Sparrows join the throng.
The mourning doves wait with grace.
The backyard bird buffet.

Moving together,
the flock of valley quail
hustle and bustle
around the backyard.
They run past the trees
to hide under the lilacs.
Mama clucks softly,
gathering her family.
Birds of a feather
rest all together.

The bumblebees fly
like they are drunken sailors
without their sea legs
or any destination.
The honeybees fly
with purpose and direction.
There's work to be done
and a hive to be maintained.
The yellowjackets fly
only to cause trouble,
because thugs do that.
The ladybugs fly
wherever they damn well want,
because nobody
bosses a lady around.

Fawns and does on tippy toes,
moving through the grass,
They find rest in the deep shade.
Dark eyes watching.
Alert ears listening.
Fawns and does away from foes,
serene and quiet.

MEET THE CONTRIBUTORS

Tamelia Aday

Tamelia Aday loves books and has been writing stories since grade school. After trying various jobs (including a disastrous stint in banking), Tamelia realizes she's happiest at home crafting novels and raising her family. Her debut novel is *The Filbert Ridge Miracle*, and she's currently working on a cozy mystery and another novel. When not writing or tackling laundry, she attempts to knit and crochet—preferably with coffee and chocolate nearby.

Find out more about Tamelia at:
Facebook – https://www.facebook.com/profile.php?id=100091125939443
Instagram – https://www.instagram.com/tameliaaday

Kathy Appel

Kathy Appel is a Florida native who has called the Pacific Northwest home for nearly five decades. An avid reader, gardener, and ukulele player, she enjoys yoga, walking, and being grandma to six great kids. She has published a personal memoir, but her story for this anthology marks her fiction debut. Kathy lives in Saint Helens, Oregon with her dog, Biscuit, and her chicken, Henny Penny.

Find out more about Kathy at:
Facebook – https://www.facebook.com/kathy.appel

Kathrin Classen

Kathrin Classen writes thrillers from the Pacific Northwest, where she hikes through old-growth forests with her family. Her previous publications include a short story in HellBound Books' Anthology of Horror. She is the creator and host of the Writers in the Wilderness Podcast and the My Little Library of Lost Short Stories podcast.

Find out more about Kathrin at:
Instagram – https://www.instagram.com/kathrin.classen.writerreader
Substack – https://substack.com/@kathrinclassen

Cate Cross

Cate Cross writes and illustrates stories for children, creating picture books and middle-grade adventures with heart and humor. A Pacific Northwest native with a medical background, she has coauthored peer-reviewed research articles for medical journals. When not writing, Cate enjoys painting and spending time with her beloved cat, Hero.

Find out more about Cate at:
Website – https://catecross.com/

Estella Edgewater

Estella Edgewater creates immersive fantasy worlds, both on the page and online. The founder of Foxbridge Fantasies, an interactive literary roleplay at foxbridge fantasies.com, Estella writes collaboratively with their wife. Estella devotes every free moment—waking and dreaming—to crafting stories. They live in the forest with two cats, Asmodeus and Little Foot.

Find out more about Estella at:
YouTube – https://www.youtube.com/@estellaedgewater
Website – foxbridgefantasies.com

Mike Exinger (Buxton Manning)

Mike Exinger spent the '90s as a freelance writer and reporter, longing for the day he could skip the facts and make stuff up. Since retiring to Warren, Oregon, he's done exactly that. As Buxton Manning, he creates stories for adults. As Rex Michaels, he invents tales for younger readers. Under his own name, he continues producing a popular series of gaming guides. Mike spends his "off" hours playing in the dirt.

Find out more about Mike and Buxton at:
Website – https://www.buxtonmanning.com/
Substack – https://mikeexinger.substack.com/

David Fryer

David Fryer is an author and engineer from Portland, Oregon. His short stories, including "Snow Diagnosis" in *Witcraft Magazine* and "221C Baker Street" in *Ellery Queen Mystery Magazine*, blend mystery with imagination. When not writing, he hikes Oregon's waterfalls—he's conquered half of the best ones and looks forward to tackling the rest.

Find out more about David at:
Substack – https://dsfryer.substack.com/

Sharon Hughson

Sharon Hughson loves cats, books, and spoiling her grandchildren. She's published short stories and novellas in multiple genres. Themes of faith, family, and friendship populate her writing as she encourages her readers to be the hero of their own story. Her perfect day involves reading in the sun or hiking near her Columbia River home in Oregon.

Find out more about Sharon at:
Amazon – https://www.amazon.com/stores/Sharon-Hughson/author/B00T8O3B0A
Facebook – https://www.facebook.com/sharonlhughson

Ellen Jacobson

Ellen Jacobson is a chocolate-obsessed cat lover who writes cozy mysteries and romantic comedies. After working in Scotland and New Zealand, she returned to the States, lived aboard a sailboat, and traveled in a tiny camper before settling in northern Oregon with her husband and an imaginary cat named Simon. She is the author of the Mollie McGhie Cozy Sailing Mystery series, the North Dakota Library Mystery series, and the Smitten with Travel Romantic Comedy series.

Find out more about Ellen at:
Website – https://ellenjacobsonbooks.com/
Instagram – https://www.instagram.com/ellenjacobsonwriter

K.D. Jewell

K.D. Jewell writes young adult fantasy that invites reader participation. Author of *Angel in Repose*, she creates interactive literary worlds where readers help shape storylines and explore characters more deeply. A Warren, Oregon resident for nearly four decades, she enjoys training and showing horses, biking with her dogs, and watching horror movies.

Find out more about K.D. at:
Amazon – https://www.amazon.com/stores/K.D.-Jewell/author/B0FP9TV7HR

Elaine Kelley

Elaine Kelley advocates for environmental protection, Middle East peace, and social justice through her nonprofit work. For over 50 years, she has served in development roles supporting Palestinian Christian organizations and contributing to publications on Middle East affairs. She has managed grant research and proposal writing for universities and advocacy centers promoting nonviolence and interfaith cooperation. Elaine currently serves on the board of the Oregon Conservancy Foundation.

Find out more about Elaine at:
Facebook – https://www.facebook.com/SisterElaineKelley

Shaun C. Kennedy

Shaun C. Kennedy, husband and father, lives in Southwest Washington. He writes speculative science fiction, fantasy, and theological reflections. His deep thinking leads him to explore history, philosophy, and faith through both fiction and nonfiction. A student of Biblical Hebrew and Greek, he is working on *The Corrected King James Bible*, a project correcting textual variations, before undertaking his own translation.

Find out more about Shaun at:
Website – https://shaunckennedy.wordpress.com/
Facebook – https://www.facebook.com/ShaunCKennedyAuthor/

J. LaRiviere

J. LaRiviere translates the abstract vibrations of reality into comprehensible words—or tries to. A concept occupying a mortal vessel, J. writes speculative fiction that blurs the boundaries of perception and existence. J. dwells in the woods with cat shapes Little Foot and Asmodeus, and alleged humans Icarus and Estella.

Find out more about J. at:
Tumblr – @jadynlariviere
Instagram – https://www.instagram.com/jadynlariviere/

Kevin Lay

Kevin Lay has been writing stories since his teenage years in rural Ohio—many told through guitar, composed scores, and now prose. A composer and president of Cascadia Composers, he produces concerts of new music throughout Portland while exploring Deep Listening, poetry, mathematics, and Vajrayana. Kevin is currently developing a software application to help writers access their entire body of work as they create.

Find out more about Kevin at:
Website – https://www.kevinbryantlay.com
Facebook – https://www.facebook.com/kevin.b.lay

Jana Mann

Jana Mann grew up in a family of storytellers—like her gifted Grandpa. After spinning an outlandish tale about recess shenanigans, her mother advised: "Don't be a liar like your grandpa. If you're going to tell lies, write them down and turn them into stories instead." Jana has been doing exactly that ever since. She leads the St. Helens Writers Guild and lives in St. Helens, Oregon, where she loves to fish.

Find out more about Jana at:
Substack – https://janamanna.substack.com/

Linda Paul

Linda Paul is a writer and musician residing in Saint Helens, Oregon, who works across multiple genres. Her monologue *Semper Fi* was performed on stage and TV in Portland, and her play *Halloween in the ICU* was a finalist at the Midwest Dramatists Center Conference. Her poems, essays, memoir, and short stories have appeared in *The Oregonian*, Brevard Scribblers' anthologies, AGS Magazine, and on Amazon. Her first novel is nearly complete.

Find out more about Linda at:
Website – https://boomerbabeblog.com/about/

Dawn Shipman

Dawn Shipman has dreamed of writing since Mrs. Juell's 10th-grade Creative Writing class. She wrote hundreds of articles, short stories, poems, plays, and blog posts before launching her YA fantasy series, The Lost Stones of Argonia, in 2021.

Dawn lives in the Pacific Northwest with her long-haired, IT-guy husband and a roving band of dogs, horses, and cats.

Find out more about Dawn at:
Website – www.dawnshipmanfiction.com
Facebook – https://www.facebook.com/profile.php?id=100063338973694

ABOUT THE COLUMBIA COUNTY AUTHORS ALLIANCE

The mission of the Columbia County Authors Alliance (CCAA) is to support Columbia County, Oregon writers through educational and networking opportunities, local author events, anthologies, regular creative gatherings, and building connections with readers. The real goal: building connections between writers—because when writers support each other, everyone's work gets stronger. And when the writing community thrives, readers are drawn to the magic, too.

Find out more at www.columbiacountyauthors.com

CONTRIBUTOR COPYRIGHTS